LOVE IS A
FOUR-LEGGED
WORD

Love is a
FOUR-LEGGED
WORD

31221000724455

· KANDY SHEPHERD ·

BERKLEY SENSATION, NEW YORK

THE BERKLEY PUBLISHING GROUP
Published by the Penguin Group
Penguin Group (USA) Inc.
375 Hudson Street, New York, New York 10014, USA
Penguin Group (Canada), 90 Eglinton Avenue East, Suite 700, Toronto, Ontario M4P 2Y3, Canada
(a division of Pearson Penguin Canada Inc.)
Penguin Books Ltd., 80 Strand, London WC2R 0RL, England
Penguin Group Ireland, 25 St. Stephen's Green, Dublin 2, Ireland (a division of Penguin Books Ltd.)
Penguin Group (Australia), 250 Camberwell Road, Camberwell, Victoria 3124, Australia
(a division of Pearson Australia Group Pty. Ltd.)
Penguin Books India Pvt. Ltd., 11 Community Centre, Panchsheel Park, New Delhi—110 017, India
Penguin Group (NZ), 67 Apollo Drive, Rosedale, North Shore 0632, New Zealand
(a division of Pearson New Zealand Ltd.)
Penguin Books (South Africa) (Pty.) Ltd., 24 Sturdee Avenue, Rosebank, Johannesburg 2196,
South Africa

Penguin Books Ltd., Registered Offices: 80 Strand, London WC2R 0RL, England

This book is an original publication of The Berkley Publishing Group.

This is a work of fiction. Names, characters, places, and incidents either are the product of the author's imagination or are used fictitiously, and any resemblance to actual persons, living or dead, business establishments, events, or locales is entirely coincidental. The publisher does not have any control over and does not assume any responsibility for author or third-party websites or their content.

PRINTING HISTORY
Berkley Sensation trade paperback edition / July 2009

Library of Congress Cataloging-in-Publication Data

Shepherd, Kandy.
    Love is a four-legged word / Kandy Shepherd.
        p. cm.
    ISBN 978-0-425-22784-8
1. Mutts (Dogs)—Fiction.   2. Women cooks—Fiction.   3. Attorney and client—Fiction.   I. Title.
PR9619.4.S543L68   2009
    823'.92—dc22   2009009998

PRINTED IN THE UNITED STATES OF AMERICA

10   9   8   7   6   5   4   3   2   1

To all the four-legged friends
who bring such joy to my life.

Acknowledgments

My thanks to my wonderful editor, Allison Brandau, and the team at Berkley who helped craft my manuscript into this beautiful book. Thanks also to my agent, Miriam Kriss.

Top of the list of writing friends for me to recognize for their encouragement and help is Cathleen Ross. Thanks also to Anna Campbell, Elizabeth Lhuede, Isolde Martyn, and Christine Stinson—who always loved my mutt story. My gratitude also to Simone Camilleri, Beth Orsoff, Annie West, and Sandy McPhie, and to my critique group cheer squads. Thank you, too, for the incredibly supportive network at Romance Writers of America.

A special mention to Melinda and Luke Booker for always making me feel so at home in California.

To my neighbor Brutus Kell who—unlike my fictional Brutus—is a silky terrier of impeccable pedigree, thanks for the inspiration.

Most heartfelt thanks of all to my husband, James, and daughter, Lucy, for their unflagging faith in me.

· One ·

Madeleine Cartwright didn't look at all the type of female who'd boink an old man to death for his money.

Tom O'Brien saw that the second she opened the door of her apartment. His imagination had let him down big-time. How could he have got it so wrong? This woman was more girl next door than vamp. No silicone-enhanced breasts, skintight dresses, or big, bleached hair.

Rather, her slender shape was enveloped in a white chef's apron smeared with chocolate, and she had flour streaked on her pretty, heart-shaped face. She didn't have big hair. She had, well, small hair—short and feathery and kind of mussed. It looked natural, not out of a bottle; her hair was the color of marmalade.

"You must be Tom O'Brien, Walter's lawyer." Her voice was sweet and musical, not sultry and seductive. "I'm Maddy Cartwright."

She held out a hand to him in greeting. As she was wearing a blue-and-white-striped oven mitt, Tom hesitated to shake it. For a moment her eyes widened in surprise at his lack of response, then she glanced down at the offending mitt, flushed, and laughed as she slid it off.

"You're early," she said with a hint of accusation that Tom thought was quite unwarranted. "I'm right in the middle of testing a new recipe for brownies."

Was she serious? Tom stared at her, speechless, still unable to reconcile the mental image he had of the sexy seductress with the reality of this engaging, fresh-faced girl talking about, of all things, a chocolate dessert.

"Come on in," she continued. "I've got to get the brownies out of the oven at just the right moment or they won't be nice and gooey in the middle."

She turned and headed into her apartment. Her apron was tied in back with a pert bow; the long tails of the bow pointing to a nicely rounded rear end hugged by faded blue jeans. Despite his preconceived opinion of her, Tom couldn't help but admire the view as he followed her inside.

She stopped suddenly and turned back toward him. Caught in mid-stride, he nearly collided with her, his briefcase banging into her thigh.

For a second she braced her hand against his chest to steady herself, and he could feel her warmth through the fabric of his suit. She only came up to his shoulders—probably five-six to his six-two—and this close he noticed her eyes were green and that she smelled of lavender and chocolate.

"Sorry," he muttered, disconcerted by her closeness and his body's instant and surprising reaction to her.

"My . . . my fault," she stammered as she stepped back from

him. "I . . . I stopped because I wanted to ask if . . . if you liked brownies."

What was this woman up to? Tom was shaken at how exciting he'd found her sudden nearness. Shaken and annoyed.

Was this disarming, down-home-girl image some kind of ploy? A clever strategy to part gullible old men from their money? Madeleine Cartwright didn't look the part he had mentally cast her in—but that didn't mean she hadn't played it.

No way would he be sucked in by her wiles. He knew what ruin lay at the end of that particular path.

"Who doesn't like brownies?" he said abruptly. "But, Ms. Cartwright, I—"

"Good. Then you can help me test them. The kitchen's through here."

Delicious, chocolaty smells wafted toward him, and for a moment Tom was tempted. Very tempted. He was aware he'd only had a tuna fish sandwich for lunch. But he had practice at resisting temptation. A man as determined as he to be a partner in a law firm before he turned thirty-one didn't let much get in his way.

He braced himself. "Ms. Cartwright, I am not here to eat brownies. I am here to talk to you about the will of the late Walter Stoddard."

Maddy Cartwright stilled. "I know," she said, and it was as if a fizzing glass of soda had instantly gone flat. Even the brilliance of her hair seemed to dim. "I've been dreading it."

Dreading it? Tom looked intently at her face, watching for excitement, anticipation, gloating greed. But all he saw was a profound sadness in her eyes and a downturn of her bow-shaped pink mouth.

"I still can't believe he's gone," she said in a voice that wasn't quite steady.

Tom's eyes narrowed. Why would she say that? Shouldn't she be turning cartwheels of joy?

"Is there somewhere we can discuss this? Now. It's important," he said.

She gestured with the oven mitt around her living room. "We could talk in here, but I really have to rescue the brownies first. Just let me dash to the kitchen, I'll be back in a minute."

Still stunned by the reality of Madeline Cartwright—oven mitt and all—Tom paced impatiently as he waited for her. Not that there was much room for pacing.

Her living room was small and decorated in a style Tom could only call twenty-first-century girly. It was way too cluttered for his taste. The walls were painted pale blue; the squashy old sofa covered in a faded floral print; and blue-and-white-patterned china was propped on every surface. On the narrow mantelpiece, tucked between a small vase of pink rosebuds and a framed photo of a smiling older woman, was a china statuette of a pony.

There were piles of cookbooks and copies of *Martha Stewart Living* and *Bon Appétit* magazines stacked haphazardly on the floor. A well-thumbed copy of food writer Anthony Bourdain's *Kitchen Confidential* lay on the dollhouse-sized coffee table alongside an ancient, yellowing *The Lily Wallace New American Cook Book*.

The room made him feel distinctly uncomfortable.

So did Madeleine Cartwright.

She wasn't at all what he'd been expecting. Not cunning but cute. Pretty, not predatory. More Reese Witherspoon than Paris

Hilton. In fact, if he were meeting her under any other circumstances, he might have been tempted to ask her out.

But, although as a lawyer he strove to be impartial, he found what he suspected she had done despicable. And he couldn't get past that. She couldn't be more than twenty-five or twenty-six, and his client Walter Stoddard had been eighty-two. Yech! It made his thirty-year-old flesh crawl to think of it.

A sudden thought had him abruptly stop his pacing. Where was the dog? That all-important dog. He looked around the room for evidence of canine occupation.

He detected a gnawed corner of the sofa and a much-chewed toy gorilla that could indicate the animal was in residence.

But thoughts of the dog fled as Maddy Cartwright came back into the room. Her face was free of flour. She had discarded the apron. While her breasts weren't pumped up as he'd expected, they rounded out her pink T-shirt nicely. *Very* nicely. He tried not to look. Or at least make it not too obvious he was looking.

She was carrying a plate of brownies. Cholesterol city. They looked like they were studded with macadamia nuts. His favorite. Tom felt his mouth water. How long since he'd allowed himself an indulgence like that?

"I thought you could try one of these with coffee after we'd had our discussion," she said in that gently chiming voice.

After? So she was not only a temptress but also a torturess. "Right." He nodded. "After."

He steeled himself not to drool at the luscious chocolate squares. Or the equally luscious woman who had baked them.

★　★　★

Maddy perched on the edge of her favorite white cane chair opposite Tom O'Brien as he maneuvered himself onto her love seat. Her caller was way too big and rugged to look at ease in her tiny room.

He looked more like a soccer player than a lawyer, his expensive suit slightly rumpled, his silk tie a bit askew as if he would be more comfortable in sweats kicking a ball around than discussing the legal ramifications of an old man's will. His muscles were the serious kind—she hadn't failed to appreciate that when she'd held on to him for balance.

With his strong-jawed face, hair the color of richest dark chocolate, and deep brown eyes, he was so good-looking he'd made her heart flip like an expertly turned pancake when she'd opened the door to him. Made her completely forget she was wearing that darn oven mitt.

She forced herself to sit still and to look attentive for Tom O'Brien. What a ditz he must think her. Stupid, stupid, stupid to try to shake a guy's hand while wearing an oven mitt. And she hadn't realized she had flour all over her face. To top that off she'd nattered on about her brownies. Like some kind of retro housewife. Only without the house or the husband.

The oven mitt had blown it for her. She suppressed a sigh of regret. Too late to explain that when she was feeling down she found solace in the familiar rhythms of baking. Too late to make a good first impression on Tom O'Brien.

Surreptitiously she checked him out as he pushed away a pretty beaded cushion from the sofa as if it would contaminate him.

On the handsome hunk scale, Tom O'Brien's needle was

soaring past a ten. Pity he had to be so . . . disapproving. In the minutes since they'd met, the lawyer hadn't smiled once. He seemed way too grim for a man his age—which she guessed to be perhaps a few years older than herself. Maybe he'd majored in grim at law school.

He hadn't actually said anything, but she didn't need to be super-perceptive to sense that Tom O'Brien disapproved of her—disapproved of the way she looked, disapproved of the way she decorated, even disapproved of her brownies. She caught him casting sideways glances at the plate as if it were stacked with squares of poison.

Heck, there was something untrustworthy about a man who could pass on a brownie. Especially her super-duper new recipe—star of her next magazine feature, "The Ultimate Chocolate Fix."

She was hoping readers of *Annie* magazine would succumb to their triple-chocolate charm and take her another step toward her goal: to be the cooler, more hip Martha Stewart for a new generation.

But her special recipe wasn't making a good impression on Walter's dour lawyer. Why did Tom O'Brien have to be so humorless? Maybe he was one of those guys who took himself and his career so seriously there was no time for indulgences or fun. She'd met too many of that type since she'd found herself floundering in the dating pool again.

Studiously ignoring the brownies, Tom O'Brien hauled his briefcase onto the small coffee table between them and pulled out some official-looking papers.

At the sight of them her spirits fell like a mistimed soufflé.

There could be only one reason why Walter's lawyer should want to meet with her—to evict her from the apartment. She dreaded what he would say.

She tried to fill the silence with small talk. "I ... I didn't know Walter had left a will until your phone call yesterday."

"Really," he said, shuffling with the papers.

She was startled at the obvious disbelief that underlined his voice. "Why would I know anything about it?"

"You were close, weren't you?" he said, tight-lipped.

Close? Of course they were close. Walter had been like a grandfather to her. But there was something odd about Tom O'Brien's tone. And she disliked the way he didn't meet her gaze when he spoke.

She steeled herself to speak calmly. "Walter is ... was my landlord. You probably know he lived in the house above—this apartment used to be the maids' quarters years ago."

Number 23A was small, inconvenient, and being in illustrious Pacific Heights, away from most of her friends who lived in hipper, cheaper parts of town. Two years ago she'd seen it as a temporary refuge, a place to hide and salve the wounds from her broken engagement.

Now the pretty apartment tucked underneath the once-grand old house had become home. She felt like weeping at the thought of leaving. Instead she took a deep breath. And then let her words out in a rush.

"So. Hit me with the bad news. Straight. I guess the house will be sold—and this apartment with it. How long have I got before I have to move out? I hope you give me a decent notice period—it won't be easy to find somewhere where I can keep a dog."

Tom O'Brien leaned forward, his carefully schooled face finally showing some animation. "The dog? You've got Walter's dog?"

She bristled. "Well, of course I've got him. And it's not against the terms of my lease if that's what you're implying. Walter asked me to look after him when . . . when he . . ."

She intended to sound tough, assertive. But she choked up at the memory of Walter's concern that his pet would end up in a shelter. Or worse.

Tom O'Brien shifted uncomfortably on the sofa. Officious as he was, she felt a twinge of pity for him. It must be difficult having to evict people. He probably hadn't realized he'd be evicting a bereaved dog as well as a human tenant.

He watched her intently through narrowed eyes. "So you knew about the will after all."

His suspicious tone instantly destroyed any sympathy she had felt for him. Why didn't he just get to the point and do whatever lawyers did when they evicted people? And dogs.

"I told you I knew nothing about Walter's will." Why would she? This guy was beginning to bug her.

Tom O'Brien's words were scored with disbelief. Of the scathing variety. His mouth was set in tight lines. "So, Ms. Cartwright, you're seriously telling me that you didn't know Walter Stoddard left his fortune to his dog, Brutus? Because I'm finding it very hard to believe you."

· Two ·

Tom O'Brien's words came from left field. Maddy stared at the big, handsome man taking up so much room in her apartment. "What?" was all she could manage to say through her shock.

Then she felt a bubble of laughter starting in her throat. It burst into a peal of giggles. "He what?" She giggled again. "His fortune? To Brutus? You're kidding me."

The lawyer's stone-faced expression told her that he was not.

"What a hoot! Is there enough for him to go wild and buy a new collar?"

Still Tom O'Brien didn't crack a smile. In fact, he looked affronted at her laughter.

"Brutus could buy himself a diamond-studded dog collar if he wanted to, Ms. Cartwright." He cleared his throat. "That is, if a dog could, er . . . shop."

He looked annoyed at himself for making such a flippant comment. "Walter Stoddard was a very wealthy man."

Maddy tried not to laugh again. Tom O'Brien was looking so serious that she felt she couldn't give in to the grin that was tugging insistently at the corner of her mouth.

"Are you sure you've got the right Walter? This one didn't have a cent to spare."

Of course she'd never inquired into his finances—she wouldn't have dreamed of doing that—but her elderly landlord had always been very careful with his spending and she'd assumed money was tight.

Tom O'Brien's sober brown gaze didn't falter. Nor did his carefully paced words. "Walter Stoddard was a multimillionaire."

"A . . . a millionaire? No way," she said, shaking her head again, "you've got it wrong."

Tom O'Brien laughed a short, not-very-nice laugh. "Believe me, Ms. Cartwright, Walter was worth a *lot* of money. That's why I'm here."

All of a sudden Maddy didn't want to laugh anymore. And she couldn't speak. Was this guy for real?

Tom O'Brien cleared his throat. "Uh, are you all right, Ms. Cartwright?" He reached out a hand to her and then, as if he thought better of it, withdrew it.

Maddy shook her head slowly from side to side. "I . . . I think I'm in a state of shock. Tell me that again. Walter—a wealthy man?"

"A multimillionaire," Tom O'Brien stressed.

"You're sure about that?" She was glad she was sitting down.

"There's no doubt."

Was she going crazy? "But he lived so simply. Frugally even. Why would he have done that if he had lots of money?"

Tom O'Brien shrugged his broad, soccer-player shoulders.

"Beats me. Eccentric, I guess. He only confided in me as his attorney on the condition I kept his financial affairs secret until after he died and his will was read."

Maddy's mind was reeling. She forced herself to sift back through her memories for a clue to Walter's wealth that she may have missed.

She thought of her old landlord, remembering his gentle wit, his keen observations, and his kindness. How she'd get cranky with him for spending more on the dog than he did on himself. He'd worn the same shabby old cardigan the entire time she'd known him.

"Walter asked me to adopt Brutus after . . . after he went. Of course I agreed, though to tell you the truth, I'm more into cats. But he never said anything about money."

"Yeah, well. For his own reasons, he didn't want anyone to know." Tom O'Brien paused. "Maybe he wanted to be liked for himself."

Was that a loaded question? "He shouldn't have had any doubts on that score. He was a real sweetie . . . I miss him terribly."

Maddy bit down on her bottom lip to stop it from quivering. She'd cried buckets over Walter in private. She wasn't about to make a public display of her grief in front of this person who seemed to be implying that there was something untoward about her relationship with her landlord.

The lawyer cleared his throat. "He seemed a charming gentleman."

"He . . . he was. And compos mentis until the very end. I still can't believe he was rich and left it all to his dog."

She started to twist around the antique amethyst ring she wore on the fourth finger of her right hand.

"So," she said slowly, thinking out loud. "I guess this changes things, doesn't it? For me, I mean."

Tom O'Brien nodded.

Maddy continued to muse out loud. "If Brutus is a millionaire dog, he won't need to live with me. I've gotten really fond of him. But, truth is, not having an animal in tow will make it easier for me to find another apartment."

She felt sad at saying good-bye to Brutus. Really sad. But there was relief, too. San Francisco landlords weren't known for their fondness for dogs. Much as she loved animals, there wasn't really room for a pet in her lifestyle.

She braced herself. "So, when do I have to pack up and go?"

"You don't," Tom O'Brien said.

"I don't?"

He stood up. Maddy stood up, too, so they were more evenly matched. She didn't like him towering above her, though even when she stretched herself to her full height he was still a lot taller than she was.

"Ms. Cartwright, let's cut to the chase." His expression didn't change. In fact, it turned a further degree of grim. "Under the terms of Walter Stoddard's will, you are Brutus's legally appointed guardian. Trustee of the fortune Walter left for the upkeep of his dog."

Maddy stared at him. Again. Her eyes opened even wider than the last time.

"Now you're really putting me on. Dogs don't have guardians."

"This one does." He put up his hand to forestall any further interruptions. "If the dog survives Mr. Stoddard by twenty-one days, as trustee you will have full control of his fortune."

Maddy felt as though the breath had been punched out of her body.

"What?"

She sat right back down on her chair feeling light-headed, dizzy.

"What did you say?"

"Do you want me to repeat it?"

Maddy nodded. Tom O'Brien repeated.

"I . . . I still don't understand." Walter had been a just and honest landlord and a friend. Or as good as a friend could be with a fifty-six-year age difference. But why this?

"Mr. Stoddard's fortune is held in trust for the dog—a trust administered by you, with provision for you."

"For me. I don't get it? Why me?"

"Let me read the will to you." He rustled the pages and—rather self-importantly, Maddy thought—cleared his throat.

Tom read out the terms of the will in careful, measured tones, trying not to let his disgust filter through. Through her guardianship of the dog, this redheaded gold digger was set with a fortune.

The straightforward document didn't take long to read. Apart from a sizeable bequest to his church, Walter had left the bulk of his fortune in trust for Brutus. When the trust ended—on the death of the dog or after ten years—the residual funds went direct to Madeleine Cartwright.

"That's it?" Maddy asked.

He nodded.

"I . . . I'm still in shock . . ." she said.

He had to give it to her. She did sound shocked. And her face had drained of all color. But then she might be a very good actress. Heaven knows what she'd done to convince Walter Stoddard to include her in his will. Had she had to feign passion for a man that age? Or had it come naturally?

"What if I don't want . . . want the responsibility?"

What? The Miss Innocent act was going too far.

"Give up an inheritance like that? Surely not."

"But it's Brutus who's inheriting."

"Didn't you understand? It's you who will control the money."

She covered her face with her hands. "I'm still trying to take it in. Why me?"

"Only you know that," he said, not letting his thoughts stray to what this pretty young woman might have done to gain such a windfall. Had she gone all the way? Or just performed other . . . services?

She dropped her hands from her face and looked over to Tom, forehead screwed up. "Walter said in the will I was the granddaughter he never had. He . . . used to say that when he was alive . . ."

As if, thought Tom.

"He didn't have any children," said Maddy, her voice hesitant. "His only child died when she was a toddler. Once I asked him if he had any relatives; he said none he cared to know about."

"So he said in his meeting with me." Walter had been very clear about that. Even naming names.

Maddy seemed to be thinking out loud. "Brutus was his baby. I'm not surprised he wanted his dog looked after. But . . . I would have happily done it for nothing. He knew that."

Sure he had.

"Are you certain this isn't a joke? I still can't believe it's happening."

Tom nodded. "Believe it."

"Are you sure it's legal?"

"Yes. California law allows trusts for pets as a provision in a will."

She shook her head disbelievingly. "It's still sinking in."

"You heard the terms of the will—as executor, it's my duty to make sure Brutus survives the twenty-one days. Well, seventeen now."

Maddy Cartwright chewed on her bottom lip. He had to admit she was very convincing. "Tell me again what happens if Brutus doesn't survive?"

"You get a very substantial inheritance and the rest goes to a dogs' home."

The color flooded back into her face. "So it's a win–win situation for me?"

Yes, and that's the way Walter Stoddard had wanted it. He'd made that very clear to Tom on the one and only occasion they'd met just a month ago. Tom had assumed that the lucky young woman in question had been the old man's mistress.

Walter Stoddard had been clever. Leaving his fortune in trust for the dog rather than directly to the young girlfriend made it more difficult for disgruntled relatives to contest the will. It was difficult for a dog to be seen as having undue influence over an old man's dying wishes.

"You do understand that during those seventeen days I have to assess your suitability as Brutus's guardian?"

Maddy was silent for a long moment, looking down at her

sneaker-clad feet. When she looked up at him again, Tom was surprised at the tight set of her face and the downward twist to her mouth.

"You think I influenced Walter with his will, don't you?" she said.

"I didn't say that."

"You don't have to," she said.

Tom was glad he wasn't the type to blush. His imaginings had definitely been of the lurid variety. He knew how foolish an older man could be over a pretty young face—and body. His father had been proof of that.

He cleared his throat. "One way or the other, whatever the reason, Walter Stoddard wanted his money to be yours."

Her chin went up at a tilt. "Huh! And you disapprove. I sensed your hostility the second you got here."

"Hostility? I'm not hostile toward you, Ms. Cartwright."

Her mouth twisted. "Don't bother lying. You're entitled to think what you want. And I'm sure you won't be the only one . . ."

He tried to interrupt, but she spoke over him.

"I'm not naïve. A rich old man. A poor young woman. Well, not poor, but living-from-paycheck-to-paycheck type average. For heaven's sake, Walter was eighty-two! But some people have sick minds. I know what they'll say when they hear about the will."

Tom stopped fiddling with the catch on his briefcase. He was surprised at the sudden sympathy for her that surged through him. Somehow, he wanted to believe in the girl next door she gave every appearance of being.

"Walter was so kind to me. If I was the granddaughter he never had, he was the grandfather I never had. But I'm stunned beyond belief that he's been so generous to me."

She got up from her chair. Tom was shocked at how pale she was. Her fair skin looked almost translucent, the scattering of freckles across the bridge of her nose standing out starkly in contrast.

In a nervous gesture, she pushed her marmalade-colored hair back from her face. "But I don't expect you to believe that. You've obviously made up your mind about me."

Tom wasn't as sure of her motives as he'd been before he'd knocked on her door. But he was still suspicious enough of her not to deny her accusation. Instead he made a noncommittal, lawyerlike murmur.

Her hands were trembling as she picked up the plate of brownies. "I need to think about all this. I'll go get a snack to take out to Brutus. Try and tempt him to eat."

Without really looking at him, she halfheartedly offered the plate to Tom. "I'm not hungry. You have one if you like. They're good." Her words were stilted, as if speaking to him were an effort. As if maybe she were fighting against tears.

Tom swallowed against a dry mouth. He took the plate. But all of a sudden he didn't feel like eating. Even a macadamia-studded, chocolate-laden brownie.

What if he really was wrong about Madeleine Cartwright? Like he had, people would think the worst of her. There would be gossip, speculation. A millionaire dog and its beautiful young guardian would make news. The newspapers would want to dig for dirt.

If she was as innocent of intent as she said she was—hell, even if she wasn't—the next weeks would be unpleasant ones for her. "Uh, no, thanks. I'll pass," he muttered.

But still, he had his duties as executor to consider. And that meant not being sucked in by her story until he could be 100 percent sure of her good intentions. Apart from his desire for moral justice, it was in his own best interests to do so.

Walter Stoddard had insisted that if Brutus survived the twenty-one days, a substantial bonus would be added to Tom's fee. The dollars should impress the senior partners in Jackson, Jones, and Gentry enough to elevate him to partner. And that promotion was what he wanted above all else.

Brutus had to live.

He watched her as she headed for the kitchen, unable to stop himself again from admiring the view. But when he saw what she brought back as a snack for the dog, all such thoughts fled. Alarmed, he stood up.

He looked at the pink-frosted cupcake in Maddy's hand. He thought of the dog's arteries. "Are you sure you should be giving that to Brutus?"

Maddy Cartwright's smile was tight. "He's got a serious sweet tooth. I want him to think it's a human cupcake—like Walter used to give him for his birthdays. But this one is stuffed with grated apple, alfalfa, and dog vitamins."

"As well as butter and sugar and eggs?"

"Eggs are good for dogs. Don't worry, I'm not trying to poison him."

"Uh. I didn't say that."

Damn! What was the matter with him? Where was his lawyer

cool? He was getting confused here. There was something about this woman's candid green eyes and lovely face that was turning his thoughts upside down.

"Come outside with me and check I don't lace the cupcake with arsenic on the way, why don't you," she said, much too sweetly for the look of loathing she was casting his way.

"Yes, I will. Well, not to check up on you but to—" Mentally, Tom slammed himself on the side of the head. What a dumbass thing to say.

He followed it with worse. "But to meet Brutus. Yes, to meet Brutus. He is—in a manner of speaking—my client after all."

Did that sound damn pompous or what? Why did being around this girl make his words come out so wrong? Was it because he was finding it impossible not to notice that her body-hugging T-shirt didn't quite meet the top of her low-slung jeans and the gap revealed a few tantalizing inches of creamy skin? Or to keep from staring at the arching fullness of her mouth?

But Madeline Cartwright just looked at him with a smile so cool it was almost pitying.

"Brutus is trained to shake paws," she said. "I'll tell him to behave in a businesslike manner."

Brutus. Great name for a dog. A German shepherd? Doberman? Not a Rottweiler, Tom hoped. Too big and unpredictable. After all, he'd be working with him for the next seventeen days. He'd like him to be a breed he felt happy with.

Damn! His fists clenched by his sides. This was a dog he was talking about. A four-legged dumb animal. How had a corporate attorney fast-tracking to the top gotten mixed up with this weirdo will? And stuck with a dog named Brutus for a client?

Tom hadn't studied any protocol regarding a canine client in law school. And nothing he'd learned since graduating had taught him how to handle the contradictory and much-too-appealing Madeleine Cartwright.

He had a feeling that the next seventeen days might not be as straightforward as he had imagined.

· Three ·

Maddy was way too aware of Tom O'Brien following her out of her apartment. After all, six feet two inches of broad-shouldered hunk didn't come knocking on her door every day.

She had a weakness for good-looking men. And Walter's attorney—or was he Brutus's attorney?—was so handsome he should have warning bells attached that went off when she found herself admiring him for longer than a second or two.

In her experience, excessively good-looking men were too interested in themselves to have anything much left over for the women in their lives. Next time around she'd be seeking out bald, tubby, glasses even. A man who would support her ambitions. And who she wouldn't have to fight for space in front of the mirror.

But that didn't stop her from appreciating a prime male specimen. Pity this one appeared to be so humorless and officious. Why had Walter picked an attorney like Mr. Takes-Himself-So-Seriously Tom O'Brien?

Mentally, she answered her own question. Because he was the son of Walter's friend Helen O'Brien from his church. On the occasions Maddy had met Helen, the older woman had never failed to boast about her super-successful—and single—lawyer son.

Maybe Walter hadn't realized what a stuffed shirt the boy wonder was when he'd decided to consult him for legal advice.

Maddy fought off an errant thought—Tom O'Brien's shirt was actually stuffed with the most amazing muscles. The guy was built.

Not that she should be noticing. Or touching. Men had a nasty habit of getting in the way of what she wanted to achieve. And she wanted to achieve a lot.

Her plan was in place: step one, food editor on a glossy magazine; step two, her own television cooking show. Why not aim high? Right now she was getting the kind of career break she'd only ever dreamed of.

Her success as chef at one of San Francisco's most fashionable restaurants had brought her to the attention of the editor in chief of bestselling young women's magazine *Annie*.

The magazine was published in San Francisco and had become a real player in the national market alongside titles published in New York City. She'd been approached to stand in as food editor while the regular food editor was on maternity leave. That was nearly a year ago. Now that editor had decided to resign and stay home with her baby, and Maddy was being considered for the permanent appointment. She was raring to go. And nothing—certainly not a man—was going to get in her way.

Until she'd gotten where she wanted to be, she'd sworn off

all but the most casual of dating. Since her split from too-handsome Russell—who had only pretended to support her ambitions—she hadn't broken her two-date-max rule. Or been tempted to.

Tom O'Brien politely opened the door for her and ushered her through the back door of her apartment. Her best friend, Serena, and she always rated the new men they met. For manners, she'd give this one ten out of ten. For manner—zero. Undeniably gorgeous—but way too stiff and formal for a guy his age. No temptation at all.

She paused at the top of the back porch steps, knowing that he would want to gasp at the view. People always did.

He gasped.

Wow, what a view, she whispered in her head.

"Wow! What a view," said Tom.

There wasn't a trace of fog and the view from Walter's back garden encompassed San Francisco Bay right through to the Golden Gate Bridge. Maddy never tired of admiring the scene. She was a country girl from the mountains close to the Oregon border, but now she'd tasted city life, she was hooked.

"Talk about a million-dollar view," said Tom O'Brien, with a whistle of admiration. "Correction. More a multimillion-dollar view."

Maddy was taken aback at his mercenary comment. "I guess so. I hadn't actually thought to put a value on a view. I just enjoy it."

He looked at her through narrowed eyes. "Come on, this is Pacific Heights. How could you think Walter Stoddard was poor when he lived in a house like this?"

Maddy felt herself flush. She was disappointed and angry at

Tom O'Brien's inference. It was insulting to both herself and to Walter's memory.

"I actually didn't give it much thought except to be grateful that my rent was so reasonable for such a great part of town. And if you look a little closer, you'll see the house is very run-down and shabby."

She was gratified to see that he looked uncomfortable at her reply, shifting from one foot to another. "He probably bought the house years ago, anyway," he mumbled, "before prices really boomed."

"He did," she said. "When he got married, he told me. His wife loved the view, too, apparently. But that's not getting me anywhere with Brutus, is it?"

It was crazy to feel hurt by what Tom O'Brien had said but she did. She had to bite on her bottom lip to stop it from trembling. She turned her back on him so he couldn't see what she was feeling.

"I'll see if I can tempt Brutus out with the cupcake," she said, walking down the stairs.

"Tempt him out?"

She stopped and turned back to him. "Don't you know? Brutus is in mourning. I'm worried sick about him."

"The dog is in mourning?" Tom O'Brien's brows drew together in a frown.

"Ever since Walter passed away. Brutus howled and howled the day his master died. He knew before anyone else did. Animal intuition, you know."

"Uh, right," said Tom.

She didn't like the way he said that. But then lawyers were a skeptical lot, she supposed. And judgmental if this guy was an example.

"He hasn't come out of his kennel. And he won't eat, no matter what I tempt him with."

"Have you sought help?"

She couldn't stop herself from a sharp reply. "Of course I have. I got the vet here the next day. Her diagnosis was that Brutus is suffering from a broken heart."

"A broken heart," Tom spluttered. "A dog with a broken heart?"

"Is that so stupid?"

"Yes," he said, "it sounds damn stupid to me."

"The vet didn't think so. She said there's also another problem. Brutus is missing his alpha male."

"His alpha male? What kind of garbage is that?"

Maddy felt affronted at his reply. Was rudeness also part of his lawyer's stock-in-trade? "Brutus's vet happens to be a leading expert in animal psychology if you must know. She even has a *Pets on the Couch* program on the radio."

Tom groaned. "So Brutus is seeing a shrink. This I've got to see."

Maddy gritted her teeth. "It's true. The alpha-male thing, that is. I checked it on the Internet. A dog is a pack animal. All the dogs in the pack are subservient to the alpha male. In the human world, Walter was a kind old man. But to Brutus he was leader of the pack."

"Leader of the pack? Well, now I've heard everything."

"Not quite. The vet said Brutus could pine away and die of grief if he didn't soon attach to another alpha male."

Tom made a sound that could have been disgust or could have been a smothered laugh.

"Well, that's what the vet told me," she said. "I'm no expert on dogs."

"Die of grief? If this is true, it could be serious—especially in light of Walter's will."

"Tell me about it. But right now all I care about is this poor, sad animal and how I can get him to eat something."

Maddy followed the length of the porch and turned the corner of the house to where Brutus's kennel was located under the shade of a magnificent jacaranda tree. A sprinkling of purple jacaranda flowers had fallen onto the roof of the kennel. It was very quiet.

Her heart sank. No Brutus rushing up to meet her, sniffing around for snacks. This dog was normally a trash can on legs. With an overdeveloped sweet tooth. He must really be sick not to have sniffed out the treat she held in her hand. The hunger strike thing was a worry.

"C'mon, Brutus, C'mon, boy, I've got a nice snack for you," she coaxed. But there was no response.

She was conscious of Tom O'Brien behind her, imagined she could almost feel his warm breath on the back of her neck.

"Is he in his kennel?"

Maddy nodded. "But he won't come out for me. Not even for a frosted cupcake. Why don't you call him? If the vet is right, he might respond to a man's voice."

Tom O'Brien approached, giving the large kennel a wide berth. "Is it vicious?" he asked.

"Vicious? He's a good watchdog. Barks a lot."

"I'd better approach with caution then."

Approach with caution. From the little she knew of Tom O'Brien, Maddy suspected those words just might sum up his entire attitude to life. But did he really need to tippy-toe around the kennel like that?

As she watched him, a suspicion began to form.

"What kind of dog do you think Brutus is?"

"With a name like that I thought maybe a German shepherd."

"Right. Or a Doberman, perhaps?"

"Yes. Or Rottweiler. Uh, he's not trained to kill, is he? Like, he won't go for the throat if I call him?"

"You can only try it and see," said Maddy, her stifled laugh making Tom O'Brien cast a sharp glance at her.

Self-consciously, he cleared his throat. "Uh, here, Brutus. Come on." His voice was sufficiently deep and commanding.

Maddy could hear a shuffling and a clinking of dog tags from the kennel.

"Here he comes!" she said, her voice rising in excitement. "It worked, the male voice worked."

Tom O'Brien stepped cautiously back.

Brutus slunk slowly on his belly out of the kennel, making little whimpering noises as he fixed his black button eyes on the tall, well-built man who stood in front of his kennel.

Maddy had to put her hand to her mouth to kill her laughter at Tom's disbelieving expression.

"*That* is Brutus?" he said.

"Meet your new client."

Tom paused for a long moment before he spoke. "Walter must have had a real sense of humor to christen this animal Brutus."

"You could say that."

Maddy could only guess at what was going through the lawyer's mind as he stared at the little dog's long, low-slung body, pugnacious face, and scruffy black-and-ginger-brindled fur.

His face wasn't giving much away. "I guess I'll have to rethink Rottweiler," he said.

"Walter used to call Brutus a Heinz type of dog—you know, fifty-seven varieties."

"At least fifty-seven by the look of him."

"He's slung so low to the ground he must be part dachshund."

"The coloring looks bulldog."

"But I think there's a lot of shih tzu in him, too."

"What? You're saying the dog's full of sh—?"

"I said shih tzu. A Tibetan lion dog. See the way his bottom teeth jut out from beneath his top teeth? The vet says that's a fault of the shih tzu breed."

Miracle of miracles, a smile was beginning to tug at the corners of Mr. Way-Too-Serious Tom O'Brien's mouth. It lit up his eyes with humor and changed his face completely from grim to gorgeous.

And for a moment Maddy was so entranced by the dimple that formed in Tom O'Brien's cheek as he smiled that she didn't think about Brutus at all.

Until Tom spoke again. "Brutus is the ugliest dog I have ever seen," he said.

Maddy glared at him. "Hey! You didn't hear that, Brutus. Avert your ears," she said, bending down to stroke Brutus's head.

Then she glared again at Tom. "That doesn't help matters, does it? We're trying to build up trust here."

Again the grin pulled at his mouth. "As if the dog could understand me."

"You never know. He might have."

"Huh," said Tom. "But you've got to admit I'm right. About how ugly he is, I mean."

"Weeell," Maddy said. "He's quite a mix. But I wouldn't call him ugly. Exactly. More . . . unusual, perhaps?"

"Ugly." Tom snorted.

Brutus slunk on his belly right up to Tom and sniffed his feet in their well-polished business shoes. Then he wagged his long, plumed tail so vigorously his whole body moved.

Maddy couldn't keep the amazement from her voice. "Hey, in spite of you insulting him, I think he really likes you."

"Well, I don't like him," Tom said. "I like big dogs. Man-sized dogs."

"How can you say that?" Maddy's voice rose in accusation. "This is so great. It's the first spark of interest the little guy has shown in anyone since Walter died."

She had to stop herself from dancing around the dog—and Tom O'Brien—in excitement.

"C'mon. Speak to him like an alpha male. That's what the vet said to do. How are you at growling?"

"Growling?" he said.

"Like the top dog in the pack. You know, like this." She tried to growl deep in her throat. "Grrr. It won't work for me. I'm a girl. You need to talk to him like dogs talk to each other. Establish you're the boss."

Tom looked at her as if she should be certified. But his smile hadn't quite disappeared. Neither had the dimple.

"C'mon," she said. "You try it. Growl."

"Are you out of your mind? I'm not going to growl like a dog to a dog. No way."

He bent down and put his hand out for Brutus to sniff. "Hi there, fella."

At his deep tones, Brutus promptly rolled over on his back, panting, tail wagging madly.

"That's a pose of submission!" Maddy practically shouted. "Oh, this is so good. That means he's acknowledging that you're an alpha male. You didn't even have to growl."

The unbidden thought flashed across her mind of what she'd do if Tom O'Brien growled at her in a deep, sexy voice. And what he would do if she rolled over on her back in response.

To hide her sudden blush, she knelt down and rubbed the little dog's tummy. "Oh, good boy," she crooned.

Brutus squirmed excitedly and licked her hand.

Tom O'Brien didn't look the slightest bit impressed.

"What do you mean, 'good boy'? I'm *not* his alpha male."

"I was saying 'good boy' to Brutus, not you. But I can say it to you, too, if you like," she said, risking a flirtatious tone to her voice.

Since he'd encountered Brutus, Tom O'Brien had switched right out of grim lawyer mode. Now he was acting like a regular too-handsome-to-be-true thirty-year-old guy. And she liked it. A lot.

It was a major flaw in her character to only be attracted to handsome men. She knew that. But she just couldn't do ugly. Or even ordinary. And Tom O'Brien had never been anywhere near the ugly stick.

"You'd call me a good boy even though I didn't growl?"

"You didn't need to. He probably responded to your scent."

She liked the scent of him, too, she realized, a citrus after-shave mingled with something uniquely warm and male.

"My scent? Isn't that a bit far-fetched?" he said.

"No. It's all about instinct. Animal instinct. Do you realize that now Brutus has found a new leader of his pack he'll snap out of his mourning? That's what the vet said would happen, anyway."

Tom O'Brien was looking charmingly disconcerted, obviously not at all certain of how to react. It suited him so much better than his too-straight lawyer look. "Look here, I am not this dog's pack leader. I'm his lawyer . . . uh . . . that's not right, either.

"Dammit, I'm the executor of Walter Stoddard's will, and my responsibilities toward this animal only extend as far as making sure it stays alive and well for the next seventeen days. That's all."

"And that I'm a fit dog guardian. Don't forget that," Maddy prompted. She was discovering this big, so-serious guy responded beautifully to a bit of teasing.

He groaned. A loud how-the-hell-did-I-get-into-this-situation type groan that, surprisingly, endeared him to Maddy.

"That's right. That you're a fit guardian. But I am not—repeat—not this dog's alpha male or the leader of its pack."

She looked up at him, wide-eyed. "I'm afraid you are," she said. "Brutus has chosen you and that's that. You don't have a say in the matter."

She tried very hard not to laugh at the expression on Tom O'Brien's face.

Tom looked down at Maddy as she knelt by the dog. Her hair was burnished copper by the spring sunshine and he noted that she didn't wear any makeup. She didn't need to.

As she leaned over Brutus, her T-shirt pulled right up from her jeans and Tom couldn't keep his eyes from the enticing stretch of gently curved tummy it revealed. She had a great body—slim, but rounded in all the right places. He wondered what her legs were like.

Brutus was rolling his eyes in ecstasy as she energetically patted and stroked him, crooning endearments as she did so. Lucky dog. He wondered how it would feel if she—

Tom refused to let his thoughts go any further. He wrenched his gaze away from the sight of her hands caressing the dog's fur. Her fingers were long and slender, topped by practical, short-filed nails. Brutus obviously thought they felt great as he whimpered his appreciation.

Was she serious about this alpha-male thing? Tom couldn't be quite sure. She seemed earnest enough but her green eyes were dancing with mischief.

Or was it challenge?

Right. He was taking control of the wheel here.

He cleared his throat. Maddy's eyes widened with quick interest. "That was not a growl," he said.

"Oh," she said, "I thought you were going to try it."

"No!" He assumed his best lawyer voice. "You will never—I repeat—never hear me growling at a dog."

She pulled a disappointed face and again he couldn't be sure how serious she was.

"And furthermore, if we're to keep that dog alive, you can start by feeding it proper dog food—not cake."

"What? You're not serious? Brutus has such a sweet tooth."

"No cupcake," he said.

She glared at him. "That's ridiculous. He's been snacking on my baking ever since I moved in here."

As she argued, she held the cupcake up out of the little dog's reach. But it wasn't high enough. With surprising speed for an animal with stumpy, cabriole legs, Brutus suddenly leapt up, twisted in midair, and expertly snatched the treat from her hand. Maddy gasped and stepped back.

Brutus gobbled the snack down in one gulp and then looked up expectantly for more, begging with his black button eyes. He whimpered. He held up his paw to shake.

Maddy laughed triumphantly.

"Bad dog," said Tom.

"Sorry, Brutus," Maddy said to the animal, "No more. You've got a new leader of your pack now and he says no. How's about some yummy kibble instead?"

A dog whose favorite food was frosted cake? Spoiled and yappy, too, he'd bet. And that was on top of being the ugliest-looking animal Tom had ever seen. Had he done something terrible in a former life to be saddled with responsibility for its welfare?

Tom led his life according to plan—a carefully constructed five-year plan, in fact. He figured out goals and targets and went for them with unrelenting purpose. He'd started the first plan the year he turned eighteen. The year his father had left the family. Those carefully scripted plans had helped him restore order to the sudden chaos his life had become.

He didn't like to be diverted from the objectives he'd set himself. Not by an ugly, greedy, pint-sized dog. And certainly not by the maddeningly cute Maddy Cartwright, who might or might not be a coldhearted seductress of wealthy old men.

"Let's get this straight, I am not this dog's boss. I'm just—"

"His lawyer. I know. But I . . . uh . . . think he sees you as more than that, though right now he seems a little confused." Maddy's green eyes danced as she looked meaningfully toward Brutus.

Tom jerked back as he felt a movement around his ankles. He looked down. He swore. Brutus the millionaire mongrel was enthusiastically humping his leg.

· Four ·

Late the next morning, Tom walked slowly toward the small group of mourners gathered outside the grand old church. He felt uncomfortable at funerals—too much sentiment—but knew he had to pay his respects to Walter Stoddard.

He spied his mother, tall and elegant in a dark hat. She broke away from the people she was talking to and hurried over.

"Glad you could come, darling," she murmured as he gave her a hug. "Everything's on schedule. Walter's other friends from the church are here, too. And Maddy, of course, sweet thing."

Tom followed his mother's gaze across to where a slim figure clad in black stood near the arched entrance to the church. A slim, yet very shapely figure whose short skirt showed off amazingly long, slender legs. Yeah. He'd guessed that under her blue jeans she'd been hiding great legs. Now his conjecture was confirmed.

"You know Maddy Cartwright?" he asked.

"Of course I do. She's lovely, isn't she?"

"Hmm," he grunted.

"She was so kind to Walter. She's a professional chef, you know—and a magazine food editor. Spoiled him with her wonderful cooking."

"I'm sure she did." Tom's words were underlined with irony, but his mother didn't seem to notice.

Obviously she didn't share any of his suspicions about Maddy Cartwright's "kind" treatment of Walter Stoddard. But then Helen O'Brien always saw the best in people. Had even taken back his dying father to nurse him, years after he'd run off with a much-younger woman and squandered the family's money on her. To this day Tom could not understand why she'd done that.

"Don't sound so grumpy about it, darling. I know doing Walter's will wasn't really your line of business, but when Walter found out my son was a lawyer—"

"It's okay, Mother, I didn't mind. Really."

He hardly heard his mother as he stared over at Maddy. Her hair glinted and shone in the sunshine, like a flame dancing around her head.

Tom had always had a thing for olive-skinned brunettes. But he had to admit that Maddy's unusual coloring was eye-catching. Witch's coloring. He'd read somewhere that the most dangerous witches of all had red hair and green eyes. She was looking up to her companion and chatting. But suddenly she dipped and swayed as if she were being pulled by some invisible force. Tom narrowed his eyes against the sun. Not an invisible force but a leash. And an animal straining against it.

"I don't believe it! She's brought that disgusting dog to the funeral."

Helen O'Brien laughed. "Father Andrew isn't too happy

about it, I can tell you. Brutus has been lifting his leg on every-thing he can see. Including Father's cassock. Hope he doesn't try it on the casket . . . you know, to say farewell."

This time Tom heard his mother loud and clear. He frowned. "Mother, I can't believe you said that."

Helen O'Brien laughed again. "Oh, loosen up, darling, you take everything so seriously these days."

Tom chose to ignore her. They'd had this conversation be-fore. Didn't his mother realize someone had to be the responsi-ble one in the family? Next she'd be trying to match-make him with some "very nice girl" she'd come across.

The race for a partnership at Jackson, Jones, and Gentry was all-important to him. It was vital both to prove something to himself and—deep down in a part of his psyche he didn't care to visit too often—to his father.

Before he'd gotten ill, his father had been a larger-than-life-sized character. Raymond O'Brien was forceful, always running toward risk, and Tom had hero-worshiped him. But when Tom reached adolescence, his dad grew scornful that his smart, serious, thoughtful son was not a chip off the rough-hewn, only-kind-of-man-to-be block. He became overly critical. *Stop thinking, son, and start doing or you'll never amount to anything.* Over and over he'd said that.

To be a partner at one of San Francisco's most prestigious law farms was *something*. Now Tom had the ball at his foot and nothing was going to stop him from putting it into the net. Why couldn't his mom realize that left little room for frivolities? Or for serious girlfriends.

He narrowed his eyes again. "Who is that guy Maddy is talk-ing to?"

His mother peered across. "The rather gorgeous dark-haired fellow? Don't have a clue. He's not from church. Maybe he's one of the undertakers. But he's not wearing a suit."

Tom didn't like the way Maddy was smiling at the stranger. Or the way he was standing so close to her.

Duh. Again Tom mentally slapped his forehead. Somehow he'd just assumed Madeleine Cartwright was single. But maybe she'd had a boyfriend in on the scam on the old man. And he'd come with her to the funeral to gloat.

"Hmm," said his mother, following his gaze. "Doubt he's an undertaker. I wonder who he is? Maddy doesn't have a boy-friend as far as I know."

Perhaps conscious of their combined scrutiny, Maddy turned in their direction, saw them, smiled, and waved with the hand that was not trying to rein in Brutus.

Tom scowled and gave an awkward kind of salute in return. He didn't like being caught gawking at her. Didn't want her to get the wrong idea. Like that he was attracted to her.

He was just checking her out because he was so suspicious of her. If she insisted on wearing such short skirts, he couldn't help staring at her legs.

The man next to her also turned and looked across. But he didn't wave. Or smile. It seemed all his smiles were directed to Maddy.

"Why don't you go over and find out who he is, Tom? I've got to look after a few of the old dears from Walter's bridge club. It's getting a bit hot for them to be standing around."

Tom walked as nonchalantly as he could across the church-yard. Damn! Why should he feel so self-conscious? What was it about this bewitching redhead that made him so concerned about how he appeared to her?

Yes, she was cute and funny and very different from the women he usually met. Maddy was the girl next door who stood out in a world of ambitious businesswomen jostling to bust through the glass ceiling. But that was no reason for him to let her turn his thoughts upside down the way she was doing.

As he neared her he caught his breath in surprised admiration. Makeup and a body-hugging black suit added a surprising sophistication to her homey image. Double damn. She looked more appealing than ever.

And, he realized, more seductive. More, perhaps, the type of woman who would go after what she wanted from an old man? His mouth was suddenly dry and he knew he was going to find it hard to rustle up casual words of greeting.

As it turned out, he didn't need them. Brutus caught sight of him. The ugly mutt jerked so vigorously away from Maddy that she let go of the leash. His stumpy legs moved with amazing speed toward Tom. Within seconds Brutus was yapping hysterically as he jumped up on Tom's legs, claws scrabbling painfully.

"Get down!" snapped Tom, pushing him off.

Great. What a sight. The deceased's lawyer, a soon-to-be (he hoped) new partner at Jackson, Jones, and Gentry, having his leg humped by a horny little mongrel in front of all the mourners.

Where was Maddy with the bucket of water? That's what it had taken yesterday to rid him of Brutus's attentions.

Maddy quickly covered the distance between them and grabbed the dangling leash.

"Sorry, I couldn't hold him." Her voice shook with repressed laughter, and her cheeks were flushed pink.

"Get him off me," Tom snapped, struggling with the tenacious animal. "And shut him up."

Maddy reached down and grabbed the little dog's collar.

"C'mon, Brutus," she said, hauling him away. The little dog danced around on his back paws, still yapping. "At least he didn't lift his leg on you like he did the priest."

Tom stepped back. "Didn't this damn dog ever go to puppy school?"

"He was, uh, expelled."

"Why doesn't that surprise me?"

Her green eyes were dancing. "Don't be so mean. The little guy's just excited to see his alpha male."

"For God's sake, don't say that when anyone else can hear," hissed Tom.

"Okay. His leader of the pack, then."

Tom groaned. "Don't say that, either. Keep the damn animal under control."

"But . . ."

"No buts. Just do it."

Maddy's eyes flashed. "Order the dog around, but don't think I leap to your command," she snapped, surprising him.

Nonetheless, she took the leash and tugged Brutus closer. "Can he sit by your feet? I think he just wants to be with you. You know, because you are his—"

"I said, don't say it," Tom warned through clenched teeth. "And keep him away from my legs."

She made to protest again but then obviously remembered

what had happened when the dog last got an intimate distance from Tom's leg. "Yeah. Okay. Sit, Brutus," said Maddy.

Brutus ignored her.

"Sit," said Tom. Immediately, Brutus shut up and sat down, his button eyes gazing up at Tom in devotion.

Maddy twisted the leash around her wrist to keep Brutus on a tight rein.

"Brutus, be good," she hissed at the dog. And stop treating Tom O'Brien's leg as if it were a girl dog. She couldn't blame Tom for scoffing at her alpha-male theories when Brutus persisted in that kind of gender-confused behavior.

"So, who is your date?" asked Tom.

"Date?" she said, surprised by the tight set of his mouth. "Who brings a date to a funeral?"

"The guy you were talking to."

She frowned. "He's not my date. I only just met him today. He's Walter's great-great-whatever-nephew. Jerome Stoddard. He's very nice."

Nice was an understatement. Jerome was gorgeous, with a sexy British accent that made her knees weak. The drought had definitely broken in San Francisco. From the sky had fallen, in as many days, two of the best-looking men she'd ever met.

"Hmm," said Tom in an undertone. "Walter warned me about him."

"What d'you mean, 'warned you'?"

"Confidential client information."

There spoke pompous Tom O'Brien, all right. She bristled.

"You can't just say that."

"Sure I can. I'm a lawyer, remember." Surely that wasn't a gleam of humor in his eyes?

"But you're also a human being, right? And it isn't fair to say things like that without following up on them. I want to know why Walter warned you against him."

"Just called him a leech."

"A leech?"

"After his money," said Tom. "He's heading over. You'd better introduce me."

Maddy did so, comparing the two men as they shook hands. Tom was so much bigger—taller and more broad-shouldered, his face strong jawed, his hair a little unruly.

Jerome—shorter, leaner—was way more sophisticated; sleek black hair, so good-looking he was almost beautiful with eyes so blue she wondered if he wore colored contacts.

In food terms, Tom was a hearty porterhouse steak, Jerome an escalope of salmon—each very different but equally delicious. Hmm. She'd find it difficult to choose if they were offered to her on a menu.

But, immediately, she sensed the men didn't like each other although it wasn't apparent in their polite exchange of introduction.

No, it was more in the way they sized each other up in a completely nonverbal way. The set of Tom's shoulders; the narrowing of Jerome's eyes. The two men reminded her of a wildlife film she'd seen of two stags circling each other in confrontation. Only the stags had been fighting over a doe.

"So you didn't know your uncle well?" asked Tom.

"No," said Jerome, "the English side of the family lost touch some years ago. I haven't been in the United States long but managed to track Uncle Walter down. How fortunate I managed to meet with him before he passed away." He sounded very sincere to Maddy.

"Indeed," said Tom, and Maddy was surprised at how noncommittal he was.

"Jerome's great-grandfather and Walter's father were brothers, isn't that right, Jerome?" she said.

"So that's the connection," said Tom in an icy tone.

Maddy looked from one man to the other, puzzled. She found Jerome charming not least because he resembled Walter. He didn't seem at all leechlike. In fact, he looked very like photographs Walter had shown her of himself as a young man.

But Tom obviously wasn't impressed and she wondered why. She'd have to quiz him further on what Walter had said about his great-great-whatever-nephew.

She noticed people starting to move inside the church. "I think we'd better be going in," she said.

"What about Brutus?" asked Tom.

"Ah, the millionaire mutt," said Jerome.

Maddy looked up sharply. Was it appropriate to call Brutus that?

Jerome leaned down to pet Brutus, but Brutus backed away from him and cowered behind Tom's ankles. His movement tugged on the leash and pulled her closer to Tom, right up against his rock-hard biceps. Her heart started racing at the contact. She felt light-headed as she breathed in his already-familiar male scent.

"Sorry. Brutus . . . he's shy with strangers," she found herself explaining awkwardly to Jerome as she extricated herself from the too-close proximity to Tom and his too-appealing muscles.

But Brutus hadn't been at all shy with Tom. Quite the opposite. For the little dog it had been hero worship at first sight.

"I'm sure he'll get used to me," said Jerome.

Get used to him? Maddy felt a little shiver of excitement. Was the gorgeous Jerome planning to get to know her better?

"Uh, sure," she said, forcing herself to sound nonchalant. "But right now we have to be going into the church."

"I'll join you in a moment," said Jerome, pulling his cell phone from his pocket. Odd. Why would he be calling someone when the funeral service was about to start?

His face inscrutable, Tom watched the other man walk around the corner. Then he looked pointedly down at Brutus.

"Are you going to tie him up outside the church?"

"No way," said Maddy. "Walter would have wanted him to be here."

"But would Father Andrew?" asked Tom, glancing to where the priest stood guard at the door.

Father Andrew glared at Brutus and then at her—even though she had offered to pay for the dry cleaning of his cassock.

"I know how much the dog meant to Walter so I'll let him inside. But keep him under control or he's out," warned the priest.

"I will, Father," she said meekly. "I should have brought a muzzle, I guess."

"It's the other end I'm worried about," said the priest, turning with a flourish of his robes.

Maddy could have kicked Tom for his smothered laugh.

· Five ·

Tom hadn't been inside a church for some time. The last time he'd been to this particular one had been for his father's funeral ten years ago.

He looked across the aisle to where his mother knelt serenely in prayer, lit by a shaft of sunlight streaming through the stained-glass windows. Was she remembering that long-ago service? His stepmother—if you could call someone barely older than himself a stepmother—hadn't even bothered to come.

And now here he was sitting beside another young woman whom he suspected of using her looks and youth to bamboozle a fortune out of an older man. He shifted uncomfortably, thinking he should excuse himself and go over to sit with his mother.

But there was Brutus. Subdued now, the dog sat on the pew between Tom and Maddy, and Tom had to admit that the animal was behaving impeccably.

Had Maddy been right that Brutus was in mourning for his

master? Did he instinctively know that Walter lay at rest in the imposing casket that sat beneath the altar? Or was this heartbreak thing, as Tom suspected, just so much hogwash?

As the priest commenced the service, Brutus maintained a reverential silence except for the odd clinking of his dog tags as he scratched behind his ears. Tom shifted uncomfortably at the thought of fleas.

His father's funeral service had been unbearably sad. Death had come prematurely from the same high cholesterol that Tom dreaded developing. The messy family situation had cast a pall over the proceedings. Tom had been racked with guilt over the anger he'd felt for his father and the pain at his loss.

Before his dad had discovered the stock market and the prizes his gambling instincts could net him as a trader, the family had lived in Denver, Colorado. Tom's happiest times had been when his dad took him horseback riding. Tom was a natural and basked in his dad's approval. All that stopped when they moved to San Francisco.

Tom took a deep breath, unaware that he had done so. Father and son had reached a shaky reconciliation before Raymond died. But that had not made the funeral any easier. His mother had sobbed nonstop through the service. His sister had refused to come, having disowned their father when he'd run off with wife number two.

But today was a very different funeral. Walter Stoddard had lived a long and fulfilled life. The church was packed with his friends and there was even laughter during the eulogy. Though no one seemed to know about the old man's millionaire status.

But Tom scarcely heard the words of the service. He rose, kneeled, and sang hymns on automatic pilot.

He was way too aware of Maddy, rising, kneeling, and singing hymns beside him. Of the swell of her breasts against her
sleek-fitting black jacket. Of the elegant curve of her calves outlined by fine black hose. Of her lavender scent now blended not
with chocolate but something else. Strawberries? What had she
been cooking? Even if it was onions he was convinced it would
smell good on her.

As they sang "The Lord's My Shepherd" he noticed her
beautiful full mouth tremble and tears escape and roll down her
cheeks. She sniffed and wiped them away with her fingers.

Tears unnerved him. He wanted to do something. Comfort
her. But what could he do? He was Walter's lawyer, and she was
shedding tears for a man old enough to be her grandfather.
Great-grandfather, for heaven's sake.

She sat down and, with shaking hands, pulled some crumpled
tissues from her purse. Tom sat, too. Brutus laid his head on
Tom's thigh and whimpered deep in his throat. Poor little devil.
His over-jutting jaw gave him such a pathetic appearance.

For the first time Tom felt a pang of sympathy for the animal.
He went to pet him. Maddy went to pet Brutus at the same
time and Tom found his hand on top of hers. He left his hand
there, hers warm and smooth beneath his palm. Her fingers
curled into Brutus's fur.

Tom turned to face her and found her looking mutely up at
him, her eyes puffy with tears, her nose red. She seemed fragile
and alone. Something seemed to turn deep inside him and he
felt overwhelmed by the urge to hug her and comfort her. To
stroke her hair and kiss away her tears.

He held her gaze for a moment longer than he knew he
should. Then he stopped himself. He must not get involved in

any way with this woman, not when he had such grave misgivings about her.

But he couldn't resist gently squeezing her hand before he took his away. For a moment longer, she left her hand on Brutus's neck where his head lay on Tom's leg.

As she caressed the dog, her fingers trailed along Tom's thigh. Tom felt himself respond—that surprising arousal he'd felt before at her touch. He felt a mixture of relief and disappointment when she took her hand away and folded both hands together on her lap.

He was angry with himself. How could he let himself get sexually aroused at a funeral? It wasn't right. Awkwardly he propped the hymnbook over his lap to disguise the evidence.

He stared straight ahead at the altar. The service was ending and the pallbearers were lifting the coffin onto their shoulders. Suddenly Brutus was gone, scrambling off Tom's lap and up the aisle. Maddy started forward but, on impulse, Tom stayed her. He wasn't sure why.

The little brindle dog trotted purposefully toward the casket and then sat on his hindquarters at its head. Startled, the pallbearers stopped their procession. Brutus began to howl—a long, heartrending howl that made the hairs stand up on the back of Tom's neck.

Maddy clutched Tom's arm. There was a stunned silence in the church so that Brutus's wailing reverberated around the walls. Then he gave a final whimper and was still, laying his head on his front paws. Shocked murmurs rose in a wave around him.

Tom got up and walked up the aisle. "Brutus," he said in his best alpha-male voice. Brutus looked mournfully up at him.

Then he trotted obediently to Tom and rested his head against his leg.

Tom picked the animal up and carried him back to his pew. He left him on his lap, unable to say anything for the emotions that were churning inside him.

Maddy was right. This ugly, greedy creature, which humped inappropriately, peed indiscriminately, and had who knew what other dreadful habits, had suffered a very real loss.

But while Maddy had been empathic enough to sense the innocent animal's pain, Tom had ridiculed it. Tom, partner-to-be, always prided himself on developing a good understanding with the people he dealt with on a professional basis. So far, he'd bombed out badly with his new canine client.

Sniffing back her tears, Maddy ruffled and caressed the dark fur around Brutus's neck in silence as the church emptied respectfully around them.

She didn't speak until everyone else had gone.

"Poor little guy," she whispered to Brutus, "but it's all right, you've got me now." She turned to Tom. "Thank heaven you were here," she said.

"Yeah," he said. "I guess."

Aware of being in church Maddy spoke in a hushed voice. She wouldn't tease Tom about the leader-of-the-pack thing. They were past that now. She could see the hunky big lawyer was shaken by Brutus's performance.

"You . . . you were right about the mourning," he said.

She nodded in agreement. "Incredible wasn't it? Pure instinct.

Cathartic." Her voice caught. "I . . . I think we all feel like doing that when we lose someone we love. But people are too inhibited to let go."

Her mother had died when she was sixteen, and Maddy'd never forget how she'd wanted to howl her pain to the heavens. She twisted her amethyst ring around her finger. The ring had been her mother's and Maddy rarely took it off.

"Do you think he'll be all right now?"

Tom's face tightened and she wondered if he had lost someone he loved. He was silent for a moment. Then, with a nod, he indicated Brutus. "Yes," he said, "I'm sure he'll be fine."

She sniffed back the last of her tears. "Remember the vet said once he met a new alpha—?"

He cut her off. "I remember."

She took a deep, steadying breath. "It went well. The funeral service I mean. But don't you think it's weird that out of all those people, no one knew Walter was a millionaire?"

Tom nodded. "It's not uncommon for eccentric people to hide their wealth. But usually they're more reclusive than Walter appeared to be. Yeah. As his lawyer I shouldn't really say it, but I think it's weird."

"I wonder what they'll think when they find out." Surely they would react with the same disbelief she had.

"Well, the will is not public knowledge yet. And it still has to go through probate. Other than you and Father Andrew, no one outside my office knows who Walter's beneficiaries are."

Uh. And Jerome. He was Walter's family. She'd answered his questions about the inheritance quite happily.

"It was a good send-off. For Walter." She looked around the now-empty church and focused on a stained-glass image of a dove of peace in the large window above the altar. She found it comforting. "Eighty-two was a good age."

"It was."

She patted Brutus again and stood up. It was time to be joining the cortege to the cemetery. Tom stood up, too, holding Brutus in his arms. He seemed a bit stunned by what had happened.

"Well," she said slowly, "Walter's gone, but we're still here and I've got Brutus. I guess . . . I guess it's all part of the great circle of life."

"As Mufasa said to Simba."

Shocked, Maddy looked up at Tom. "Like . . . like in *The Lion King*, you mean?"

He shifted uncomfortably from one foot to the other as if regretting what he'd said. "Yeah."

She looked at him, frowning. "You like animated movies?"

He shrugged. Brutus licked his chin. Tom wiped it on his suit collar. "I . . . uh . . . watch them with my young nieces sometimes."

"Really?" Maddy said, unable to mask her surprise.

"*The Lion King* is one of their favorites."

"Mine, too," she said. "*Shrek*?"

He shrugged again. "The kids like him."

"What about *Aladdin*? I love *Aladdin*."

"Only the ones when Robin Williams voices the genie." He paused. "I, uh, mean the kids prefer those."

"Me, too."

She couldn't believe she was having this conversation. Not with stuffy Tom O'Brien. She found herself unable to resist teasing him.

"What about *The Little Mermaid*?"

His laugh echoed around the empty church. "That's pushing it. Even for the fondest of uncles."

Maddy couldn't help smiling a secret smile. So. She'd suspected there was a sense of humor lurking somewhere under all that stuffiness. But she couldn't believe Tom O'Brien admitted he watched animated movies. Even if it was just to keep his nieces company. Her passion for the genre certainly wasn't something she as a twenty-six-year-old admitted to everyone.

She found herself looking at him with new eyes. She noticed his silk tie. Like the first time she'd seen him, it was impeccably tied, though it was now sprinkled with dark hairs from Brutus's shedding winter coat.

She wondered if Tom ironed his underpants.

The final straw with her former fiancé, Russell, had been when he'd demanded she iron his boxers. With a crease down the center just so. She had decided then and there that she hadn't been put in this world to iron a man's underpants.

But Maddy didn't want to think about Tom O'Brien's underpants. Because that might lead her to thinking about what might be inside his underpants. And how she . . .

She didn't want to go there. Really she didn't.

She looked away, terrified he might somehow be able to read what was going on in her mind. "C'mon," she said. "I'm not sure how to get to the cemetery and I'll need to follow the cortege."

She was so anxious to get away from her wayward thoughts about Tom's underpants that she pushed past him and Brutus in the pew to get out. Her breasts skimmed his arm and she felt her nipples harden in response.

What the heck was going on here? Just because he said he

liked *Shrek* didn't give her body permission to get turned on by Walter's lawyer. She rushed ahead of him and outside the church.

She blinked in the sunlight. There seemed to be a lot more people in the churchyard. A gathering of men and women at the gates. Had they mistaken the time of the service? Jerome seemed to be talking to them, explaining their error, she supposed.

She sensed Tom come out of the church behind her. He stopped beside her and put Brutus down on the step. "Give me his leash," he said, "and I'll—"

He followed her gaze. "Who the heck are they—?" he started to ask. Then he groaned as the group of people rushed toward them. Maddy blinked against a sudden flash.

"There it is," a woman shouted, "it's the millionaire dog."

"And his mistress," a man sneered.

Mistress? Whose mistress? Brutus's?

Beside her Tom groaned again. He swore. "Hell, it's the press," he said.

· Six ·

The reporters surged toward Maddy where she stood with Tom on the church steps. There were only about six or seven of them but it seemed like a mob as they simultaneously hurled questions at her. And though they were asking about the millionaire dog, they seemed more interested in her than in Brutus.

She felt unnerved by the unexpected attention, intimidated by the microphones thrust in her face. There was even a television camera, for heaven's sake. She longed to appear on TV but not like this.

Instinctively she moved closer to Tom and the haven of his broad chest. She snuck a glance up at his face. Her heart thudded into overdrive. Yep, that strong profile was a ten out of ten. Maybe even a twenty out of ten. But gone was the charming smile and the dimple. Back in full grim mode, he was standing rigidly to attention and glaring at the gathered media over the top of Brutus's scruffy little head.

"Don't say a thing," he hissed, without looking down at her.

"I don't know wh—" she started to reply before being bombarded with questions.

"Hey, Maddy, what was your relationship to the late Walter Stoddard?" called a reporter.

"And how does it feel to be a millionaire?" asked another.

How did they know her name? That fact registered among the barrage of questions. And hadn't Tom said the will wasn't public knowledge? She blinked at a camera's sudden flash.

"I . . . uh . . . I'm not a millionaire. It's . . . it's Brutus who—" she stuttered but Tom cut her off.

"Ms. Cartwright has no comment," he said, bundling Brutus into her arms and holding out both his hands to ward off the photographers.

"Could I have your name please, sir?" asked a reporter from a daily newspaper. "And what is your relationship to Miss Cartwright?"

Tom snorted in disgust but did not reply. Brutus struggled to get down, scrabbling with his claws. He started to bark, urgent, yapping barks. Maddy held his squirming little body tightly but she couldn't manage to quiet him.

"Hey, the dog's talking instead," said a smart-aleck reporter from a radio station, thrusting a microphone toward the little dog. "Anyone here understand dog speak?"

Brutus bared his teeth and snarled, an effect more comical than threatening. The reporter chuckled, "Guess I don't need a translation for that." The other reporters laughed.

Maddy found herself wanting to laugh, too. Especially at the way Tom was glowering. Did he have to take everything so seriously?

She still felt bewildered by the presence of the press. And she had no intention of discussing anything about Walter's will with them. But personally she didn't have anything against the media.

Heck, she had a degree in journalism and was part of the media herself—though working as a food editor on a glossy women's magazine hardly qualified as hard-core news reporting. Someone had tipped these people off and they were following up the lead. Her journalist colleagues would do the same.

She petted Brutus in an attempt to soothe him. Out of the corner of her eye, she saw Jerome making his elegant way toward a sleek Jaguar parked nearby.

She felt a little miffed that he hadn't made any attempt to talk to her again after being so attentive before the church service. But he didn't turn back, didn't seem curious at the unexpected media intrusion.

Suspicion shot through her. She remembered his call on his cell phone. Could he be responsible for this melee?

The reporters started throwing questions again. "About the will, Ms. Cartwright? Does it—?"

Tom cut them off. "Ms. Cartwright has no comment," he repeated. Maddy felt a surge of irritation at the way he seemed to be taking over.

"I can speak for myself," she hissed to him in an undertone. Then—taking a deep, steadying breath—she spoke to the reporters. "Guys, I know you're trying to do your job, but this is a funeral. Please, show some respect."

Grasping Brutus tightly she walked down the final steps from the church and went to walk around them. "I have nothing to say to you. If you'll excuse me, I have to get to the cemetery."

There was a rumbling of dissent. "I have no comment," she said, walking away.

"So why did you have to be so nice to them?" Tom muttered as he strode along beside her, so close his shoulders brushed hers. Too aware of his maleness, she neatly sidestepped away.

"Because I'm not in the habit of being rude to people," she said between clenched teeth.

"They'll hound you now. Won't let you alone."

"And I'll keep telling them I have nothing to say."

"They'll dig for dirt."

Maddy felt sick at the implication of his words. She stopped and looked up at him, over Brutus's head. "There is no dirt to find," she said, unable to keep her voice steady.

His words were an unpleasant revelation. She'd begun to warm to Tom O'Brien. When it came to rating men, a sense of humor ranked as high as a good butt. Higher even. How could someone who appreciated the humorous satire of *Shrek* judge her so harshly for something she hadn't done?

She turned on her heel and walked on, stomach churning with disappointment and anger. She reached her too-old, in-need-of-a-service Honda hatchback.

"Why don't we go in my car?" he said, gesturing to a recent-model BMW parked a few spaces over.

"We?"

"You. Me. Brutus."

"Brutus and I are fine, thank you. We don't need a ride." She made her voice as chilly as a freshly churned sorbet.

"You do if you want help getting away from that lot," he said, gesturing at the reporters following them.

"I can manage on my own, thank you. Now if you don't mind, I don't want to be late to the cemetery."

Tom's voice rose with frustration. "For crying out loud, Maddy, I'm just trying to help here. Protect you. I hadn't even intended to go to the cemetery. I've been away from the office long enough as it is."

At his tone of voice Brutus whined sympathetically and leaned over to lick Tom's hand. Maddy expected Tom to snatch his hand away, but with a pained look on his face, he left it there for Brutus's slobbery ministrations.

"Uh, anyway, isn't it obvious Brutus wants to be with me?" he said.

"Because you're his alpha—"

"I didn't say that," Tom said. "And for heaven's sake, keep quiet about that dumb theory in front of these reporters." He wiped his hand down the side of his trousers. "Now come on, are you getting in the car or not?"

Brutus looked appealingly up at her with his black button eyes and then back to Tom. She didn't need a degree in dog speak to know what he wanted.

Maddy thought for a minute. She could evade the reporters just fine by herself. But it would do Brutus good to bond further with Tom. He still wasn't eating very well. Was only just out of mourning. What harm could it do to accept a ride with Tom? Give Brutus what he wanted.

It wasn't what she wanted. Of course it wasn't. She wouldn't even think about how comforting it had been to have Tom by her side during the church service, how appealing the thought of having him with her at the cemetery.

"Okay," she conceded, "for Brutus's sake."

She climbed into the BMW, appreciating its leather luxury. She noted its showroom condition, quite different from her own car, which hadn't been cleaned for months and was full of cooking equipment and props for food photography. She prayed Brutus wouldn't do anything untoward to damage Tom's car. Like lift his leg against the expensive sound system and short-circuit the electronics.

"Nice car," she said.

"Yes," Tom said with the doting look men reserved for their boy toys. She wouldn't have been surprised if he'd lovingly stroked the dashboard. "I've only had it a few weeks."

Brutus went to scramble onto Tom's lap, but she dragged him back to her side of the car, studiously avoiding coming into contact with Tom's legs as she did so. She fastened her seat belt and settled Brutus on her lap as Tom gunned the car away from the church.

"I know this area well," he said. "We'll easily lose those guys before we head out to the freeway."

Maddy found there was something disconcertingly intimate about being alone with Tom in his car. She couldn't help noting the interesting play of muscles in his thighs as he used the brake. And it was kind of, well, sexy the way he pushed the Steptronic stick shift when he changed gear.

The citrus male scent of him seemed to intensify in the confines of his car and she felt suddenly short of breath. She remembered how her nipples had hardened as she'd brushed against him in the church and willed them not to do it again. He was undeniably gorgeous. And yet he seemed to have such a bad opinion of her.

They'll dig for dirt. His words kept going over and over in her head. She got more and more annoyed as she thought about their implication. She would start to hyperventilate if she didn't say something in her own defense.

"Stop the car," she said, surprising herself nearly as much as she surprised Tom.

"What?" he said.

"I said pull over. Please," she added. "We've lost the reporters."

"Uh, okay," he said, sounding puzzled, "you're not going to—"

"No, I don't get carsick. Though I don't know about Brutus. I *did* give him a peanut butter cookie—uh, a healthy one of course—before we left home and I suppose he could be feeling a bit nauseous . . ."

"Don't even think about it," Tom groaned. "Let him bark, not barf. Not in my new car." He pulled over to the curb and killed the engine.

"Well?" he said, his brow creased with annoyance. "I thought you didn't want to be late to the cemetery?"

"I don't. But this won't take long."

"Hmph." He sounded unconvinced.

She took a deep breath. "Tom, what you said. About dirt. Digging for it. There isn't any. I mean, I appreciate your good intentions. But I can't accept any help from you if you continue to think . . . to think that I . . . that I had a . . ."—it was so distasteful it was almost impossible to say it—"any kind of . . . of sexual relationship with my friend Walter." Her final words came out in a rush.

Tom stared at her for a long moment, his deep brown eyes incredulous. Then he exploded into a paroxysm of coughing. His face went red under the bronze of his tan. His eyes watered.

Maddy resisted the urge to slap him on the back to stop him from choking. The way she was feeling at the moment about this stuffed-shirt lawyer—gorgeous as he was—she might slap him just a bit harder than was warranted.

Tom managed to control his coughing and get his breath back. But, momentarily unable to speak, he continued to stare at Maddy where she sat next to him in the passenger seat of his car.

She turned to face him, looking directly with those clear green eyes, her cheeks flushed, her chin tilted upward, her mouth set in a stubborn line. Hell, even the tips of her ears looked angry. She certainly didn't pull any punches. He couldn't believe she'd been so direct.

"I . . . I . . ." he finally managed to stutter, stunned at how she'd put him on the spot. "I never . . . I never thought . . ."

"Oh yes, you did," she stated. "And don't try to deny it."

How could she possibly have guessed what he'd been thinking about her? In his dealings with her he'd been subtle, discreet, lawyerlike. "I . . . uh . . . don't make judgments on people before I . . ."

"That's bull," she said. "It was obvious you'd made up your mind about me before you'd even met me."

Obvious? How obvious? He cleared his throat. "That's not true," he said.

"Ahem," she said, holding his gaze. Brutus looked at him from her lap, equally accusingly. The dog snuffled as if to agree with its mistress.

Mistress? He hadn't meant to even *think* the word *mistress*. In any context. The two pairs of eyes met his unflinchingly and Tom began to feel a totally unaccustomed panic. As if she had him on the witness stand.

He couldn't prevaricate any longer. She demanded the truth, and dammit, he'd give it to her. "Yeah. Okay," he said. "I thought you were the old man's mistress."

As soon as he said the words he wished he could take them back. Her face seemed to crumple. Her beautiful full mouth began to tremble and she bit down on her lower lip.

Her eyes misted. "That . . . that's what I thought you thought," she whispered. "Yet . . . yet it sounds dreadful to hear the actual word." She closed her eyes. *"Mistress."*

What had he got himself into? Where was his lawyerlike cool? His caution? His next words seemed to spill out of their own accord. "But as soon as I met you I knew that couldn't be true."

Her eyes snapped open. "Really?"

That wasn't 100 percent the truth but he couldn't bear to see her face crumple again. Couldn't bear to witness tears. Didn't know how he'd stop himself from gathering her into his arms to comfort her if she cried.

"Really," he said. And was surprised to find that if he hadn't meant it the first time he'd met her, he certainly meant it now. She'd never fitted the femme fatale image he'd built up in his mind.

"You . . . you mean that?"

"Yeah, I mean that," he said. "You . . . you didn't seem the type."

Her mouth twisted. "I don't know whether I'm meant to be flattered by that or not."

"Feel flattered," he said.

"Thanks," she said with a watery smile. There was silence for a moment. "Tom?"

"Yes?"

Her eyes widened and he thought again how candid they were. "I swear to you that there was absolutely nothing . . . nothing untoward about my relationship with Walter. He truly was like a grandfather to me. I even tried to fix him up with my grandmother when she visited with me from upstate. She's a widow. Still very attractive."

Typical female. Never satisfied with leaving a guy alone. Even at eighty-two. Tom swallowed a retort. But he couldn't help rolling his eyes.

"Yeah," she said with a wry smile, "I know. Neither of them was interested."

"Right," he said, knowing any other comment he made could get him into trouble.

"And . . . and about the will. I was clueless about the money."

"Yeah. I believe that."

He really did. He didn't know why. His gut instinct told him she was honest. Was innocent of plotting to gain a fortune. But he didn't know why he should feel so relieved. Or so glad that they were now on a level playing field.

"Great," she said, "I'm pleased we got that sorted out. I . . . I didn't like you thinking badly of me." She glanced at her watch. "We'd better get going or we'll lose the cortege."

Then she cried, "Oh no!" and yanked on Brutus's collar to jerk his head upward.

"What now?" asked Tom, thinking wearily of regurgitated peanut butter cookie on his pride and joy: custom-dyed leather upholstery. Made especially for him in Germany.

Maddy looked at him, her eyes wary as she clutched the dog defensively to her. "Don't get mad but I . . . uh . . . I'm afraid that while we've been talking, Brutus has been, uh, chewing on the edge of the car seat. Not much. Just a nibble really. A teensy, weensy nibble. That's all. Really."

Tom felt the blood rush to his head. Now Maddy would really hear him growl.

As soon as they reached the cemetery, Maddy leapt out of the car and rushed away from Tom. She wanted to put as much distance as she could between Brutus and his attorney until Tom cooled down about the car seat.

It had set back the cause of the alpha-male bonding by quite a bit. Why were some men so obsessed with their darn cars?

Brutus could afford to get the leather upholstery fixed once he inherited. She'd explained that to Tom but he didn't seem at all impressed. She'd actually had to scramble into the backseat with Brutus to get the little dog away from him. It was only a car, for heaven's sake.

She attached Brutus's leash. She'd shoot over to where the other mourners had gathered around the graveside. Surely Tom wouldn't make a scene in front of them.

Jerome was among the twenty or so people congregated around the graveside. He saw Maddy and came over to her with his elegant stride.

"So sorry, I missed you back at the church," he said in that smooth-as-double-cream voice. He had taken off his jacket and his eyes were as blue as the beautifully cut striped shirt he wore.

"You mean among all the reporters?" she said.

He looked charmingly abashed. "My fault, I'm afraid. I was chatting to a journalist friend and the news about the dog just slipped out."

"Just slipped out," she repeated, not convinced, looking back distractedly over her shoulder to see if Tom was coming after her.

"Well, you must admit Brutus's, ah, inheritance makes a good story," said Jerome. "My words were like a bone to a dog to a journalist, so to speak." His teeth gleamed as white as a toothpaste ad as he smiled.

"So to speak," she echoed, not finding the analogy at all amusing and wondering why she was suddenly doubting the Englishman's sincerity. Probably something to do with Tom telling her Walter had called Jerome a leech. But leech or no leech, he was incredibly handsome. And the way he tilted his head when he smiled reminded her so much of Walter that her heart ached.

Brutus huddled around her ankles as she spoke and she wondered why he didn't rush to Jerome like he had to Tom. Whatever made a dog sniff out an alpha male, Jerome obviously didn't have it.

"Ah," said Jerome, nodding his head in the direction of the graveside, "the . . . uh . . . business is at hand."

Maddy realized that the other mourners were gathering solemnly around the graveside where Father Andrew was officiating. Tom towered above a group of women, and she noted he was chatting to his mother.

Good. Maddy liked Helen O'Brien. She had recently bought a very cool dress from Helen's boutique on Fillmore Street. It would be nice to catch up with the older woman; maybe she could enlist her to Brutus's side if Tom was still upset about the car seat.

She made to move closer when she halted suddenly. There were the reporters—more of them now—circling around the group of mourners. Her sympathy for them dissipated. Surely they wouldn't take photographs of so private a proceeding?

Her respect for the media's right to do their job slipped down a notch.

Tom broke away from the group and headed toward the reporters. She could tell by his stride and the rigid set of his body how angry he was at the press disruption.

But it was her they were after. Her and Brutus. What did they want? A shot of her weeping and Brutus whining? She couldn't trust herself not to cry at this final farewell to her old friend. No way would she give them that photo opportunity.

Without Brutus she would attract less attention. She handed the leash to Jerome. He'd said he wanted to get to know Brutus better. Now was his chance.

"Mind him for a moment, would you please?" she murmured, and stepped briskly away from the cameras to the protection of a cluster of palm trees. From there, she could see the proceedings without visibly taking part in them. She couldn't bear to think that her presence would detract from the dignity of the final rites for Walter.

There, in privacy, she choked back her tears to offer her own prayer of thanks and remembrance of her old friend. "You must have had your reasons for leaving me this inheritance," she whispered. "I just wish I knew what they were."

She stood in respectful silence, thinking of how kind Walter had been to her and hoping he was reunited with his beloved wife, Isobel, and the child he had never ceased to mourn.

Then, hearing the final blessings come to an end, she wiped her eyes and waited for the mourners to move away. She turned around and slowly made her way back toward the graveside. Some distance away, Jerome was standing alone, smoking a cigarette.

"Where's Brutus?" she asked.

Jerome shrugged his shoulders. "He ran off."

"Ran off? What do you mean, he ran off?" Her voice started to rise. "I asked you to look after him."

He shrugged again. "Couldn't hold him I'm afraid."

"You couldn't hold him? A small dog like that?" Her heart started to thud. She looked anxiously around her. Brutus was nowhere in sight. The cemetery was a big one. And unfamiliar territory to the little animal.

A shiver ran through her. Surely Jerome hadn't let him off the leash on purpose?

"Brutus," she called. "Brutus, here, boy."

Suddenly Tom was by her side. "Is there a problem?" he said, looking pointedly at Jerome.

Hurray. She didn't try to mask her relief at seeing him. Somehow Tom O'Brien seemed the kind of man who would be good in an emergency. "Jerome let Brutus run away," she said, looking at the Englishman through narrowed eyes, expecting support from Tom.

"*Jerome* let Brutus run away? But *you* were looking after him."

He was blaming her, not Jerome? "Jerome was watching him for me while I . . . while I went over there . . ."

"Slipped the leash I'm afraid," said Jerome in his plummy

British voice. He blew out a stream of smoke that made her wince. "Not a well-trained dog."

"So where is Brutus now?" Tom demanded.

Jerome shrugged his shoulders again. Once okay, two maybe, but three times was beginning to bug Maddy. She glared at him. He reminded her of the salads set in aspic she'd made at culinary school—beautiful to look at but when you bit into them they didn't taste so great. No substance at all.

Not like Tom, who she was beginning to think would be satisfying in every way.

"Brutus!" she called again, scanning the rows of headstones.

Tom scowled. But he was scowling at Maddy, not Jerome. "Why didn't you bring Brutus over to me?"

She hunched away from him. "I thought you'd, uh, strangle him."

"Strangle the millionaire mutt?" asked Jerome with a sudden show of interest. "Surely not?"

"He chewed up Tom's car and—oh, never mind," said Maddy. Her heart was pounding. Not because she knew how important legally it was to keep Brutus out of harm's way for the next seventeen days but because she couldn't bear the thought of anything happening to the little animal. "Come on, we've got to go look for him."

Jerome ground out the butt of his cigarette with his heel. "By all means."

"Which way did he go?" asked Tom, looking around.

"Tom, maybe you could try gro—"

"Don't say it," he said in a passable imitation of a growl.

"Why, isn't that the recalcitrant pooch itself?" said Jerome with a languid wave.

Trailing his leash, Brutus came bounding through the rows of headstones, followed by a sweet-faced Border collie. The dogs came to a halt nearby and then cavorted playfully around each other. The Border collie was way bigger than Brutus, but size had never daunted him when it came to female playmates.

"I might have known." Maddy sighed, exasperation mingling with the relief that flooded her.

"Might have known what?" asked Tom.

"That he'd find himself a girl dog from somewhere."

"Huh?" She liked the way he looked puzzled, the tough lawyer suddenly lost for words. "I don't get it."

She stooped to grab Brutus's leash and pulled the protesting animal toward her. She looked back up at Tom.

"Didn't Walter mention it? Brutus is a lady's man, uh, dog. If there's a doggy word for a womanizer, that's him. He's a little dog with big appetites. And not just for cupcakes and peanut butter cookies."

Jerome laughed. Maddy nearly laughed at the expression on Tom's face. Was it fair to tease a man at a funeral?

Tom scowled. "That damn dog. It gets worse by the second. I wish you'd told me this before."

"Why? What good would it have done?"

Tom scowled some more. "I could have made more sense of the message that I've just got from the office. A poodle named Coco is slapping a paternity suit on Brutus for support of her five puppies."

· Seven ·

Coco the poodle was proving to be as determined a litigant as Tom had ever encountered. Its owner just wouldn't let up. The damn woman was bombarding Tom with constant phone calls, asking ridiculous questions that only Maddy would be able to help him answer.

That was why, early the next afternoon, Tom found himself again at the door of Maddy's apartment. He knocked loudly and tried to ignore the delicious aromas that wafted through the keyhole. What was she cooking today? He inhaled, trying to identify the taste. Pastry perhaps? Buttery, cholesterol-laden pastry.

Inwardly he groaned. Did that mean that today Maddy herself would smell of her own sweet femaleness, lavender, and hot apple pie? The combination could prove to be irresistible. And that wasn't good. Because he intended to resist his attraction to the too-cute Maddy Cartwright. All the way.

With her appealing homey ways she had "commitment"

written all over her. He was certain she was not—in spite of his earlier way-off-the-mark imaginings—the type for a no-strings affair. In fact, it was likely, with all that brownie baking going on, she was in the market for a husband.

Hell, he was only two years into his current five-year plan. At age thirty-three he would commence a new one—and would seriously consider writing "marriage" into the goals for that sector of his life. But that was three years away and right now the partnership at Jackson, Jones, and Gentry was his priority. His absolute priority. He had to prove to himself that he could achieve what his father had doubted he could.

Where was she? He rapped again on the door—impatiently this time. He could hear music coming faintly through the door. Was that the soundtrack from *Shrek*? She showed good taste in movies and music. Yet another reason he found her so appealing.

He felt—no, he feared—Maddy Cartwright would be dangerously easy to get attached to. But subsection 2a of the five-year plan stated "no serious girlfriends." And he wouldn't want to hurt her by bailing if he saw signs she was starting to get attached to him—as per strategy outlined in subsection 2c of the aforesaid five-year plan.

Tom tapped his foot against the doorstep. What was he doing here? Right now he should be downtown in the Financial District attending a meeting involving a billion-dollar corporate takeover. Instead he was wasting time on this ludicrous poodle paternity case.

He could have called Maddy about the poodle of course. He could even have gotten his secretary to call her. But these kinds of meetings were better conducted face-to-face.

Who was he kidding? He raked his hair back from his forehead with his fingers, something he tended to do when he was agitated. Stop fooling yourself, O'Brien. Truth was, he hadn't been able to stop thinking about the green-eyed witch since the funeral yesterday.

This was just an excuse to see her again and he knew it. Unfortunately there was no relevant subsection in the five-year plan to deal with these inconvenient, unscheduled feelings that had been bothering him almost from the moment he'd met her.

Where was she? The entrance to her apartment was down a narrow pathway leading from the road. The gate had been open when he'd come through. Had she gone out? Or might she be out back?

He turned the other way and walked down into the garden. An early fog had lifted and the bay was gleaming blue under a brilliant sky. Brutus's kennel under the jacaranda tree was empty. In front of it sat a big ceramic water bowl painted with the words "One Spoiled Dog Drinks Here" and a single purple jacaranda flower floating in it.

"Anyone home?" Tom called, but the only reply was the distant sounding of the horn of a ferryboat on the bay.

He strode around the other side of the house to find the second, larger gate also stood open. He made his way up onto the sidewalk. And there he saw her, walking on the opposite side of the road coming toward him.

He sucked in a breath of admiration. This girl was hot. Wearing a tight, apple green sweater that showed off her curves and a short denim skirt, her pale, slender legs seemed to go on forever. Her hair gleamed copper in the sunlight. Pow! His body's reaction was instant.

"Maddy!" he shouted, trying to keep the excitement he felt at the sight of her out of his voice.

Startled, she looked up and saw him. Fearfully, she dipped her head. For an astonishing moment he thought she might run away. He stared.

Hey, this wasn't the reaction he'd been daydreaming about when he'd engineered an excuse to see her again. In fact, it seemed like he was the last person on earth she wanted to see. But she crossed the road to meet him just the same.

Close up he could see that she looked agitated, her gaze darting up the road, over his shoulder, anywhere but at him. So much for subsection 2c and letting her down lightly if she got too attached to him.

"Is something wrong?" he asked. Okay, maybe he'd over-reacted to the car-seat-chewing incident yesterday—although wait until Brutus got the bill for the repair. But there was no need for her to look at him like he was an ogre.

She wrung her hands together. Her lashes fluttered. Reluctantly she met his eyes. "Oh, Tom, I've lost Brutus again."

He stared at her in disbelief before he exploded. "You what?" What gave with this woman that she could be so careless with a millionaire dog?

She looked up at him. Her eyes widened. She bit down on her lower lip with her two neat, white front teeth. "Don't be angry. You know I wouldn't have done it on purpose. I don't know how he got out."

"Got out?"

"He was safe in the backyard. I was in the kitchen cooking—I do most of my recipe testing at home. Jerome was upstairs looking through some of Walter's things."

"Jerome was here?" Jerome alone with Maddy? Tom didn't like the sudden jealousy that jolted him.

She nodded. "He came by. Asked me if he could get some family photos and mementos of Walter."

Tom groaned. "Maddy, you don't even know this guy. And probate hasn't been granted yet. Nothing should be removed from the property."

She wrinkled up her nose. "Maybe you're right, but he . . . well, he looks so much like Walter it only seemed right to give him access to Stoddard family stuff. And he can be very convincing."

Convincing? How convincing? Convincing with words, kisses? He supposed women would find the Englishman attractive, though he thought him too slimy by half. He couldn't bear to think of Jerome kissing Maddy, touching her . . .

Tom gritted his teeth. He wasn't jealous. Of course he wasn't. And Maddy could kiss whomever she liked. It was no business of his.

He just didn't like Jerome. Walter had warned him about his great-great-nephew, and his own observations had done nothing to make him disagree with Walter's canny assessment.

The incident at the cemetery had worried him. But there'd been no proof that Jerome had had any evil intent.

"So, did he let Brutus off the leash like he did yesterday?" he asked.

"No. Maybe. I don't know. He told me he went down to the garden for a cigarette and found the gates open and Brutus missing."

"And you weren't suspicious of that?"

"Well, yes, I was. I never leave the gates open, I swear to you.

I told you what a wanderer Brutus is. And quite a lot of traffic comes along this road."

"So what happened then?"

"I asked Jerome to help me search for Brutus, but he said he had an urgent appointment and had to go."

"How convenient."

"That's what I said. And do you know what he did? He shrugged."

"He shrugged? And that's a problem?"

Maddy's chin tilted upward and she looked as fierce as a pretty girl with a heart-shaped face could look. "A little dog is in danger and all the guy does is *shrug*. He's a shoulder shrugger of the first order and it bugs me. I told him to get out and never come back here again. I am so over Jerome."

Good. If Jerome never went near Maddy again, Tom would be a happy man. But he wrote himself a mental memo never to shrug his shoulders in Maddy Cartwright's presence.

He looked up to the end of the sidewalk. "We'd better go look for Brutus." He thought again of his mauled custom-dyed-in-Germany leather car seat, but somehow it wasn't as painful as imagining Brutus squashed somewhere on the road. Annoying as the animal was. "Come on."

"Wait." Maddy held up her hand to halt him. "I need to think for a moment. I've searched all around these streets. Hang on. He may have gone to Coco's house. I hadn't thought of that. He adores her."

"Coco? You mean the litigious poodle who is, uh, the mother of his puppies? The alleged mother, that is."

"Right. I bet he's there. Come on, she lives on the next street. Up this hill and turn left."

Tom strode along beside her, easily taking the steep slope. "So, if Brutus is a doggy womanizer, where does Coco fit in?"

Maddy giggled. She had the most delightful, melodious laugh. "She's his number one girlfriend, I guess. In fact, I think he'd be happy just with her if Coco's owner would let him hang around instead of putting the hose on him."

"Huh," snorted Tom, "a monogamous dog. That's a new one. Which crazy canine psychology theory of yours does this fit into?"

Maddy stopped. She looked up at him, wide-eyed. He noticed the green of her sweater emphasized the color of her eyes. "You don't believe in fidelity, Tom?"

Was she serious? He couldn't be sure. "You mean for dogs or for humans?"

"Humans of course. Men and women."

"Of course I believe in fidelity. Uh, at the right time, that is."

Her brow furrowed. "What do you mean at the right time?"

Hey, who was the lawyer around here? How come she kept putting him on the spot? "When the time is right for . . . for well, you know, commitment."

He felt uncomfortable talking about this kind of stuff. Very uncomfortable.

"Ooh." She drew the sound out in a long, teasing way. "You mean marriage."

"Marriage? Yes, I suppose I do." How in hell had the conversation gotten around to the dreaded *M* word?

"But until then?"

He started walking again; she had to skip two steps to his one to keep up. He couldn't help noticing how her breasts bounced when she did so. "Uh. Well, I don't intend to settle down for a long time yet so I, uh, guess I hadn't given it much thought."

"So, you wouldn't be faithful to a steady girlfriend?"

"I didn't say that, but dammit, Maddy, I don't have time for a serious girlfriend."

"Oh," she said.

They'd reached the midsection of the hill and they paused, waiting to cross the road. Her eyes were gleaming with mischief.

"What do you mean, 'oh'?"

"Well, that's not what your mother told me when we were chatting after the funeral. She said you never got to meet any nice girls in that cutthroat law firm of yours."

"She *what*?" He loved his mother but he hated her relentless matchmaking. And he'd never had trouble finding a girlfriend for himself when he wanted one. "What else did she tell you about me?"

"Oh, nothing much," she said. "How smart you are, what a great athlete you are, how adorable you look in your baby photos, especially the naked ones. That sort of thing. Then she told me how you needed—"

"Stop! I don't want to hear another word."

Maddy laughed her delightful laugh as they crossed the road. "Don't worry. You're safe. She tried the baby photos on me once before. I told your mother I wasn't interested in a serious relationship. I thought about telling her I only ever date a guy twice but decided that would be giving her more information than she needed."

What? Tom reeled at her words—it was more information than *he* needed. Had he misjudged her again? So she wasn't on a husband hunt?

"So why is that? The two-date thing?"

This new piece of information was disconcerting. He'd bet she wouldn't be able to stop at two dates with him. That is, if he ever asked her on a date. Which right now didn't look in any way likely.

She looked straight ahead as she walked along. "I was engaged once. But . . . but it didn't work out."

"I'm sorry to hear that," Tom said. But he wasn't. He didn't like to think of Maddy with another guy.

"Don't be. In some ways I'm glad. He didn't support me in my career. It's . . . less complicated to stay single while I establish myself."

That last sentence could have been words coming from his own mouth. So why didn't he like the sound of them from hers?

She turned around. Again her eyes were wide and guileless. "I, uh . . . am assuming you're interested in girls. You know, sometimes mothers can be blind to that kind of thing."

She was trying to look serious but her mouth kept quirking upward and betraying her. Now Tom knew for sure she was teasing him. He put out his hand and took her arm to stop her.

"I am definitely interested in girls," he said slowly and deliberately, letting his gaze roam across where her sweater hugged the swell of her breasts.

He lingered there and was astounded and aroused to see her nipples firming under his scrutiny. With his thumb he made little circles on her arm through the fabric of her sweater and felt her quiver in response.

His gaze slid down to the gap of taut tummy where her

sweater stopped and her skirt started, and then to her firm, bare thighs. "Yes," he said, bringing his gaze back up to her face, "I am *very* interested in girls."

He'd started by responding to her teasing in kind. She'd met his gaze defiantly. But now, subtly, the atmosphere between them changed, became charged with awareness.

She flushed pink under her redhead's pale skin and stuttered into silence when she attempted to speak. He found he was powerless to drag his eyes from her. She stared back as if mesmerized.

Then she swayed ever so slightly toward him and, before he could think about what he was doing and why he shouldn't, Tom was kissing her, claiming that enticing mouth that had fascinated him from the get-go, tasting her honeyed sweetness, pulling her soft curves to him with a strangled sound that was somewhere between triumph and capitulation.

Kissing her was invalidating every subsection and sub-subsection of his five-year plan. But she felt so good in his arms he wondered why he hadn't done it sooner.

Maddy was melting like the finest Belgian chocolate. Tom O'Brien was kissing her, and she was rising on her toes to kiss him back, sighing with delight at his firm, warm mouth on hers, the slight roughness of his chin against the softness of her skin, the fresh citrus smell of him mingled with his own maleness.

She wound her arms around his neck, reveling in the firmness of his muscles against her curves, her breasts tingling as she pressed them against the hardness of his chest. She was so close to him she could feel his heart pulsing in time to her own. Her eyes closed as she savored the sensation.

"Mmm," she murmured as he twined his hand in her hair, tilting her head back as he deepened the kiss, pushing against her lips with his tongue. Eagerly she parted her mouth to welcome him, meeting the tip of his tongue with hers, tangling with it, taking it inside her.

He tasted of toothpaste, fresh, sharp. Yes, Tom O'Brien would be the type of man who kept toothpaste in his desk drawer for an after-lunch brush. It was thoughtful, considerate. She liked that. She liked this. A kiss had never felt so good. In fact, this kiss took kissing to a level she never thought she'd reach.

Who would have thought stuffy Tom O'Brien would be such an amazing kisser? Or that she would respond with shivers of delight coursing through her body, her nipples hard, her knees all wobbly? She felt dizzy with the pleasure of it.

She could feel his heat through the layers of his jacket and shirt and felt her own heat rise in response. She slid her hand up his back, caressed the back of his neck between his collar and his hair. The feel of his bare skin made her want to tug on his tie, loosen it, unbutton his shirt, feel more than this tantalizing taste of his body. Test the strength of those muscles, discover if they felt as good as they looked.

His hands moved down her shoulders, traced the side of her breasts. She trembled, gasped within the kiss, pressed her mouth hungrily to his, demanded more.

Then was blasted into reality by the slowing of a passing car and a male voice yelling, "Woo-hoo! Get a room!"

Her eyes flew open and she pulled away from the kiss, mouth swollen, heart pounding, gasping for breath. She was kissing Tom

O'Brien in the street? Where her neighbors could see her and passersby yelled ribald comments? How could she have let herself go so out of control?

Tom did not step back from her. "Wow," he said, sounding dazed.

"Double wow," she echoed, giddy from the aftereffects of his kiss. She looked up at him, speechless. He seemed in an equal state of shock.

She licked her lips. They tasted of him. "That . . . uh . . . that shouldn't have happened," she whispered, still looking up into his eyes, still light-headed with an inexplicable excitement.

"True," he said in a deep, husky voice. "Not a good idea."

But his gaze was not repentant or regretful. She found herself unable to look away, her heart thudding in anticipation.

With one long, strong finger he traced the outline of her mouth where his mouth had been just a minute before. Still looking into his eyes, she took his finger between her teeth, lightly nipped it and curled around it with the tip of her tongue.

With a husky laugh, he withdrew his finger. Then he leaned forward and claimed her mouth again in a kiss that made her gasp and was over too quickly.

He smiled. Ohmigod, that dimple! It was irresistible. She wanted to reach up and plant a kiss on it.

Kiss Tom O'Brien's dimple? What next? This was way too confusing. She braced herself against his chest and pushed herself away from the too-alluring circle of his arms.

"You . . . you just said that wasn't a good idea," she managed to get out, her breathing ragged. "So why did you do it again?"

"It was you who said it shouldn't have happened. I just agreed."

Maddy was pleased to note that his voice was as unsteady as hers.

"And I kissed you again because you're beautiful and I couldn't stop myself."

Tom sounded as though he were surprised at his own words. He even shook his head as if to clear his thoughts.

She swallowed hard, willing her voice to sound normal. "Well, you certainly proved your point."

"My point?" His brow furrowed.

"That you're interested in girls."

His dimple deepened. In such a strong, masculine face that dimple was a surprise. Like the special touch of seasoning that transformed an ordinary recipe into a culinary masterpiece.

Maddy couldn't look at him; she couldn't trust herself not to reach up and kiss him again. She looked down to the sidewalk, noting where a youthful hand had chalked a red heart with "K & J forever" entwined within it.

Huh. Forever love. She'd given up on that idea some time ago. Love brought strings she wasn't willing to entangle herself in. Strangle herself in.

She cleared her throat. "It isn't a good idea," she said. "The kissing I mean. You being Brutus's lawyer and all."

Truth was, she was shaken by how much she'd enjoyed Tom's kiss, how disappointed she'd been when it stopped. Wanting more kisses—and more than kisses—from Tom O'Brien did not fit into the strict two-date regime she'd imposed on herself.

"What? You see a conflict of interest?"

Trust him to use such lawyerlike words. "No, it's not that." She looked up. "It was just . . . unexpected. And . . . and . . ."

"And . . . ?" Tom prompted.

She didn't want to say, *I liked it so much it frightened me.* She sought frantically in her brain for the right words. And didn't find them. "And ... we shouldn't be spending time kissing or talking about kissing when Brutus is missing."

Tom looked as bemused as she felt at her lame choice of words. "Well, that's one way of putting it I suppose."

She nodded emphatically.

The dimple disappeared. He was switched back into grim mode. But it looked suspiciously more like pretending-to-be-grim mode. "You're right, of course. Doesn't fit with my plan at all."

"Your plan? What plan?"

"We haven't got time to talk about my plan when Brutus is missing," he said, turning her own words back on her. A smile hovered at the edges of his so-sexy mouth.

She blinked. Was he teasing her now? She wasn't so sure she liked having the tables turned. "I can't argue with that," she said. And vowed to find out about that plan. All about it.

He turned businesslike. "Hadn't we better go find Brutus? I've got a legal obligation to keep that dog alive."

A legal obligation? Was that all Brutus was to him?

And her? Was kissing her just something to keep her sweet until the will was finalized? She felt a funny little pain at the thought of it.

But in her heart, remembering the dazed look on his face after their kiss, she couldn't believe that was true.

She mustered up a bright tone of voice knowing it sounded strained to her own ears. "Right. I'm convinced he's at Coco's house or I wouldn't be standing around here ... uh ... talking."

"Of course you wouldn't," he said, and again she wasn't too

sure how serious he was. "Or kissing. Now let's get going on a dog hunt."

She moved into step beside him, trying to match his rhythm, being careful to avoid brushing her shoulder against him, amazed how hard she had to fight the impulse to slip her hand into his. "To Coco's house then."

"To Coco's house," he echoed. "What's Mrs. Porter, the owner, like? She sounds like quite a character on the phone."

Maddy grasped the opportunity to change the subject. "A character? You wait 'til you see her. Try not to laugh. Just don't look at me when she opens the door or I won't be able to stop myself from laughing. Because I'm telling you, she looks just like a poodle herself."

She was gratified to see Tom's dimple reappear as he threw back his head and laughed. And stunned at the way her heart went into double-quick time at the sight.

· Eight ·

Tom didn't dare catch Maddy's eye when confronted by Coco's owner, Mrs. Porter. She was short and skinny, and with her black curly hair clipped back from her long face with two red plastic bow-shaped barrettes, she bore an uncanny resemblance to a poodle. Worse, she looked ready to snap.

He'd barely introduced himself when the forty-something woman glared at Maddy. "The little brute is here if that's who you're looking for," she said. "I kept him inside instead of dispatching him with the hose because I wanted Mr. O'Brien to witness him trespassing on my property."

Maddy screwed up her face in a passable attempt at penitence. "Thank you, Mrs. Porter, I can't tell you how glad I am that he's safe. I'm so sorry. I don't know how he got out, I promise you."

Maddy looked adorable in her unaccustomed meekness—how could Mrs. Poodle—uh, Porter—resist her apology? He certainly wouldn't be able to. In fact, he just wanted to kiss her again. If they were alone, he would. In spite of subsection 2a.

"Hmph," muttered Mrs. Porter. She glared at Tom. "I think you'll agree with me that there could be no doubt as to paternity when you see Brutus with the puppies."

Maddy's face lit up. "Oh! The puppies are here? I'm dying to see them. May I?"

Mrs. Porter led them through a small house cluttered with more dog figurines than Tom had ever seen. Even the sofa was covered in a poodle-print fabric. Gross. He liked a sparsely furnished room—stark, modern, with nothing on display. And certainly not scented with the doggy aroma that permeated this place.

They emerged to a small courtyard dominated by a large, open kennel. A black miniature poodle lay on her side suckling five plump, wriggling puppies. Curled possessively around Coco's back was Brutus.

"Brutus, you're a naughty boy for running away and frightening us," chastised Maddy. "Don't even think about doing that again."

Think? Brutus? As if the dog understood a word of it, thought Tom. Women. His mother talked to her cat as if it were human, too. If only they realized how dumb it sounded.

Brutus lifted his head in acknowledgment of the people and thumped his plumed tail. But he didn't get up. He nestled a little closer to Coco.

Maddy dropped down to look more closely at the puppies. "Oh, they're adorable!" she cooed.

Mrs. Porter's face softened. "Yes, they are dear little things." Her face tightened again. "But not worth a cent to me. Coco is a champion with a pedigree a mile long and should have been put to stud with her equal. I had her booked in with another champion—Lagrange Midnight Claude the Seventh. Until Brutus beat him to it."

"Uh, sorry about that, Mrs. Porter," said Maddy again with unaccustomed meekness. How did she keep a straight face at the elongated name of Coco's thwarted stud?

"Hmph," said Mrs. Porter, not sounding at all mollified.

"But these little things are so cute. And don't they look like a real family?" said Maddy. "How does it feel to be a daddy, Brutus?"

"Considerably poorer, Ms. Cartwright," said Mrs. Porter. "I expect compensation to the tune of what a litter of pedigree puppies would have netted me. I heard on the radio how Brutus had come into money."

Tom rolled his eyes heavenward. How had he gotten himself into this bizarre situation? Bonus or no bonus, representing a millionaire mutt in a paternity suit was not going to go down as the pinnacle of his legal career. Though it had introduced him to Maddy and that was certainly a bonus of sorts.

"Before we discuss your claims, Mrs. Pood—um—Porter, I need proof that Brutus, uh, sired these puppies. I'll have to seek veterinary advice. Blood tests, perhaps."

Mrs. Porter reached down to one of the puppies and picked it up. She thrust it up toward him—a squirming, brindle bundle with a distinctive jutting lower jaw. "Surely this is all the proof you need. This and the rest of the litter."

Tom looked from Mrs. Porter to the other puppies. Even he could see they looked more fifty-seven varieties than pedigree poodle.

"Uh, Tom, I think she might be right. This one could be Brutus Junior," said Maddy, her mouth quirking up in that already-familiar way of suppressing laughter.

Tom didn't dare meet her eye for fear he would laugh himself. Especially when he noticed Coco was wearing red satin ribbons tied at the top of each ear to match the barrettes in her owner's hair.

Maddy held out her arms to Mrs. Porter and the puppy she was holding. "Please, can I pet him?"

"It's a her, actually," said Mrs. Porter, handing over the puppy.

Maddy cradled the puppy in her arms, crooning endearments to her in her melodious voice. "Ooh, a little girl are you? Who's a precious sweetie?" The puppy energetically tried to lick her face. "You're a friendly little thing, aren't you?"

Unconsciously Maddy rocked, swaying rhythmically as she cuddled the puppy, and her face as she looked down on her was tender and glowing with delight.

Suddenly Tom had a terrifying vision of Maddy cradling a baby in just such a way. His baby. With a little fuzz of ginger hair and its mother's green eyes. It was terrifying because for a crazy, surreal moment he felt warm and mushy at the thought, when he should have run screaming from it.

She was mortar attacking a part of his heart that up to now had been totally bombproof.

Sirens went off in his head, screaming a warning of defenses about to be breached. Sweat broke out on his forehead. There was no provision at all for, gulp, children in the five-year plan. That was so far off the screen that it wasn't even in draft mode.

He must be hallucinating. He was working way-too-long hours. Skipping meals. Drugged by honey-flavored kisses.

He blinked rapidly to clear his head.

But then his horror at being catapulted into a vision of fatherhood was overtaken by a lawyerlike panic at what Maddy was saying to Mrs. Poodle.

"I agree there's no doubt as to who fathered these puppies, Mrs. Porter. As trustee of Brutus's fortune I consent to pay you the value of five pedigree poodle puppies plus some extra to cover the wonderful care you're giving them."

"Maddy." He glared at her. "This needs to be considered."

She ignored him. "Is that okay with you?" she asked the other woman.

"Maddy," he said more sternly, "think about this before you commit to anything."

"I can handle this myself, thank you, Tom," she hissed in an exaggeratedly polite tone.

Then, with the hand that wasn't still clutching the puppy to her breast, Maddy shook Mrs. Porter's hand. "I have to wait until funds become available, but I assure you that you will be paid as soon as possible."

Beaming now, Coco's owner nodded her agreement. Tom could see the dollar signs flashing in her eyes. He gritted his teeth. Did Maddy not have any idea of the possible legal consequences of her rash action?

He was determined to have his say. "You understand you will be required to sign an indemnity that assures us you will make no further claim against the estate," he told Mrs. Porter, glaring at Maddy as he did so.

Mrs. Porter nodded again. "I'll be happy with compensation for the litter Coco should have had."

Maddy flashed Tom a glance that made him suddenly remember that redheads had a reputation for having bad tempers. And become aware that he might very soon see a demonstration of it.

"It's a deal," she said to Mrs. Porter. "Now before we go, can I pet the other puppies, please? I'm aching to cuddle them."

Maddy had scarcely put the poodle house behind her when she whirled on Tom, nearly tripping on the borrowed hot pink leash that attached her to Brutus.

"How dare you boss me around back there? You were making a fool of me in front of that woman. Contradicting every word I said."

"Making a fool of you? I thought I was trying to give you informed legal advice. Stop you from exposing yourself to years of demands from that greedy woman."

"Greedy? I think she had a perfectly reasonable claim."

"Huh," he said in a tone that made her blood boil. "Make sure she signs that release or you'll have her on your back for years."

"I doubt it. But then you're very good at thinking the worst about people, aren't you, Tom?"

She scowled at him, remembering how he'd assumed she was Walter's mistress. Then didn't know whether to feel triumphant or sorry at the obvious discomfort her words caused him.

"Guilty as charged," he said, tight-lipped.

Her flare of anger fizzled as fast as it had flamed. How could she stay angry with the man who'd sent her senses soaring to heaven less than an hour ago? A man who was quite possibly the best kisser in the country. The world. The universe.

She yanked Brutus back from his investigation of interesting smells against a lamppost.

"Well, I guess you were only trying to do the right thing," she conceded. "But I need to handle this Brutus-and-his-money thing my own way."

"Granted," he said. "But I wouldn't trust Mrs. Poodle as far as I could kick her. Didn't you see the dollar signs in her eyes?"

Was she imagining things? She looked at him in amazed delight. "Mrs. Poodle? Her name is Mrs. Porter. You just called her Mrs. Poodle."

"I did not. I called her Mrs. Porter," he said, affronted.

She loved it when he lost his lawyer cool and looked so disconcerted. Instead of weakening him it somehow made him seem even more masculine. She had to fight the urge to reach up and kiss the spot where his dimple appeared when he smiled.

"You didn't. I distinctly heard you call her Mrs. Poodle just then. And you nearly called it to her face inside her house, by the way."

"I did not."

"Did so." She laughed. "I particularly noticed because I can't help thinking of her as Mrs. Poodle myself."

The dimple was back. "Oh, really?"

She nodded. "I warned you about how she looked, remember."

"What a weirdo," said Tom. "Thank God we're out of there. I would have killed you if you'd accepted the coffee. I couldn't have spent a second longer in that awful room."

"Yeah, well, the poodle-print sofa was a bit over the top. But I kind of liked all her doggy decorations. She's obviously crazy about dogs. I think her decor shows character."

"Character? You've got to be kidding," he said. "More an excess of bad taste, I would have thought."

Maddy tilted her head on one side. "Let me guess. Your place doesn't have a tchotchke or knickknack anywhere. Sleek, slick, and everything in its place."

"How did you know that?" he asked, his eyebrows raised in surprise.

"Just a lucky guess," she said, thinking back to how uncomfortable he'd looked in her pretty apartment full of her favorite things.

"Yeah, I like things plain. No clutter." He cleared his throat. "It's the way I am."

"No need to apologize. I wish I was neater—and less sentimental about the stuff I have all over the place."

"But you're creative; you're allowed to be like that."

"And you're logical and orderly; I admire that."

She laughed and so did he—his laugh warm and rich with good humor. He was nice—really nice. And that was on top of being the handsomest hunk she'd ever seen.

"I'm sorry I lost my temper, Tom," she said on impulse.

"Apology accepted, and no offense taken," he said.

"Thanks," she said. "But seriously, I have a thing about being ordered around by men."

"A thing?" he said, his brows drawn together.

"If you met my family you'd know why. I love them madly but my father is just plain domineering, and my brothers—two of them, both older than me—have ideas about women that passed their use-by date about a hundred years ago."

"What about your mother?"

"She . . . she died when I was sixteen."

"I'm sorry," he said.

"Thanks. I . . . I still miss her." She paused before she continued. "We have a cattle ranch upstate in Fall River Valley—that's eastern Shasta County. I kind of had to step into her shoes. Look after my father and brothers. Luckily I liked cooking. But—I still get mad when I think about it—they seriously thought I should leave high school."

"But you didn't?"

"My grandmother stepped in and made them get some paid help. And then, thank heaven, when I was eighteen, my brother Mike met a girl whose only ambition in life was to be a farmer's wife."

"Some ambition."

"Don't knock it. It works for some, including my beautiful sister-in-law. She convinced the menfolk to let me move into town and live with Grandma. That way I got to go to college."

Behind a fence a dog started barking. Brutus pulled frantically on the leash. Maddy's arms felt like they were being wrenched from their sockets as she tried to hold him in check. "Here, will you take him? He needs the alpha-male touch."

Tom took the leash. "Brutus. Heel," he said in a commanding voice. Brutus immediately did as he was told.

Maddy looked from the dog to Tom. "It's the alpha-male thing, all right," she said. "Brutus recognizes it."

"I don't know about that," said Tom, "he's just spoiled rotten and knows he can get away with murder around you."

"Hmm," she said, not willing to concede her theory.

Wouldn't anyone think Tom was an alpha-male type? Physically, he stood head and shoulders above other men and he had an undeniable air of authority. His voice was deep and strong.

And when it came to kissing he was without a doubt 200 percent, hot-blooded, testosterone-powered male. Her cheeks flushed warm at the thought of it.

They reached home and Maddy was grateful for the chilly breeze from the water, both to cool her face and to blame for the way her nipples had tightened thinking about Tom's testosterone.

"Thank heaven we found this naughty dog," she said in a forcedly light voice as they walked down through the yard. She hoped Tom wouldn't notice her breasts and folded her arms in front of her. Which actually only drew Tom's gaze to her chest.

He looked, she flushed deeper, but then Tom turned away and unclipped the dog leash. Brutus scampered toward his kennel.

Deep breath, deep breath, try to act normal, she urged herself. "He can have a drink of water. Then I think I'll take him into my apartment with me where I can keep an eye on him," she said. "I've got to finish my recipe testing—I'm due in the office by three for a meeting."

"I've got back-to-back meetings for the rest of the day," said Tom, sounding anything but enthusiastic at the prospect.

"Poor you," she said. "Before you go, why not come in and taste the pie I'm working on? I'd like some feedback on it."

"Pie?" said Tom, a look of yearning on his face. "I thought I smelled pie."

"I'm experimenting with a new recipe, pear and pecan with a honey glaze."

It was Tom's eyes that looked glazed. "You tasted like honey when—"

He fell silent. So did she and the silence hung between them.

"When I kissed you," he slowly finished.

He was only kissing distance away and Maddy found herself gazing in fascination at his mouth. His lips were full and firm, the top one with an uneven curl she found most intriguing. She remembered how he tasted. How he felt. The heat of his body.

"I . . . I thought we weren't going to talk about kissing . . ." she managed to get out in a voice that was barely above a whisper.

"Or about why we shouldn't be kissing," he said, his voice deep and husky.

She was melting like chocolate again. Her lips parted, she found herself swaying toward him—when she saw movement from Brutus's kennel.

"Brutus! What is he eating?"

She dashed over to the little dog who was wrestling with a steak nearly as big as he was. He'd managed to chew off a sizeable chunk.

"I didn't give him that; did you?" she said, snatching it away from the animal. Brutus yapped his outrage.

"No, I didn't," said Tom, standing beside her. "Let me see it."

She handed the steak over. Cautiously, he sniffed at the meat. "It smells okay."

"Jerome might have given it to him," she said.

"That's what I'm afraid of," said Tom.

"Surely Jerome wouldn't—?"

"We don't know the guy, Maddy. Walter warned me about him. He specifically said that he didn't want him inheriting, he thought so little of him."

"He reminds me so much of Walter, it's hard to believe . . ."

"It's in our best-interest to keep Brutus alive, but Jerome might have another agenda altogether."

"If you think—"

She stopped mid-sentence. Brutus had suddenly gone quiet. She looked down. He lay on the grass with his legs collapsed under him.

"Brutus!" She dropped to her knees. The little dog raised his head, his button eyes glazed with pain and confusion. "Brutus, what's wrong?" Her voice felt strangled with fear.

Tom grabbed his cell phone. "Call his vet."

Maddy's hands shook as she took his cell. "Oh God, I don't know the number. It's in the house. Brutus, I'm so sorry." She felt paralyzed by terror and panic.

"Call nine-one-one."

She started to punch out the numbers. "Does nine-one-one help dogs? Of course they help dogs." She knew she was babbling but she couldn't stop herself. Guilt. Fear. Anxiety. All were churning so fast in her head she could scarcely think.

As she punched the final number, Brutus hauled himself up from the grass. He staggered. Then started to retch so violently she could see the muscles straining under his fur.

She dropped the cell. "Ohmigod, Brutus." Her mouth went dry with terror.

"Don't panic," said Tom. "If that steak was poisoned, this is good."

"You're right." Maddy stroked Brutus encouragingly on the back of his neck. "Come on, baby. Get rid of that nasty stuff."

After what seemed like an agonizingly long period Brutus barfed, expelling chunks of barely chewed steak. He retched until there was nothing left.

When it ended, Tom heaved an audible sigh of relief. "I never thought I'd be glad to see a dog do that. If the meat was poisoned, it wasn't inside him for long."

"Oh God, I hate Jerome. How could he have done this?" Maddy scooped Brutus into her arms and cradled him like a baby. She looked to Tom. "The vet. Now. C'mon."

Was it the word "vet" that perked Brutus up? Maddy couldn't be sure but the next moment he was wriggling and squirming. His eyes were as bright as ever and his tail thumped against her arm. He gave a put-me-down-now bark.

Maddy pressed kisses to his furry little head. "Thank heaven! But you still have to go to the"—she spelled out the word— "V-E-T." Brutus twisted and turned to get out of her arms but she held him firm.

Maddy looked from Tom to the ground and back again. "Tom, the vet might want to inspect the . . . the . . . puke."

Tom's face went so green she wondered if he might be the next to perform.

"Quick. There are some doggy-doo bags behind the kennel," she said.

Still holding the protesting Brutus, Maddy dashed inside her apartment to pick up her purse. When she came back out, Tom was waiting outside the door, a small plastic bag held at arm's length.

She followed him, two steps to his one, as he strode up the side path toward the street. Only to bump into his back as he came to a sudden halt. She blinked at the flashes that exploded in her eyes. Then peered at the two men who stood outside the gate.

Tom's arm restrained her. "Remember. No comment."

She recognized the cameraman from the media posse at the church steps. The one who had made the offensive mistress remark. She didn't know the other one.

He leered at her. "Cozy up to your boyfriend for me, Maddy. C'mon, give me a good shot."

Horrified, intimidated, and sick with anxiety at the delay in getting Brutus to the car, she shouted, "Leave us alone!" She pushed open the gate. "Let me through. This dog has been poisoned. I have to get him to the vet."

She didn't have to hear Tom groan beside her to realize that it was completely the wrong thing to say.

· Nine ·

Maddy was helping her friend Serena into a bathtub full of chocolate sauce when her cell phone rang. Darn! Since yesterday's incident with the reporters she had been wary of answering it. But she had to pick up. She was expecting some last-minute props to arrive by courier at the studio and it was already well into the afternoon.

Her heart thudded into double-quick time when she heard Tom's voice.

"You okay? No more harassment?"

"I left really early this morning to avoid them."

Then her revved-up heartbeat nearly stopped at his news.

"The steak was poisoned? Jerome. I hate him."

"We have no proof it was Jerome," came Tom's reasoned lawyer tones.

"Only a heck of a suspicion."

She felt sick at the thought of what might have happened if

Brutus—never known for his discrimination in choice of food—
had eaten more than just a bite of the T-bone. As it was, the vet
had dosed the little dog with charcoal to stop any poison ab-
sorption. Then, after a few hours' observation, she'd pronounced
him okay.

"Where is Brutus now?" Tom asked.

"With me. I'm on a shoot, and I brought him along. After
yesterday I didn't want to leave him home alone."

"Good girl," said Tom. Surprisingly, Maddy found herself
basking in his approving tone, rather than bristling at being pa-
tronized as she would have done before he'd kissed her.

"Maddy," complained Serena, sliding down into the tub, "this
chocolate stuff is cold. Could you get off the phone?"

"Tom, I'm working," Maddy said, not even attempting to explain what that work entailed, "I've got to go."

"We need to talk about this, Maddy." His tone was urgent.
"Can we make a time to meet?"

"I'll be finished here soon, why not come over?"

"Where's 'here'?"

Maddy gave him the address of the photographic studio in
the SoMa District and then disconnected her cell phone.

"The ten-out-of-ten lawyer?" quizzed Serena. "The one who
is hotter than hot? I saw him on TV with you outside the
church."

"Tell you later," said Maddy in an undertone, aware of Joel
the photographer by her elbow. Joel had tried to hit on her several times, and she guarded her privacy around him.

Actually, she wasn't sure she wanted to share even with
Serena the irrational, bubbling excitement she felt at the thought
of seeing Tom again. It was too new, too unexplored.

"Right," said Serena with a lift of her perfectly arched brows. "Later. And I'll hold you to that."

"C'mon, girls," said Joel, "let's get on with it. Serena's boobs are nicely covered in chocolate and ready to shoot." He leered and made exaggerated licking motions in Serena's direction.

Maddy groaned and Serena pulled a face before they both laughed and told Joel to shut up.

It was great fun working with Serena. She was a part-time model, a part-time veterinary technician student, and Maddy's best friend. They'd met when Serena was waitressing in a restaurant in North Beach where Maddy was sous chef.

When Maddy had come up with the girl-in-a-tub-of-chocolate idea to illustrate her "The Ultimate Chocolate Fix" feature, naturally she'd booked Serena for the job.

"Right," Maddy said to her friend. "I'll get the triple-choc brownie. I want you to look at it as if—"

"As if it's your lover, darling," said Joel.

Tom climbed his way up the stairs of the huge old building, once a warehouse, now converted to photographic studios.

He managed to get past the heavily made-up girl manning the desk at the entrance of studio five. She had a pierced tongue that he'd found it difficult not to stare at while she spoke. In his dark business suit and carrying a briefcase he felt totally out of place.

The smell of cooking welcomed him as he made his way into the cavernous, white-painted room. Chocolate again. His mouth watered. How would Maddy taste to kiss when she'd been eating chocolate?

Not that he'd be kissing her again to find out, he told himself. He'd been distracted yesterday, but now he was back on track, his five-year plan firmly in mind. And he wouldn't let himself forget it.

He hadn't been too sure what to expect at Maddy's "shoot." He wasn't surprised at the stainless steel, open-plan kitchen. Or the tall, white windows flooding the room with afternoon light.

But he sure as hell hadn't been expecting to find a beautiful dark-haired girl reclining in an old-fashioned claw-footed bathtub full of liquid chocolate. Was she naked under there?

The tub was surrounded by photographic lights and reflectors. Maddy stood with her back to him peering at an image on a computer screen and discussing it with a short blond man whom Tom presumed was the photographer.

Tom cleared his throat to get her attention. Maddy spun around at the sound. He was gratified at the look of pleasure that lit up her face. "Tom! You got here so quickly we're not quite finished yet. We're having trouble with this final shot and—"

"Enough of the chitchat, Maddy," cut in the gorgeous girl from the bath. "I want out of this chocolate ASAP. Let's get on with it."

"She's worried that calories can be absorbed via the skin," explained Maddy in the same teasing tone she used on him. "Guys, this is Tom. Tom, this is Serena and Joel."

Joel nodded a terse greeting. Tom had the distinct feeling that Joel was guarding his territory. Who was he interested in— Serena or Maddy? It had better not be Maddy. He found himself ready to growl at the thought. Though lifting his leg to mark his territory might be going too far.

"Hi, Tom," said Serena in a voice as rich and sultry as the chocolate she was bathing in, "I've heard all about you."

She had? Tom felt like his jaw was dropping to the floor at the vision of the chocolate-coated goddess. With dark hair tumbling to her shoulders, smooth olive skin, and topaz eyes she was a picture of his "ideal woman" come to life.

So why did his gaze stray immediately to the slender redhead wrapped in a chocolate-smeared white apron?

Goddesses, he decided, could be quite boring when compared to a feisty, funny girl with freckles across the bridge of her nose, a girl whose kisses tasted of honey. Not that he was going to allow himself to dwell on how she tasted, how she felt in his arms . . .

The photographer spoke, "I think we've got it this time, Maddy. I'll shoot off a final set, and we can finish."

Maddy nodded to another girl hovering behind the photographer. Tom noticed with a shudder that she was pierced not only through the nose but also below each eyebrow. "Amy, Joel's assistant," Maddy said briefly by way of introduction. "And over there in the kitchen is Jane, who is helping me with the cooking."

She called across to Jane, "We're ready for another brownie, please."

All these people—and Maddy confidently in charge, her passion and commitment to her job shining from her. Tom found himself fascinated at seeing her in action in her world—a world so different from his own. There were not many opportunities in a law firm to work with chocolate-coated women.

Serena took the brownie and posed with it, her eyes heavy with mock desire as she held it to her mouth.

"Perfect, darling," said Joel as he photographed her.

Tom turned to Maddy. "Can I ask what this is all about?" he asked, unable to contain his curiosity.

"Remember that brownie recipe I was testing the day I first met you?" she explained in a low voice, not taking her eye off Serena. "Hang on—Joel, stop." She dashed over to Serena. "A piece of hair has fallen too far forward." Gently she smoothed it back from Serena's face. "That's okay now, thanks, Joel."

She stepped back to Tom. "Where was I? Yes, the brownie. It's one of a series of chocolate recipes for a feature I'm calling 'The Ultimate Chocolate Fix.' We've photographed the other recipes like a regular food shoot but I wanted this one to be really spectacular. This is for the opening double-page spread. Don't you think it will look sensational?"

Tom looked to the beautiful woman covered to just above her breasts in chocolate. "Sensational," he echoed. With conviction.

"I'm glad you think so," Maddy said. "I hope my editor will. You know I'm not permanent in my job at *Annie* magazine. I've been filling in for the regular food editor while she's been on maternity leave. Now she's decided to resign and stay at home with the baby, and I really want—"

"Done," said Joel as he finished shooting.

"Hooray," said Serena, "now get me out of here, Maddy."

Serena started to rise from the tub, the chocolate sauce streaming from her elegant elbows.

Tom didn't know where to look. So he did the gentlemanly thing and turned his back. Hmm. How would Maddy look in a tub of chocolate, the rich brown contrasting against the milkiness of her skin and her copper-colored hair? No need for a towel when she stepped out, he could lick it off her, starting first with . . .

He tried to force his thoughts to something less arousing. And found himself wondering if all the hair on Maddy's body was the same vivid color. Which was even more arousing.

Serena really was very naughty, getting out of the tub like that in front of Tom, thought Maddy. She knew her friend didn't mean to be provocative. As a model, Serena was so used to being semi-naked in front of male photographers she wasn't even aware of the effect she might be having on a so-serious lawyer. But Tom was different. And Tom was hers.

Tom was *hers*?

Maddy beat the errant thought out of her mind. Of course he wasn't hers. She had to deal with Tom because of Walter's unusual will. That's all. The kiss had just been . . . curiosity. Or that's what she'd been telling herself for the last twenty-four hours.

So why did it twist her heart at the thought of him panting over Serena—as most men did when they first met her extraordinarily beautiful friend?

She could scarcely admit her relief to herself when Tom had immediately turned away the minute it looked like the chocolate mantle would slide away from Serena's body. She couldn't have borne it if he'd taken the opportunity to ogle.

She held up a large towel for Serena. "Wipe off what you can, then dash into the shower," she advised her friend.

Serena leaned close. The smell of chocolate was overwhelming. "What a hottie! Definitely a ten," she whispered. "And he's smitten. I can tell."

"Shush," Maddy whispered, terrified Tom might hear. "He's just a friend. Not even that. More an . . . an acquaintance."

Serena snorted. "So why are you blushing?"

"I'm not blushing," Maddy lied, feeling her cheeks get warm, "but you're dripping chocolate all over the place—and me. Could you please get into the bathroom?"

Laughing, Serena did so, leaving a chocolaty trail behind her that Maddy knew she was going to have to clean up. She also wasn't quite sure how she was going to dispose of a bathtub full of slightly used molten chocolate.

Joel and his assistant had gone home to start editing the numerous pictures he had taken. Maddy was just about to tell Tom it was safe to turn around when there was the sound of frantic barking from the other side of the large double doors at the entrance to the studio.

The doors opened and in scurried Brutus, yapping excitedly, trailing his leash, and heading straight for Tom.

"Sorry, Maddy," said Will the studio manager, looking harassed. "I took him out for a walk, but as soon as I got back up the stairs, he started scratching on the door and—"

"That's okay, Will. He must have sensed that his alph—"

"Don't say it, Maddy," said Tom, doing the growl-like thing again.

"—that his friend Tom had arrived," amended Maddy.

Brutus leapt up and scrabbled at Tom's legs. "Settle down, boy," commanded Tom.

Brutus obeyed instantly and sat panting at his feet. He was wearing a jaunty red bandanna tied around his neck.

"Doesn't he look cute in his necktie?" asked Maddy.

"Very cute," said Tom dryly. "Good dog," he said, leaning down to rub him behind the ears and unclip his leash. "I'm relieved to see he's all right. If he'd eaten more of that meat, he would have been in big trouble."

Maddy sobered. "That's horrible, Tom. I'm still finding it hard to believe that Jerome could have been so . . . so evil."

"We can't prove it, remember," Tom cautioned. "The reporter and the photographer were hanging around, too."

"Can't prove what?" asked Serena coming up behind Maddy. She was now fully dressed.

Maddy filled her in on the poison T-bone episode.

Serena glowered. "That Jerome guy should be shot. He must know dogs are so greedy they don't know what's good or bad for them." She pointed at Brutus. "Like right now. Watch him head straight for the spilled chocolate on the floor."

"So?" said Tom. "Brutus eats cake. Why not chocolate?"

"Because it can make dogs sick," said Maddy, lunging for Brutus at the same time as Serena swooped down and swept the little dog up into her arms.

Brutus, thwarted, strained back toward the floor, whimpering.

"Why not let him do mop-up duty?" asked Tom.

"Because chocolate is toxic to dogs," said Serena.

Maddy stared at her. "Toxic? I know they shouldn't eat it. But toxic?"

"There's a chemical in chocolate called theobromine that could be lethal for Brutus," Serena explained. "Eat too much of it and he could start having convulsions. And then—" She mimed a finger cutting across her throat.

Tom paled beneath his tan.

Maddy had no reason to doubt Serena; her friend was a dog nut and knew all there was to know about canine care.

"What about cupcakes and peanut butter cookies?" Tom—back in full grim mode—asked Serena.

"They've never done him any harm," protested Maddy.

Serena continued to clutch Brutus to her. "The fat and sugar isn't great for him. But so long as there are no raisins or grapes in them, the odd bite of cookie or cake probably wouldn't hurt. But let him lap up all that chocolate and it could be bye-bye Brutus."

Maddy shuddered at the sound of her words. Death by chocolate? She'd made that dessert a thousand times without ever realizing there could be some truth in the title. For dogs, anyway.

She put her arms out to take Brutus from Serena and hugged him tight. "No more naughty snacks for you, then, mister piggy in disguise as a dog," she said.

Did Tom muffle a laugh at her words? She looked up sharply but he was straight-faced.

"And this time I really mean it," she said. "Honestly, Tom, I had no idea. I've told you before I don't know a lot about dogs. They were working animals back home on the ranch and I wasn't allowed to make pets of them. I had my horse and my mom had cats."

She couldn't bear it if he didn't believe her. She bit down on her lower lip to stop it from quivering. "But I'm doing my best. Really I am."

Tom's face softened and there was a hint, just a hint, of that disarming dimple. "I know you are," he said.

Grateful, she smiled at him, then petted Brutus. "From now on we've got to really watch what you eat, little guy," she said. Brutus greedily tried to lick at a smear of chocolate on her elbow. She jerked her arm away. "I'll have to be so careful."

"Maddy, you need to do more than that," said Tom, looking very serious again. "I think—"

At that moment Will the studio manager rushed into the room brandishing a newspaper. "Maddy, you should see this. I bought it at the grocery store when I took Brutus out for a walk."

Will's expression was a mix of curiosity and pity as he handed the sleazy tabloid to Maddy.

The headline was impossible to miss: "Heiress in Plot to Murder Millionaire Mutt?"

Maddy stared so hard at the bold black type it seemed to blur before her eyes. She had to shake her head to clear her vision.

Underneath the headline was a large color photo of her and a grim-faced Tom. She was clutching Brutus to her chest. Her dazed expression made her look guilty as hell. Of what, she couldn't imagine. She read on, nausea rising in her throat. "Poisoned pooch in mercy dash to doggy ER."

Worse was the second photo on the page. Her heart seemed to stop. She and Tom were kissing on the sidewalk, straining to each other as if they were about to tear each other's clothes off. "Old man's mistress in cahoots with attorney?" questioned the caption.

How could this be happening to her? What would this do to her career? Oh God, her family. And poor Tom . . .

The blood seemed to throb, throb, throb behind her eyes.

She felt dizzy from the heat of the studio lights, the sickly smell of the bathtub of chocolate. The fear of what people might believe of her.

"Maddy, what is it?"

She was aware that Will had left the room, murmuring something sympathetic, and taking Jane with him. Could hear Serena's voice coming from a long distance away. Feel her friend's hands gently pushing her down into a chair.

"This is so unfair," she said, forcing the words out of a pinched, parched throat. She remembered Tom's warning: *they'll dig for dirt.*

Tom took the newspaper as it slid from her suddenly numb fingers. Wordlessly, she watched him as he turned to the second page. He cursed.

"It gets worse," he said, as he handed the newspaper back to her.

"Let me see," said Serena, moving behind her. "Oh, Maddy, I'm so sorry."

There was her grandmother at her front door, giving the camera the finger. Her father's tight-set face with a reported "no comment." Her high school archenemy smirking from the page with the quote: "Maddy always thought she was too good for this small town."

And Jerome. He looked impossibly handsome and evilly sincere. "I was concerned about my great-uncle's state of mind. He was too feeble to see what the vixen was up to."

"Ohmigod, ohmigod," was all Maddy could get out. She buried her face in her hands.

"This is all lies," said Serena. "Tom, can't you and Maddy sue the newspaper?"

"The story is short on facts and long on speculation," said Tom. "But they've been careful not to publish anything libelous."

He put his hand on Maddy's shoulder. She lifted her face to meet his concerned gaze. "If it's any consolation, today's headlines are tomorrow's recycling," he said. "But other media might follow this up. It could get worse before it gets better."

Without a word, Serena walked over to the television in the corner and switched on a news channel. Tom and Maddy followed her. Almost immediately the text that ran at the bottom of the screen flashed the words: "Millionaire Mutt Under Threat."

"Oh no!" Maddy cried. "How can they say that?"

Before anyone had time to comment, the elegant female news anchor started her next item. The newspaper picture of Tom, Maddy, and Brutus flashed up behind her. Then a faded picture of young Walter, in his World War II naval uniform.

Maddy gasped. "Where on earth did they get that?"

"Three guesses," said Tom, "and the clues all start with the letter *J.*"

"It's a tale as old as time," the anchor started. "A lonely, wealthy old man. A sexy young woman. But there's a twist to this tale. And it *has* a tail."

The screen changed to a close-up of Brutus. "America is fascinated by the story of this cute little mutt worth millions." Brutus's pugnacious face with its jutting lower jaw made him seem to glare at the viewer. "Well," said the anchor, playing for laughs, "maybe not so cute. Maybe more . . . characterful."

Maddy realized she was holding her breath. She let it out as she lunged for the control. "Turn it off!"

The studio seemed very silent. Maddy turned to Tom. Her heart was pounding. "So what do I do now?"

"You and Brutus move out of your apartment and go into hiding."

For a long second Maddy stared at him, uncertain she'd heard right. "Go into hiding? Why?"

Tom answered as only Tom could answer. By listing his reasons and ticking them off on his fingers.

"One: Jerome Stoddard could be trying to get Brutus out of the way to give him a better chance to contest Walter's will. Two: the media now knows where you live and will camp on your doorstep and make your life hell. Three: all kinds of lowlifes might come out of the woodwork—dognappers, blackmailers, stalkers."

Maddy was so shocked she could hardly think. "But where could I go?"

"Well," said Tom slowly, "I have—"

"You can move in with me," said Serena. "I'd love to have you, and Brutus will be company for Snowball."

"Snowball?" asked Tom.

"My Maltese terrier," said Serena.

"Boy or girl?"

"Boy."

"Good," said Tom, and Maddy couldn't be sure if he was serious or not. "We don't want to disburse any more funds to Brutus's ill-gotten progeny."

Maddy laughed, but her laugh came out forced and she knew it.

"Okay, Maddy?" Tom asked and she appreciated the concern in his eyes. She wondered if for a moment he'd been about to suggest she move into his place. In spite of herself a thrill ran through her at the thought.

Maddy hugged Brutus so tightly to her he yelped. She loosened her grip to just tight enough to keep him in check. Poor little thing had escaped death by chocolate only to nearly suffer asphyxiation by hugging. How good a dog guardian was she?

She began to feel overwhelmed by all that had happened since Walter's passing. She shivered. "Tom, I'm scared. This is all so horrible. I can't believe those reporters went after my family. And how could anyone want to harm this little animal? I'm not sure I can handle it."

Tom closed the distance between them and put his arm around her. It felt warm and comforting and she leaned gratefully against him, snuggling her head into his shoulder. It felt wonderful to be close to him again. She breathed in the heady, citrus maleness of him.

"Of course you can handle it," he said, his voice deep and re-assuring. "You're strong and you're brave. Walter wouldn't have entrusted Brutus to you if he didn't believe you could look after him."

Did she feel a light brush of his lips against her hair?

She twisted her neck to look up at him. His face was so close she could easily reach up and kiss that dimple. She started melting again. "You think so?" Her voice didn't come out very strong or brave.

"I do. And you've got friends to help you. Isn't that so, Serena?" he said.

"All the way," said Serena.

Friends? Maddy pulled away from Tom. Did he see himself just as a friend? But wasn't that what she'd told Serena he was to her? Darn it, she wanted him to kiss her again. To run his hands along her body, to hold her to his hard muscles. Not just be friends.

But do so and she might end up on TV screens all over the country.

This was all way too confusing. She put Brutus down on the floor and fastened his leash. This dog wasn't going anywhere near that chocolate, no matter how much he whimpered and strained toward it.

She turned to face Tom and Serena and took a deep breath. "Okay, I'll decamp to Serena's. But for how long?"

"Until the twenty-one days expire," said Tom. "That's fourteen days."

"I thought you'd say that," she said with a sigh. "Do you realize how awkward this will be for me? Serena's kitchen is designed to microwave frozen diet meals and make egg-white omelets."

"Oh, come on, Maddy, it'll be fun," said Serena. "I'll wipe the cobwebs off the stove for you."

"Fun. Of course it will be. And I'm so grateful you're taking me in." She took another deep breath. She had to stop thinking about those awful headlines. "Right, well, anyone got any ideas on how to siphon the chocolate into the trash?"

"We'll think of something," said Tom. "Just point me in the direction of where you need help."

Help? He was going to help her clean up? Somehow she hadn't expected that. Russell had never, ever offered to help her with her work. Or even shown much interest in it. It had been all about his career.

"Me, too," said Serena.

"Right, well, let's feed the workers first," said Maddy, feeling immeasurably cheered. "Would you like a brownie? Or a slice of chocolate fudge cake? Strawberries dipped in chocolate, maybe?"

"Okay if I scrape the chocolate off the strawberries?" asked Serena.

Maddy was amazed at the look of almost anguish that contorted Tom's handsome face. "Haven't you got anything that isn't chocolate?" he asked.

"Not today," she said. "We're talking the Ultimate Chocolate Fix here, remember."

"To hell with the cholesterol," he said finally, "I've got to try one of your brownies."

Brutus whimpered at the sound of the word. "Kibble for you, Brutus," said Maddy, "from a sealed packet that no one could have tampered with."

"Right," said Tom to Maddy. "And after that I'll take you to your apartment while you get your stuff together to go to Serena's. I want to make damn sure Jerome isn't sniffing around again. And that you don't accidentally blurt out a new headline for the media."

· Ten ·

Tom tried hard not to look at Maddy's underwear as she stuffed it haphazardly into the bright purple suitcase that lay open on top of her bed. The lid of the suitcase was up and she probably thought he couldn't see what she was doing. But he could.

He hadn't given any thought to her underwear before. But if he had he would probably have imagined something along the lines of fresh white cotton—charming in its simplicity but not really mattering much as he'd just want to get it off her ASAP.

Now he couldn't stop thinking about her underwear. Black lace bras that wouldn't hide a thing from a man's hungry eyes, thong panties in a rainbow of colors, barely there bikinis—and was that a frilly garter belt? Had she bought out Victoria's Secret?

He felt his body reacting as he imagined Maddy's milky skin peeking through black lace, her delicious curves cupped by something silky and sheer, the alluring triangle of her thong . . .

He couldn't quite suppress a groan and she looked up at him with those wide, candid eyes. A silky camisole the color of warm, naked skin dangled from her hand.

"Tom, are you okay? Are you worrying about those reporters? I—" Then she faltered. "Oh," she said reading the message of his eyes, his body. Color flooded her cheeks. She dropped the camisole.

The bed loomed between them, a white iron bed covered in a silky quilt and a heap of embroidered pillows. As soft and feminine as its owner. And as enticing. For a long moment her gaze locked with his across the expanse of flowery silk. Was she thinking what he was thinking? Because if she was—

Maddy slammed the suitcase shut. Her flush deepened. She spoke very quickly. "That's the clothes packed. Now the kitchen stuff—Serena hasn't got so much as a decent saucepan. And Brutus's things, of course, and—"

So she wasn't thinking what he was thinking. In spite of the hard peaks her nipples had formed under her snug-fitting T-shirt. "I get the picture," he said, commanding his body to a mental cold shower. "If you've finished packing, I'll take this suitcase out to the car."

"Fine. Great. Thanks," she said, making several attempts to lock the suitcase before succeeding. "Just be careful, it's got my—"

"I know what it's got in it," he said, more gruffly than he'd intended, still amazed at the surprise of the sexy underwear she owned. What did she have on now under her T-shirt and jeans? A low-cut sheer bra that barely contained her breasts? Thong panties?

"I was going to say my lucky china pony, actually," she said, obviously making an effort to look dignified despite knowing he'd seen the contents of her underwear drawer. "I would never move anywhere without it. It's wrapped in my . . . never mind what it's wrapped in."

"A lucky china pony," he said slowly, envying the figurine. Would he ever get so lucky and be wrapped in her . . . whatever? "Is that the one that sits on your mantelpiece?"

"Yes," she said, "It was a gift from my mother and it really works—got me through all my exams. And job interviews."

"And the proof of that would stand up in a court of law?" he asked, enjoying the annoyed exasperation on her face.

"It works for me and that's all that counts," she said with dignity. "Now, come on, I've got to pack that other stuff I'll need at Serena's house."

Maddy's bedroom was small and she could not get past him to the door without brushing against him. Her shoulder touched his arm and it felt like an electric shock pulsing through his body. It was all he could do not to reach out and pull her to him, to kiss her senseless, and then fall with her onto that bed, which didn't seem strong enough to bear his weight, let alone the two of them.

The precise details of the five-year plan, sections 2a through 2c, were starting to get fuzzy in his memory. "Maddy," he said hoarsely.

She looked up at him, her pupils so black they nearly obscured the green of her eyes. "I still don't think it's a good idea," she said.

"What's not a good idea?" he said, struggling to maintain his equilibrium.

★　★　★

"K ... kissing you," Maddy stammered, fighting the urge to wind her arms around his neck and claim that sexy mouth. She was finding it very difficult to find reasons why she shouldn't kiss Tom O'Brien in private and away from prying cameras. But being in such close proximity to a bed should probably be one of them.

With his shirtsleeves rolled up and the first few buttons of his shirt undone he was so handsome that just looking at him sent a shiver of desire through her. His hair was all mussed up from his habit of raking his hands through it. She didn't know whether she wanted to smooth it down or ruffle it some more.

"Who said anything about kissing?" he said.

"You did," she said, knowing that he hadn't. But he'd had a kissing look about him. That she could be sure of.

"If it's no to kissing, how about holding hands? That's harmless enough, isn't it?" A half smile played lazily around his mouth—the sexy mouth of the best kisser in the universe.

"I ... I guess," she said, struggling with the warmth that was rising in her body at the thought of just holding hands with Tom O'Brien.

Very deliberately, he picked up her hand. He started to stroke the palm with his fingers, circling it slowly round and round. Not a tickle, more a caress. Then he moved up each of her fingers one by one, stroking right to the tip. She shivered with pleasure.

Harmless? Had he said harmless? There was nothing harmless about the way Tom O'Brien held hands. If his hand felt this good on her hand, how would it feel on her body, stroking and caressing her bare skin, exploring parts of her that were just waiting to be discovered by him?

"So," he said.

"H . . . holding hands is good," she managed to get out of a suddenly constricted throat.

He took both her hands in his and slowly pulled her to him. "How about hugging? Some harmless hugging?" he said, his face very close, his voice deep and husky.

Her softness yielded to his hard strength, her nipples tingled and firmed as she pressed against his chest, then wound her arms around his back.

"Hugging is good, too," she said, finding it difficult to breathe.

He slid his hands up her arms and shoulders, found the tender nape of her neck, and pushed his hands up through her hair over her suddenly sensitized scalp and right through to the very ends of her hair. The slow, sensuous movement felt amazing. She closed her eyes to savor the sensation as he did it over and over again until she felt the consistency of the molten chocolate in Serena's bathtub.

"Head massage is good, too," she murmured finally, opening her eyes to look up into his face. "Very good," she added.

His eyes were intent on her. They were beautiful eyes for a man, brown and warm with thick black eyelashes. And she was fascinated by his mouth—firm, well sculpted with that slight curl on his upper lip that she found so darn sexy.

"Maybe . . . maybe kissing would be good, too." She sighed in surrender and, finally, lifted her mouth to his.

The kiss wasn't just good, it was bliss, his lips firm and warm, his tongue doing wonderful things to hers, practiced but tender, sure but sensual. She pressed closer to him, reveling in the sensation, thrilling to the feel of his heartbeat, deepening the kiss, tasting chocolate, breathing the intoxicating citrus male scent of him.

Eventually, she surfaced. "Kissing is very, very good," she murmured before going back for more.

His hands, warm and exciting on her bare skin, slid under her T-shirt. She welcomed them as he cupped her breasts over the sheer silkiness of her bra, gasping as he circled her tense nipples with his thumbs. She was melting, yearning; aware she didn't want to go any further than this—it was way too soon—yet not wanting him to stop.

Knowing she should leave the warmth, break the kiss, she pulled away. He held her tightly for just a second, let her feel the evidence of his arousal, then released her.

Maddy didn't want words. She just wanted to stand, resting her head on his shoulder, hearing nothing but the thudding of his heart and his ragged breathing, and try to get her own breathing back to normal.

She knew her definition of a kiss would never be the same again, and she tried not to think about what that meant. All she knew was that being in Tom O'Brien's arms was utter heaven. And that liking it so much was terrifying her.

Getting too attached to him and then losing him would be hell. She didn't want that kind of upset at this stage of her career. Couldn't take that kind of risk. She'd gone to pieces after her engagement to Russell was broken. Had come dangerously close to getting sacked from the restaurant where she'd worked at the time. She couldn't afford for that to happen again. Not when she was getting so close to her goals at *Annie* magazine. And not when she was feeling so uptight and uncertain about Brutus, Jerome, and the scary press intrusion in her life.

With her head on his shoulder, she couldn't see his face. She cleared her throat. "You . . . you never told me about your plan. You know, the one that didn't allow for kissing. Even though there is photographic, front-page proof that we already kissed."

"You don't want to hear about my plan," he said, caressing the back of her neck.

"Yes, I do."

"Not now you don't." His voice was hoarse.

She lifted her head from his shoulder to meet his gaze. "Seriously, you said you'd tell me about it."

Why was he being so evasive? Maddy pulled away from him, suddenly aware that it was important she knew about his plan before she kissed him again. She would not let herself be distracted by the tantalizing way he was stroking her ear.

"It's no big deal," he said. He started to shrug his shoulders and then abruptly stopped himself. Curious. An old football injury causing him pain on the upward shrug, perhaps?

He set his shoulders square. "It's just my plan for my life. You know, goals, ambitions. I make a new one every five years."

She felt incredulous. "You actually write it down? A plan for your life?"

"On my PC, yes. And linked to my BlackBerry of course." He looked uncomfortable at his admission, shifting his weight from foot to foot.

"You're not serious?"

"I'm very serious."

Suddenly Maddy felt like she wasn't getting enough air. She sucked in a deep breath.

"So you stick to this plan? Without deviating?"

He nodded. "That works for me."

"And the plan doesn't include kissing?"

Tom raked his hand through his hair until it stood on end. "Maddy, it's all about work. My goal is to make partner. That's what's most important to me."

It's all about work. That certainly put her in her place with a painful jolt. "You . . . didn't answer my kissing question."

"Of course it doesn't say no kissing, just—"

"I get it," she interrupted. "Just no kissing of the serious kind."

"Well, yeah, I guess you could say that." He didn't seem aware that he was raking his hair again. But she had lost the urge to smooth it back into place.

"I see," she said slowly. "The dirty *C* word. You know, commitment."

"Maddy I'm not against commitment. Just not right now."

"Not in this particular five-year plan, you mean."

He rammed his fists to his side. "Maddy, now is my time. I want to make partner. My work has to come first. I can't throw in the towel right now. I can't afford to be sidetracked."

"By a relationship you mean?" She couldn't help the slight note of accusation from creeping into her voice and was angry with herself because of it.

"You're making it sound worse than it is. Maybe it's different for girls. Maybe your work is not as important to you as it is to guys. You know, with babies and stuff . . ." His voice faltered away.

She gasped. How much worse could it get? Her work not as important as his just because she was female? In what year of the Middle Ages had she landed?

He went to put his arms around her again; she stepped back. Her hip banged on the edge of the dressing table, but she barely felt it. She laughed, hoping it sounded lighthearted, knowing it was anything but.

"You know, I might not have a written plan for my life but, like you, my work is very important to me. Even if I am a girl." She couldn't resist a note of sarcasm on the final phrase. "They're making a television show for *Annie* magazine, and I'm in the running to be the on-air cooking presenter. That is, if I don't get fired because of the Brutus publicity."

"Maddy, that's great." His enthusiasm sounded 100 percent genuine. Which only slightly mollified how she felt about his statement. "You'd be fantastic on television."

"Well, the eggs might have been broken but the cake's not baked yet. I still have to prove myself."

"They'd be crazy not to give the job to you. That brownie was out of this world. So was the fudge cake."

"Even if you did moan about the cholesterol."

"It was worth it," he said. "Every crumb."

"Thanks," she said. "I know I'm good at what I do, and I'm determined to get the job."

She stepped back from him, suddenly conscious of how close they still stood. She took a deep breath. "Unlike you, I wouldn't see a special person as a 'distraction.' I figure you can have both a commitment and a career. Eventually. When you're both ready that is, and right now I'm not."

He tried to say something but she spoke over him.

"But maybe that *is* a girl thing. You're not the only man I've known who thinks the way you do. I've told you about my family. And my ex-fiancé expected me to put his job before my ambitions."

She decided not to mention the underpants thing.

Tom looked uncomfortable. There wasn't a dimple in sight. "Maddy, I just meant that sometimes there are more important things for women that men don't—"

She spoke over him. "I know exactly what you meant." She took another deep breath. "That kind of attitude is why I broke off my engagement. And that's why I'm sticking to the two-date rule. I'm avoiding that other *C* word—complications. So you see, we're not really that different."

"So?" he said, his brow furrowed. "We're both into our careers. But we're attracted to each other. If we both went into this with our eyes wide open, it needn't affect either of our plans. So why not—?"

"Complicate things further? I don't think so. This whole business with Brutus is complicated enough. Besides," she added, "you've reached your use-by date."

If she hadn't felt perilously close to tears, she would have laughed at the look on his face.

"My use-by date?"

He looked so bemused she had to resist the urge to hug him. But he had both a plan that didn't include commitment, and an insanely outdated view that a woman's career was less important than a man's. And she had resolved that her career was more important than ironing a man's underpants.

So far Tom O'Brien, with his rigid five-year, no-serious-kissing master plan, gave every indication that he was no different from Russell. Or from her father and brothers, who had expected her to drop everything in favor of their needs. To put her own needs on permanent hold.

"Remember the two-date thing?" she asked.

He frowned. "Your two-date thing you mean? Yes, I remember. But how does that apply to me? We haven't dated."

That threw her for a moment. He had a point. She had to think hard. "You're right. Technically. But we have kissed—on two separate occasions."

"That doesn't count, surely."

"It counted to me and I'm the one doing the counting."

Tom stared at her. "Well, in that case, if you want to get pedantic about it, I kissed you more than twice."

He certainly had. Maddy went warm inside when she thought about that. How many kisses? She'd been too busy enjoying them to calculate. "You're right," she conceded. "But . . . but we're playing by my rules. We're talking . . . we're talking kissing occasions here. Two kissing occasions equals two dates. And that's where I cut out. Sorry."

Maddy didn't dare look at Tom. If she did, she'd find herself back in his arms and unable to think beyond the next kiss. She schooled herself not to give away anything of what she was feeling on her face.

She was cool and she was tough—the Two-Date Queen, Ms. No Complications, the Martha Stewart of Tomorrow. Getting that magazine job and then that television show was what she wanted, not a fling with someone who didn't count a relationship as anything important in his life.

She hardened her heart. Tom would be too easy to fall for. It was way easier to cut it off right here. "So two dates equals two kissing occasions equals one use-by date totally expired," she said, finally daring to look up at him.

★ ★ ★

Tom felt like he'd been tackled from behind. Agreed, there had been two of what she called "kissing occasions." *Kissing occasions*, for crying out loud! Only Maddy could come up with a phrase like that. But he hadn't realized that they would count against him in her date tally.

Hell, here he was trying desperately to stick to the five-year plan that had served him so well but getting waylaid by unwelcome hallucinations about red-haired babies. Not to mention fantasies of Maddy in her surprisingly sexy underwear.

Abiding by subsection 2c was getting more difficult by the minute. So difficult that he had been forced to face the fact that Maddy in his life meant he might have to make amendments to the current plan before it expired. For the first time in fifteen years of rigidly-adhered-to schedules.

She was beautiful, she was sexy, and she was smart. Not to mention funny, cute, and just a little bit crazy. But no woman was going to mess him around like that. The five-year plan was to be enforced again to the letter. And he wasn't going to be around to see what Maddy thought about it.

She was looking up at him with a mixture of trepidation and defiance. But the bomb proofing around his heart was back in place. This time with double reinforcement.

He didn't meet her gaze. "Right," he said, "your rules. Two . . . two *dates*, over and out." He couldn't bring himself to utter the phrase *kissing occasion*. "From now on it's strictly business."

"I'm good with that," she said.

He stepped toward the bed, picked up her suitcase, and hauled it over to the doorway. "Anyway, in light of the press's interest in us kissing, it would be advisable not to be seen together."

"Absolutely," she said. He sensed rather than saw that her chin was tilted skyward.

"As arranged, I'll help you get your stuff over to Serena's house."

"But—"

"I'll brief my assistant to help if you have any queries about the will, or Mrs. Pood—uh, Porter," he said.

"Right," she said, and when he finally met her gaze he saw she was calm and composed if a little wary around the eyes.

"You can go now if you want to. I don't need any help. What I'm taking is nothing compared to the props I drag around with me sometimes."

"I insist. It's important no one follows you to Serena's house."

She shrugged. "Okay. If you insist. But, Tom . . ."

"Yes," he replied, wondering if she was going to say she was relaxing the rules and what he'd do if she did. Kiss her again? Explain how there was no way he was going to forget about the five-year plan?

"You won't forget to say good-bye to Brutus, will you? He'll miss you."

Another sucker punch. Brutus would miss him?

Yeah, he guessed the little mutt had gotten attached to him. Maybe, just maybe, there might be something in this alpha-male business after all.

But would Maddy miss him? Because he suddenly knew—fight the thought as he might—that what she felt about him was important.

Really important.

· Eleven ·

Maddy let herself through the front door of Serena's house—a cute, remodeled Victorian in the Mission District. She'd been safely ensconced here for six days.

She was exhausted but buzzing. It was dream-come-true time at last. Today she'd been officially appointed food editor for *Annie* magazine. But the frosting on the cake was that she was up for an audition for the television show next week.

The editor in chief was understanding about the media attention—but only to a point. "No one who knows you could possibly believe you would boink that old man," she'd said. "But I don't want a senior editor involved in any scandal. Keep off their radar."

So far there had been no further tussles with the tabloid reporters. Maddy knew for her career's sake it had to stay that way.

She was dying to share her news about the job with Serena.

But as she walked down the hallway she could hear the faint rumble of a male voice coming from Serena's sitting room.

Tom? Her mouth went dry and her heart started to race. Although he'd called every day to check that Brutus was okay, he'd been cool, impersonal. Like an attorney doing business, not a man who'd passionately kissed her not so very long ago. Who'd held her hand in the sexiest way you could imagine and gave her a head massage that had nearly sent her into orbit.

He hadn't even let her commiserate with him when the tabloid had given him the same "dig for dirt" treatment they'd dished out to her.

But then why would he act any differently? She'd blown him off by invoking the two-date rule. And she'd been wondering ever since if she hadn't made a big, fat mistake in doing so. She'd missed him way more than she could have imagined, his company as much as his kisses.

Was he here? She stopped to listen again, more intently, before she entered the room. Disappointment swept over her. That wasn't Tom's distinct, husky voice. Already she knew she would pick it out from a roomful of conversation.

So who was the guy with Serena? Her boyfriend, Dave, was in the navy and away at sea. Serena was a one-man woman but from the laughter coming from the room she was certainly enjoying this man's company.

Maddy froze with shock when she saw who Serena's visitor was. Quite at home on the sofa and with a half-empty glass of white wine in front of him was Jerome.

He rose. "Ah, the delightful Madeleine," he said, moving to kiss her on the cheek.

Maddy ducked to avoid him and wiped her cheek where his mouth had nearly made contact. She glared at him. "Don't you mean 'vixen'?"

She signaled frantically with her eyes to Serena. How could she have let him in? How could her friend be laughing and flirting with this despicable, dog-poisoning man?

"Ah . . . that. A word I would never use. Unfortunately I was misquoted," said Jerome.

"I'd like to believe that," Maddy said through gritted teeth.

"Oh, but you must. It took me a while to track you down so I could apologize," Jerome continued in that rich, plummy voice. Only now Maddy felt it was edged with menace.

"Perhaps I didn't want to be tracked down," she said, not attempting to mask her truculence.

But the smile remained pinned to his face. "I've been enjoying the company of your charming and beautiful friend," he said, indicating Serena with an elegant wave of his hand.

"And I was just about to fix some coffee for us," said Serena. "Won't you give me a hand, Maddy?"

Maddy let herself be dragged into the kitchen. Before she could chastise her friend for letting Jerome through the door, Serena hissed, "I've kept him chatting until you got home. Now you can call the police."

"The police?"

"Yes. Get him for attempted dog murder." Serena's eyes flashed with excitement.

"Great idea." Maddy wondered how she could have doubted her friend.

She reached for the telephone. But then she seemed to hear

Tom's reasoned tones echoing in her head. She withdrew her hand. "Uh, but we don't have any proof, Serena. Tom would say we need concrete proof. Evidence."

"What about the poisoned T-bone? Tom said they had it frozen in the laboratory where he sent it for testing."

"I know, but we only suspected Jerome put it in the kennel. We don't know for sure. The police would just laugh at us."

Serena's face fell. "Darn, I thought we had him."

"Unfortunately not. We'd better get the coffee before the creep gets suspicious. Maybe we can think of something else."

She took the tray with the coffee mugs into the living room. It was disconcerting to find Jerome wandering around the room, idly picking up Serena's framed photos and examining them.

"So you've got a dog, too, Serena," he said, putting down a picture of Snowball.

Maddy swore she could hear menace again in his tone. Fear gripped her.

"No, I mean, yes, I mean, he's . . . he's at the vet," Serena lied.

"And Brutus is, too—at the vet, I mean," added Maddy, almost tripping over her words.

Jerome whipped around. "You mean Brutus isn't well?" His eyes narrowed. "The press reported he'd made a full recovery."

Maddy felt sick to her stomach as she followed his train of thought. Brutus was just fine, but that was no thanks to Jerome.

"He's at the vet to be . . . to be wormed." She crossed her fingers and hoped Brutus wouldn't start yapping from out back.

"Oh." Jerome's face fell. He sat down again. He sipped his coffee. "You're living here with Serena now, are you?"

How the heck did he know that? Had he been stalking her? The thought sent unpleasant shivers down her spine.

It choked Maddy to have to converse with him but what could she do? Accuse Walter's great-nephew with no proof?

"No. Yes. Well, tonight I'm going away for work," she invented wildly. "Upstate. On location. Picnic stuff. No one will be able to contact me . . ."

"Oh," said Serena, catching on quickly. "You're, uh, going tonight?"

"Yes. Sorry I couldn't tell you sooner. Last-minute change of plan," Maddy babbled.

"I'll help you pack," said Serena. Then, with an expressive lift of her eyebrows she added, "Jerome . . ."

"Of course," he said, putting down his mug and getting up. He was so polite, so sophisticated, his British accent so smooth and assured, Maddy wondered if she could have been wrong about him.

"But before I go," he said, "I've brought a gift for Brutus." He pulled out of his leather satchel the most enormous block of chocolate Maddy had ever seen—dark chocolate that she now knew contained the highest concentration of the dog-deadly chemical. "I know the little mutt has a sweet tooth and—"

Serena gasped.

Maddy snatched the giant chocolate bar from his hand. "Sweet tooth! You must know darn well chocolate is poison to dogs."

Anger twisted through her. She ached to hit him with the block. It was heavy enough to do him serious injury. She could hide the evidence afterward by eating it. "You . . . you dog murderer."

Jerome threw his hands up in mock defense. "Chocolate? Poison? Wherever did you get such an idea? I brought it as a treat for the pooch."

But Maddy saw his smile did nothing to warm the iciness of his eyes.

"Don't act innocent with me, Jerome. You might have fooled me at first but I know you're trying to get Brutus out of the way. I won't let you hurt him."

All pretense of friendliness fled from Jerome. He took an intimidating step closer. Maddy held her ground. He sneered. "And how would a little thing like you stop me?"

Maddy shivered at the ominous intent in those too-blue eyes. But she squared her shoulders. "I have my ways."

"Huh. Like I'm frightened." He scowled. "You won't get that money, you greedy little gold digger. You or the mongrel."

Her face flushed at the insults to both herself and Brutus. But she didn't falter. "Walter left his fortune to Brutus. That's what he wanted."

"By rights that money should be mine."

Jerome's face was so contorted Maddy wondered why she had ever thought him handsome. "My great-grandfather sold his share of the Stoddard family business to his brother, Walter's father. He was cheated; the business was a money machine, he never got his rights—"

Maddy was shaking at the venom in his voice but she willed herself to speak evenly. "That was a long time ago, Jerome. And nothing to do with me. Or Brutus."

Serena wasn't as controlled. "Get out of my house," she shrieked at Jerome.

"Or I'll call the police," added Maddy.

Jerome slung his satchel over his shoulder. "I'll be back to get that dog—when you least expect it," he threatened as he stomped out of the room.

Maddy and Serena followed him up the hallway and slammed the door after him. Maddy leaned back against the wall, shaking, staring at Serena, unable to speak.

For the first time she felt it wasn't just Brutus who was in danger.

She might be, too.

AS Tom approached Serena's house, he was astounded to see that slimeball Stoddard coming down the steps, taking them two at a time. Halfway down the steps, the Englishman paused. Then deliberately turned back to make an ugly, obscene gesture at the closed door.

It was so sudden, so vicious that Tom stopped in his tracks. The vulgarity of the gesture, the fury behind it, made him feel ill. Because he was sure it had been aimed at Maddy.

He glanced up at Serena's house. Lights shone in the downstairs windows. One or both of the girls was at home. Stoddard obviously hadn't got the reception he had hoped for.

Jerome continued down the steps and Tom quickened his pace so he arrived at the start of the sidewalk at the same time the other man did.

He blocked Stoddard's way. "Interesting to see that sign language is the same on both sides of the Atlantic," he said.

Stoddard's expression told Tom that the Englishman realized he had been observed. Malice flickered in his eyes but was quickly replaced with his usual urbane mask. "I can't imagine what you mean," he said in the unctuous tones that had grated on Tom from the get-go.

Tom kept his anger on a tight rein. "What the hell are you doing here, Stoddard?" he demanded.

"Visiting your hot little girlfriend," the other man answered without missing a beat. "And her even hotter gal pal."

Tom gritted his teeth against the innuendo that laced Stoddard's voice. "You stay away from them." He took a step closer. Let the other man know he had both height and muscle advantage over him.

Stoddard acted as though he didn't notice, even though his shoulders braced defensively. "You've got dibs on both girls, have you?" His tone was deliberately lascivious. "I knew you'd scored with the redhead but her gorgeous friend with the big tits as well? I underestimated you. I'd like a piece of that one myself." His amiable smile seemed to magnify the offensiveness of his words.

Contempt for Stoddard knotted Tom's gut. How dare he talk about Maddy and her friend like that?

The Englishman was trying to provoke him. He knew that. The temptation to swipe that supercilious look off his face was overwhelming. But he clenched his hands into tight fists by his sides.

The worst thing he could do was lose his lawyer cool.

"My involvement with Madeleine Cartwright is purely in connection with Walter Stoddard's estate." He kept his voice even, measured.

"Indeed? That's not what my cameraman friend told me."

Despite his resolve, Tom saw red.

His cameraman friend.

From the day of the funeral, Tom had been suspicious of

Stoddard's connection with the tabloids. The article that had so upset Maddy. The "in-depth" revelations about Tom himself that had done nothing but rake over the story of his parents' ugly divorce. All traced back to Stoddard.

And then there was the poisoned T-bone.

Desire for revenge twisted through him.

The stretch of street was quiet. People were either having dinner at home or eating out at one of the Mission District's many restaurants. There would be no witnesses if he decided to teach this guy a lesson.

But that would make him as bad as Stoddard.

"Madeleine Cartwright is none of your business," said Tom.

Stoddard's mask slipped. His eyes glittered and his mouth thinned with malevolence. Instinctively, Tom recoiled. Although he dealt mainly with corporate law, he'd come across enough loonies in his work to know when one was standing in front of him. Jerome was more dangerous than he'd thought.

"Oh, but that little slut and the mangy cur are very much my business. They've stolen millions that should be mine. I won't let them get away with it."

The "little slut" bit did it for Tom. He grabbed Stoddard by both shoulders and flung him against the brick wall behind him. "Touch Maddy or the dog and you won't know what hit you."

Even with the breath knocked out of him Stoddard didn't fold. He coughed and spluttered and then choked out a laugh. "Temper, temper, Mr. Attorney." Tom pushed against his chest so he couldn't move.

Stoddard continued, "I planned to seduce her, you know. Get my money that way. I knew she fancied me. But you got there first. Wish I'd known she liked it rough."

Tom glared at him, fighting to keep his temper banked down. Then, disgusted, both at Stoddard and his own lapse in control, he dropped his hands from the Englishman's torso. He felt soiled from the contact and wiped his hands down the sides of his suit jacket.

"In the morning I'll get a judge to issue a protective injunction to keep you at least five hundred feet away from Madeleine Cartwright," he said.

Stoddard brushed himself down. "Don't waste your time, O'Brien. I've beaten you to the courthouse. I've already filed a petition to contest my great-uncle's will. One way or the other I have every intention of winning against you, your whore, and that filthy mongrel."

When the doorbell rang just minutes after Jerome left, Maddy shuddered. "Don't even think about letting him back in," she said to Serena.

Serena squinted through the peephole. She turned back to face Maddy. "It's not Jerome out there, it's Tom," she said.

Tom! After nearly a week it was Tom. Maddy couldn't help the unreasonable leap of her heart. She put her hands to her chest to try and stop its sudden furious pounding. Then she went to smooth her hair. She must look a mess after a long day at work.

"Don't worry about your hair, you look lovely," Serena whispered. "Should I let Tom in?"

"Yes. Of course."

She didn't have a chance to even think about what she'd say to Tom. Whether she'd tell him she'd missed him. Whether she'd say she'd made a mistake about his use-by date, that maybe, after all, he had some more shelf life left.

Tom's dark brows were drawn in a scowl, his mouth a grim line. "You're supposed to be in hiding. Why the hell did you let Stoddard in?"

Shocked by the anger in his words, she took a step back. "I didn't. Serena did. She kept him here so we could call the police."

"The police. Why? Did he hurt you?"

She frowned. After Jerome it was such a relief to see Tom. He was so strong. So solid. So darn sane. Yet he seemed more agitated than ever. She shook her head. "No."

He closed his eyes in relief. "Thank God."

"But he did try to kill Brutus again."

Tom's eyes flew open. "What!"

"He came armed with a block of chocolate."

Tom appeared struck dumb by her words. "Chocolate. To kill Brutus," he finally managed to get out. "You're, uh, sure about that?"

"Sure, I'm sure. You heard Serena at the studio last week. Chocolate is toxic to dogs, and Jerome was carrying the biggest block you've ever seen. Wasn't he, Serena?"

Maddy turned around to seek affirmation from her friend but Serena wasn't there. She'd disappeared inside without Maddy noticing. And now she was alone with Tom in a hallway that suddenly seemed very small.

Maddy was wearing the short denim skirt that showed off her long, slender legs and a top that made no secret of the shape of her lovely breasts.

Tom tortured himself for a moment by wondering what underwear she had on. And how it would be to slowly strip it off. He took a deep breath to steady himself but all that did was to intoxicate him with her scent.

He inhaled the familiar lavender, this time blended with . . . was it lemon? Had she been baking lemon meringue pie, perhaps? Another forbidden-to-him treat with all that pastry and egg yolk. He wanted to kiss her and find out. Hell, he wanted to kiss her just because he wanted to kiss her.

He bent his head to do just that but then abruptly pulled back. In the days he hadn't seen her, he'd been working on a complicated case of corporate fraud. But thoughts of Maddy had kept intervening no matter how hard he tried to push her to the back of his mind. The senior partners didn't help, either. Every time he encountered one, they asked him about Maddy. About the dog. But most of all about the bonus. The bonus Jackson, Jones, and Gentry needed and that would bring Tom a giant step closer to his goal.

No. He could not let her distract him from the main game, tempt him with happily-ever-after-type scenarios that were not part of his five-year plan.

It wasn't that he thought his world would collapse if he deviated from the plan. But he was in no mood to test it. Back when his father had left, Tom's world *had* fallen apart. And he hadn't liked the feeling. The rigidly constructed plans had kept him steered on course ever since. And impressing the partners with that bonus was a part of it.

So he'd vowed that there would be no more *kissing occasions*. Only to find the sight of flesh-and-blood Maddy had him wanting and yearning all over again. It was too damn complicated.

He stepped back. He cleared his throat. "You're sure you're okay?"

"Fine," she said in a small voice. She seemed to have sensed his rejection, and he had to force himself not to draw her to him in a reassuring hug.

Instead he assumed his best lawyer voice. "Stoddard didn't threaten you?"

"Me?" She looked surprised. "With the chocolate? No. Chocolate definitely isn't poison to me. I figure with all the chocolate I've consumed in my lifetime that I'm immune. No matter how much theo . . . theobromine or whatever it's called is in it."

He couldn't help but smile at her words. She put the craziest twist on things. Crazy but utterly endearing.

"No. I mean did he threaten you personally?"

Her eyes were huge in her heart-shaped face. "Why do you keep asking me that? You're freaking me out."

"I met Stoddard outside on the sidewalk. The gloves are off. He told me he's going to contest Walter's will."

Maddy took a sharp intake of breath. Tom couldn't help noticing how enticingly her breasts rose on the intake.

"What does that mean?"

"He's a blood relative who was not provided for by the estate. It could get ugly. But rest assured, I bulletproofed Walter's unconventional will."

"Still, Jerome's got a chance of disinheriting Brutus?"

"Not if I have anything to do with it. But it's perfectly legal for him to have a shot at it."

"What happens to Brutus if Jerome wins? Would I get to keep him?"

"I'd make sure of it. No way could Stoddard be allowed near him."

Maddy's eyes narrowed. "That's not all, is it? You're not telling me everything."

Tom paused. So much of what he'd deduced about Stoddard this evening was just instinct. He had to be cautious. And how could he tell Maddy the Englishman had called her a slut and a whore?

"Stoddard is not a nice guy, Maddy." That was the under-statement of the year. "The point is I'm worried that having failed with Brutus he might try to hurt you now."

She paled and the scattering of freckles stood out on her nose. "Me?" she said slowly.

"The way he sees it, there's just you and Brutus between him and Walter's millions."

"But that's insane."

"Maybe. I don't like that he knows where you're living."

She put her hand up to her mouth in mock shock. "You mean he might toss a poisoned bagel into the kitchen window for me to have for breakfast?" She laughed, but it was a high-pitched laugh that didn't reach her eyes.

Tom gritted his teeth. He couldn't bear to think of anything happening to her. He wanted to protect her, make her see the seriousness of the situation, but at the same time he didn't want to distress her too much by alerting her to the psycho intent he'd seen in Jerome's eyes.

"Who knows what he's capable of? I believe it's imperative that both you and Brutus stay out of his way until the twenty-one days expire."

"You mean, like, go into hiding again?"

"That's exactly what I mean."

She chewed on her lower lip. "He did say he'd be back to get Brutus when we least expected it."

"Did he?" So now Stoddard was open in his threats. "He'll also alert his media buddies to your new address."

Maddy twisted her hands together. "My editor told me she didn't want to see my photo anywhere but on the pages of *Annie* magazine. I have to stay out of their way."

"I agree."

Maddy thought out loud. "But I don't have anywhere to go. None of my other friends have room for me and Brutus."

Tom took a deep breath. What he was going to say he would probably regret. There was no subsection in the plan to cover this contingency. "I figured as much. What you really need is access to a secure apartment with a twenty-four-hour doorman where you can hide out in safety. Where no one unauthorized can get in or out."

Her mouth twisted. "Yeah. Sure. Like they drop out of trees every day," she said.

He cleared his throat. This was no-going-back time. "Well, maybe not every day. But certainly today. Maddy, I want you to come and stay in my apartment with me. Now. Tonight."

Maddy was shocked into silence. She stared disbelievingly at Tom before she finally found her voice. "Stay with you? In your apartment?"

"That's right. I bought the apartment as part of an investment portfolio. It's registered under the name of a company, so it would be difficult for anyone to trace you there. You'll be safe."

★　★　★

Safe? thought Maddy. That depended on his definition of safety. Safe from Jerome and unwelcome reporters maybe. But what about safe from Tom and the attraction she didn't want to feel? "Just you and me?"

"And Brutus."

"Of course."

"There's just one problem."

"Yes?"

"There are no dogs allowed where I live."

"No dogs," she repeated, knowing she sounded dopey but seizing on the opportunity to distract herself from the thought of being alone with Tom in his apartment. And to stop the surge of excitement that flared through her. "So what do we do about Brutus?"

"We think of ways around the restriction."

"You mean break the rules? Are lawyers allowed to do that?"

"Well . . ." he said and the dimple appeared for the first time that evening. With a great deal of effort, she refrained from leaning forward and kissing it "hello."

"We'll have to smuggle him in and keep him completely under wraps," he said.

"Which might not be so easy with Brutus."

"Correct."

She looked up at Tom. Some of the strain had gone from his eyes. He had never looked more handsome. Her heart did a series of disconcerting somersaults.

"Brutus has a pet carrier that Walter used to take him to the vet."

"Too obvious."

"What about my suitcase?" She answered her own question

before Tom had a chance to comment. "No. Too confined. He'd panic. And when he panics he po–"

"I don't want to know about that scenario." Tom grimaced.

Maddy thought. "I've got just the thing. We'll disguise him as shopping."

Tom's eyebrows rose. "Shopping?"

"I'm a chef. I'd be bringing food into your house, right?"

Tom nodded.

"I have a big woven straw market basket. It's deep, it has air holes, it has handles. And I can cover the top with a dishtowel. No one would dream there was a dog in there. We'll smuggle him into your apartment in my shopping basket."

· Twelve ·

Brutus did not want to be stuffed into a shopping basket. He did not want to be tucked in with a dishtowel. He protested. He barked. He scrabbled with his claws and scratched Maddy's arms. She yelped. Tom cursed. Then Brutus jumped out of the basket, scampered off, and hid behind Serena's sofa. To inform the humans of his extreme displeasure he peed on Serena's rug.

Thank heaven for the wonders of veterinary science, Maddy thought as, much later that night, she found herself outside Tom's imposing apartment block on South Beach. She had parked her car at a parking garage a few blocks back.

She was carrying her shopping basket with Brutus safely inside. Protruding from one corner, for authenticity's sake, was a bunch of celery and a couple of leeks. From inside the basket emanated the faintest of doggy snores.

Tom strode beside her, carrying her hastily-packed-again purple suitcase.

"Good thing Serena still had some of the dog sedative the vet prescribed for Snowball when he travels," Maddy whispered. "But we'd better get Brutus inside before it wears off."

Tom stopped mid-stride. "Don't call him Brutus," he hissed. "The whole country knows Brutus the millionaire mutt. That would be a dead giveaway. We'll have to call him something else."

Maddy stopped, too. "You're right," she whispered. "And there's another thing. What if someone hears us calling for him and knows we've got a dog in your apartment? I mean if he escapes or something. Why don't we give him a kid's name?"

Tom nodded his agreement. "Good idea. What kind of parents would call their kid Brutus?"

"Okay. So what will we call him?"

"How about Bruce?"

Traffic whizzed along the Embarcadero, and she wasn't sure she'd heard right. She forgot to whisper. "Bruce? Would you honestly call your child Bruce?"

Tom's eyebrows rose in exasperation. "What's wrong with the name Bruce? I play soccer with a very nice guy called Bruce."

"You're not serious? You wouldn't call a baby Bruce?"

Tom looked at her uncomprehendingly. "Does it matter what I'd call a baby?"

Suddenly it did. And the realization shocked her. Why would she be thinking about baby names and Tom O'Brien in the same thought? Or arguing with him about it? What did it matter to her what he'd call his kids? That is, if he ever got around to amending his famous plan to include them.

She shook her head to clear her brain of such disturbing thoughts. She'd better concentrate 100 percent on Brutus and getting him safely away from Jerome with his poison T-bone and toxic chocolate.

"Right. Bruce it is, though I'm agreeing under protest," she said.

She looked around her, impressed, as Tom keyed in the security code to the main entrance of the apartment complex. These executive apartments overlooking the South Beach Marina were quite the thing for an up-and-coming lawyer.

She continued to be impressed by the sleek, modern, marble-paved lobby. But it was definitely not dog friendly. She swallowed hard. Could they pull this off? If they couldn't, where else could she and Brutus go where they'd be safe?

Tom nodded in the direction of the doorman as they walked past. So did she. But just then Brutus shifted around in the basket and gave a distinct snore. The doorman looked over.

Maddy froze. Then started to cough. Loud, exaggerated coughing that she hoped could be mistaken for the snore.

Tom looked mystified. "Are you okay?"

"I'm fine," she spluttered, "just coughing, you know, coughing."

"I get it," said Tom. And kissed her.

Pow! Just the touch of his lips on hers and she felt weak at the knees. For a moment she swayed forward, wanting more. But she made herself pull back. "I'm . . . uh . . . okay now."

As soon as the elevator closed in front of them she kicked Tom lightly on the shin. "Hey, what was the kiss thing all about?"

Tom's brown eyes widened. "I was just distracting the doorman. You coughed. I kissed." His gaze appeared innocent, but she couldn't be sure of his motives.

"Well, quit with the kissing."

"It was just a pretend kiss."

"Well, quit the pretend kisses, too."

Why did he have to remind her that he was the sexiest kisser in the universe? Right when she was about to be holed up with him in his apartment. Just him and her, with their only chaperone a doped-up, unconscious little dog snoring away in a shopping basket.

"Right," Tom said, "no kissing even of the pretend kind. For a moment I forgot I'd passed my use-by date." His words were heavily underscored with sarcasm.

She felt herself flushing. "You know what I mean," she muttered.

A grin tugged around the corners of his sexy mouth. "You can explain it to me later," he said. "Maybe run the 'kissing occasion' theory by me again. I'm still not quite sure how it works."

As she carried Brutus in his basket out of the elevator, Maddy had to admit to herself that neither did she.

Tom's apartment was just as she'd imagined it—large and airy, with a wall of glass facing the water with views across the palm-tree-lined Embarcadero to the marina.

It was immaculately furnished in a minimalist style with tones of black, gray, and the occasional deep purple highlight. Stylish, expensive, and undoubtedly—she thought with a heart sinking rapidly south—the most dog-unfriendly place she had ever seen.

"I bought the display apartment," Tom explained, "all the furniture included. They used a top interior designer. All I had to do was move in."

His enthusiasm demanded a response but "Mmm" was all she was able to murmur. She preferred something with more character, something that reflected the personality of the human being who lived there. On a quick glance around she could see that Tom hadn't put his mark on the place at all. Everything was probably as the designer had left it. But didn't he say it was an investment, not a home?

Still in the shopping basket, but uncovered now and with no celery for company, Brutus stirred in his sleep, nose twitching, a paw quivering. Was he dreaming of chasing imaginary girlfriends, or of his little canine family? "Good little fellow," she crooned.

She looked up at Tom. "Brutus seems absolutely fine, but I wouldn't mind keeping him in the room with me so he doesn't get too scared when he wakes up."

"Good idea," said Tom.

"So, uh, where is my room?" she ventured.

Tom looked disconcerted. "Your room? Uh, actually there is only one bedroom."

Her defenses sprang immediately to life. She put up her hands as if to ward him off. "Tom, no way am I—"

"Maddy, you can sleep in my bedroom. I'll take the couch," he said, indicating a deep, black leather sofa positioned in front of an enormous flat-screen television.

She took a deep breath. Maybe she'd overreacted. "Fine," she said, "I . . . uh . . . fine."

Even in his fantasies, Tom hadn't thought about the sleeping arrangements once he'd gotten Maddy and Brutus safely into his apartment. His only concern had been to protect them from that maniac Jerome.

But now that he had her here, suddenly all he could think of was her in his bed lying seductively across it with her hair bright against the pale gray of the pillow and him slowly stripping her of her sexy underwear.

Were Maddy's thoughts running along the same erotic lines? She looked more ill at ease than he'd ever seen her, nervously twisting the leather handles of the basket, her cheeks flushed, not meeting his eyes.

"So. You'd better show me around. You know, kitchen, bathroom . . ." She paused as if the thought had just struck her. "I guess there's only one bathroom?"

Of course. She'd be sharing his bathroom. He groaned inwardly. Naked in his shower. Standing naked in front of his sink, reflected naked in his mirror. Dashing naked across the hallway to the bedroom even? How was he going to be able to endure this? He cleared his throat. "Yeah, there's just one bathroom, but I'll stay out of your way."

"We'll be sharing the bathroom with Brutus, too," Maddy informed him. "We'll have to put some paper down on the floor for him, in case of accidents. He's used to being outside."

"Accidents?" Tom shuddered at the thought of Brutus's "accidents" in his immaculate apartment. He certainly hadn't thought things through before issuing his impulsive invitation to Maddy and the mutt. And is *that* what she'd been thinking about while he'd been entertaining erotic thoughts of her?

"Yeah. Well, that can be your department," he warned. "And keep him away from the leather furniture."

He knew he didn't need to remind her of the incident with the BMW upholstery. Her deepened flush let him know she hadn't forgotten.

"I'll do my best," she said. "I'm sure the, uh, thing with your car was a one time deal. He certainly never chewed on any of my furniture or Walter's." She leaned over to croon at Brutus still zonked out in the basket. "Did you, little guy? Maybe you were upset on the day of the funeral."

Brutus opened one round black eye but closed it again immediately and burrowed farther into the basket.

"Do you seriously believe that he understands what you're saying?" Tom was unable to resist asking.

Maddy looked up at him, her eyes wide with surprise. "What do you mean?"

He gestured toward Brutus. "The way you talk to the dog. Like he's a person. Like you expect him to answer."

"Do I?" Her eyebrows rose.

"You must know you do. My mother does it to her cat, too. I guess it must be some kind of weird female thing."

"Weird female thing? I'm not sure that I like the sound of that. Do you, Brutus?" She slapped her hand to her mouth as she realized what she'd said. Then she giggled, a sound Tom found utterly delightful.

"See what I mean," he said unable to suppress a smile at the look on her face. "It's like you expect him to answer you."

She crinkled up her nose in that so-cute way that had become so familiar. "Maybe I do. Sort of. I've always talked to animals. My mother did, too. I'll swear my horse understood every word. I guess it probably does sound a bit . . . weird."

"Hmm . . ." Tom tried to sound noncommittal. He'd enjoyed riding horses. But he'd never talked to them beyond the required "go" and "whoa."

"My mother told me that of course the animals didn't understand the words but could tell from the tone of our voices that we loved them."

"Of course. It's all in the tone of the voice," agreed Tom, now totally unable to tease her anymore. Who knew? Like the alpha-male theory, maybe there was some kernel of truth in what she said.

She looked down at Brutus. "And I have grown very fond of this little animal." Suddenly she yawned, hastily covering her mouth with her hand. "It's been a hectic day," she said. "Let's skip the tour of the kitchen and bathroom and head straight for the bedroom."

Her hand dropped and she stared up at Tom. For a long moment he stared right back at her, as speechless as she was.

"Uh, th . . . that's not what I meant," she stuttered.

If only that's what she *had* meant to say. Right now Tom couldn't think of anything he'd like to do more than make love to Maddy. Only he was absolutely sure that if a "kissing occasion" was out of bounds for this passed-his-use-by-date man, a "red-hot-sex occasion" wouldn't even be considered.

· Thirteen ·

Maddy's heart was beating a million miles an hour. Why, oh, why did she have to say such a dumb thing?

From the moment Tom had said there was only one bedroom, all she'd been able to think about was how it would be if he were in the bed with her rather than sleeping alone out on the sofa. But the more she tried not to think about it, the more the thought kept reappearing, taunting her with sensual possibilities.

She could feel the color burning her face. "Show me the bedroom. Where I'm to sleep. Alone. That's what I meant. Not . . . not . . ."

His dimple was in full evidence. Was he laughing at her? No, his eyes were giving a different message instead. A message that made her nipples tighten and her insides go all shivery. She couldn't lie to herself any longer. She wanted Tom O'Brien— badly. And unless she was misreading the signs, he wanted her.

It would be so easy to step close to him, wind her arms around his neck, press her body close to his, and pull his head down for a kiss. A kiss that would be just the appetizer for a main course too delicious to even think about.

But Brutus's basket stood as a barricade between him and her. A blessing, really, because sex without love, without commitment, wasn't her thing. And that appeared to be all that Tom O'Brien had to offer.

She faked another yawn and then forced her voice to be calm and not betray the want she could no longer deny. "So, I guess the bedroom is down the hallway somewhere?"

"Yes," he said gruffly. "C'mon, I'll show you."

Tom's bed seemed enormous, dominating the large room with floor-to-ceiling windows facing the bay. Or did it just seem enormous because she couldn't stop her eyes from straying to it and imagining Tom in it—with her? It was way too big for one person.

She was very aware of Tom's solid, manly presence behind her, of the scent of him, the warmth of him. "The room is, uh, nice," she said, aware of how stilted her voice sounded. The bedroom was as sleek and impersonal as the rest of the apartment.

"I hope you'll be comfortable," he said. "There are fresh sheets on the bed; the housekeeper came this morning."

Fresh sheets? She shivered at the thought of sheets he'd slept in, rumpled and warm with his body heat. "Uh, great," she said. "That's, uh, nice, too."

She carried the shopping basket to a spot between the bed and the door where she could easily keep an eye on Brutus. But now it was no longer a barrier between her and Tom.

Tom raked his hands through his hair, then loosened his tie

and undid the top button of his shirt. It was cool in the air-conditioned room, but he looked hot and uncomfortable. "I, uh, need to get a few things from the closet," he said.

"Oh. Your pajamas, I guess," she said.

"I don't wear pajamas."

"Oh," she said, "what do you . . . ?" Her cheeks burned. "Don't answer that question," she amended.

He stepped closer; she stepped back only to feel the bed pressing into the back of her legs. She went to sidestep but stopped. It would be way too undignified to scuttle like a crab sideways around the bed.

"I'll ask a question myself," he said, his voice deep and husky. "What do *you* wear to bed?"

She looked up at him. There was a smile hovering around that sexy, sexy mouth.

Her mouth was suddenly dry. She licked her lips. "It . . . it depends," she said.

He stepped closer, so close she could breathe his citrus scent, note the pulse throbbing at his temple. "Depends?" he said. "On what? The company you're with?"

She cleared her throat. "That, yes. But the weather, the . . . the . . . time of year . . ."

"Tonight. What are you going to wear tonight? Here in my bedroom." He reached out and trailed a finger down her cheek and past her mouth.

She swallowed convulsively. "A nightie, I guess."

"Tell me which one," he said, his voice deep and husky. "One of the ones you packed to take to Serena's house?"

His hand now traced the length of her neck and slid over her shoulder. She trembled at his touch. She'd spent six whole days reliving his kisses, missing him, trying to talk herself out of her longing to see him again.

It was becoming increasingly difficult to remember all the reasons why she shouldn't be alone with Tom O'Brien in his bedroom. She knew she was the one setting the limits here. Would it be so bad to expand them a little?

She looked up at him to meet his gaze full on. "The black one," she whispered. "The black lacy one. It's short and—"

"I'd like to see that," he growled. He took another step closer and she felt herself stop breathing. He, too, stood very still. She was conscious of the faint hum of the air-conditioning, the muffled sound of a car horn on the road outside. And the rapid beating of her heart.

When Tom spoke, his voice was dangerously husky. "This is beginning to feel like a kissing occasion to me."

She cleared her throat and filled her lungs again with air. "Uh. Yes. You could say that. A . . . a silly phrase really, isn't it?" Her gaze was still locked to his.

"You're the one who defined it."

"Defined what?"

"The phrase 'kissing occasion.'"

"Yes. I did." She swallowed again. "I, uh . . . could, of course, redefine it."

"Redefine it?"

"Well, we could replace the word 'kissing' with something else. Another word."

"So that it wouldn't become a third kissing occasion. And therefore not out of order."

"Something like that, yes."

"Any suggestions?"

"Well . . . there's 'snogging' occasion."

He thought about it for a moment. "Yes. Snogging is an acceptable alternative. Although possibly too English."

"Or . . . uh . . . 'smooching' occasion."

"Old-fashioned. And less than exciting."

"Lip smacking?"

"Sounds like fried chicken."

"Pecking?"

"Unfried chicken."

"How about . . . face sucking? I've heard kissing called that."

"Gross."

"I agree. But I . . . I've run out of ideas."

That sexy curl of his upper lip was driving her to distraction. Kiss, snog, smooch—she didn't care what they called it, she just wanted to do it with him.

"How about looking at it from a different angle? More of a description. Like a . . . a 'French kissing occasion,' say," Tom suggested.

She sighed. "I like that one. Though I've heard it called tongue wrestling, and I can't say I care for that."

"Shall we settle on French kissing, then?"

"Why not?"

She sighed with pleasure as—at last—his mouth claimed hers in a slow, sensuous kiss that made her whole body tingle with delight. His tongue tangled with hers. She slid her arms around his neck. Mmm. A French kissing occasion had a lot going for it.

He broke away from the kiss, though he held her very close. "What other kinds of kissing occasion can you think about? Or maybe something else all together?"

She didn't want to talk, she just wanted to lose herself in the kiss. And more kisses. "Uh, a different kind of occasion? I'm not sure what you mean."

"Leading on from a kissing occasion. You know, a progression."

Her brain was too fogged by passion and desire to think straight. "Uh, let's just take it one step at a time."

"One step at a time? Great idea," he said. "Step one, the French kissing occasion." He pulled her to him again and kissed her with such expertise that she could feel the excitement fizzing through her.

He slid his hands down her back and under her top. He pulled her knit top upward, breaking the kiss just for the second it took to pull it over her head. "Step two," he murmured against her mouth.

Then his hands were where she ached for them to be, cupping her breasts, teasing her nipples into stiff peaks. She couldn't suppress a low moan of pleasure.

Her knees felt weak and she didn't resist when Tom gently pushed her back and lowered her onto the bed. Then he was beside her, kissing a trail down her neck, nuzzling in the hollows of her throat, pushing back the lace of her half-cup bra to take her nipple in his mouth, sucking and tonguing first one and then the other until she was squirming with pleasure.

"Step three," he said, as he undid the back of her bra. He sighed his appreciation as her breasts sprang free from the lacy confines. "They're beautiful. You're beautiful."

Maddy flushed. "Thank you." Now it was her turn.

"Step four," she whispered as she fumbled with the buttons on his shirt, eager to feel the warmth of his skin.

She tugged the shirt from his pants and helped him shrug it from his shoulders. Then took her turn to admire him—he was magnificent, with broad shoulders, tightly defined muscles, and just the right amount of dark hair on his chest.

"You're beautiful, too, well, a man kind of beautiful," she whispered, flustered that she was too overcome to find the right word. "Well, I don't exactly mean beautiful, I mean handsome or—"

He cut her words off with a kiss. It was a powerful, hungry kiss and she met it with equal hunger. Lying facing him she felt lost in the sensation of his hands on her body, as she kissed and kissed and kissed him as if the rest of the world had faded away and there was only the two of them left. He didn't speak and neither did she, just responded to his touch with little gasps of delight and rejoiced in his quiet moans when she touched him in return.

She loved the warmth of his body against hers, her soft curves melting into his hard strength, the smoothness of her skin against the tickling, rough hair on his chest.

She uttered little murmurs of pleasure as he found the right spots to touch behind her ears, the top of her arms.

Her arms. Tom O'Brien was great at giving arm. She'd never realized the crook of her elbow could be such an erogenous zone. As he caressed her and kissed her she felt herself melting like chocolate into a puddle of sweet desire.

This was a first for her, to feel this wonderful, heady mix of tenderness and passion. This man was special. Tom, wonderful, sexy, funny Tom. Not pompous at all.

Her attraction to him made it very difficult to focus on her rules for survival as a single, to consider protecting herself from a relationship complication that would damage her career. She wasn't part of his plan. This wasn't part of her strategy.

Plan? Strategy? All she could think about was him. Them. And when he was going to move on to step five.

She stilled as his hand stroked over her bottom and onto her bare thigh. She held her breath as he stroked up to her inner thigh, made contact with the lace of her panties and then re-treated. She lifted her hips to make it easier for him to undo the zipper of her skirt and slide it off her. She trembled as he stroked her tummy. All that was between them was the triangle of her thong.

"You wear great underwear," he murmured.

"Mmm," she breathed, distracted at his finger edging under the elastic. "A chef's uniform is so boring that I like to get crea-tive with my undies."

Her breath was coming in urgent little gasps. Her face flushed with heat. Oh! Step five was unbelievable. He didn't rush, he didn't push. He just stroked and caressed her until she was on fire with want. It seemed if she had been waiting all her life to be touched like that. By him.

There shouldn't be a step six. Not yet. She knew that. It was too soon. Yet deep in a kiss, she started to fumble with his belt. She forgot time, forgot place, forgot five-year plans and career strategies and everything else. She could think only of him and the pleasure they were giving each other.

Her own gasp of impatience as she wrestled with the buckle masked the sudden intrusive sound when it first reached her ears. She stilled.

It couldn't be.

Please, it couldn't be.

But it was.

She was hearing the unmistakable sounds of retching. Dog retching.

No! Not now! She pretended she didn't hear it. But the sounds continued, and she knew she couldn't ignore them. Reluctantly, she broke away from Tom's kiss.

"Brutus?" he groaned.

She sat up to see what was going on. It was Brutus all right. Awake and retching miserably in her shopping basket.

Tom couldn't believe what he was hearing. Boy, did this dog have great timing. Maddy leapt from the bed to Brutus's rescue, a flurry of slender limbs and gorgeous bottom.

"Serena said he might have a reaction to the sedative. I'll get him into the bathroom before it's too late," she gasped, scooping the wretched, retching dog into her arms and holding him ahead of her as she dashed out of the room.

Tom groaned, flung himself backward on the bed, and cursed the interruption. That damn dog! He felt like throttling the animal. He threw his legs over the side of the bed and followed Maddy.

Maddy stood at the doorway to the bathroom and barred his way in, beautifully unself-conscious that she was naked but for a lacy white thong, her perfect pink-tipped breasts high and firm, her milky skin still flushed with passion. She was gorgeous—even more beautiful than his fantasies of her.

Down, boy, down, boy, he thought—and he wasn't referring to Brutus.

"You don't want to go in there," she said.

"Spare me the details," he groaned, feeling passion subside at the thought.

"Well, I've spared your carpet the details, so be thankful," she said.

He raked his hand through his hair. "What about Brutus? Do we need to get him to the vet?"

Maddy's face softened. "The poor little thing seems fine. I've given him a drink of water."

Tom could hear loud slurping noises coming from the bathroom. "He's not drinking from the toi—?"

"No. I put his bowl in there for him."

"That's a relief." And some.

"I suspect he'll just go back to sleep until the effects of the sedative wear off completely."

Tom couldn't help his appreciative gaze from traveling to Maddy's breasts. "So if he's okay, we can, uh—?" he suggested as he lingered there.

Maddy started, looked down at her near-naked body, and squealed. "Ohmigod!"

She whirled around, giving him an eyeful of a slender back and her sexy, curvaceous bottom defined by the sheer strap of her thong. She snatched up a towel from the rack in the bathroom and hastily wrapped it around her. "I . . . I didn't realize," she stuttered as she tucked the edge in. "Oh Tom . . . I . . . uh . . ."

"Yeah, I know," he said, her lack of enthusiasm completing the passion deflation process. "I suppose you're going to tell me that a dog barfing in the bedroom isn't exactly a turn-on."

"Well, he didn't actually barf until he got into the bathroom," she corrected him.

"Whatever," he said, fighting his frustration. "Look, I'll, uh, just bunk down on the sofa and see you in the morning."

She was silent for a moment, chewing on her lower lip. "Tom, I'm so sorry it turned out like that."

"So am I," he said. He turned toward the living room.

"Tom?" she said in a tentative voice. He turned back. She was leaning against the wall, the towel barely concealing the curves of her breasts and showing most of her slim, shapely legs. "I . . . uh . . . really enjoyed the French kissing occasion."

"Yes?" he said, thinking he knew what could be coming next.

"And steps one to five were . . . were, well, fantastic."

"They were. Without a doubt they were fantastic," he said.

"But . . . but I think we should leave it at that." She couldn't meet his gaze, was looking toward her feet. "I . . . uh . . . you . . . me . . . that is, things haven't changed, have they? Your plan I mean . . . and . . . Well, we got carried away and—" She looked up at him, imploring him for support.

If Brutus—the dog with bad, bad timing—hadn't puked when he did, would he and Maddy right now be climbing steps six, seven, eight, et cetera, toward destination ultimate pleasure?

This time Tom didn't stop the groan. "We did get carried away," he said. "But I don't regret it for one moment."

Maddy looked disconcerted but pleased. She started to say something but he stopped her with his hand placed over her mouth. "And being the 'alpha male' that I am, I won't promise that it won't happen again."

He removed his hand, kissed her hard, turned, and stomped toward the sofa.

· Fourteen ·

Tom pushed open the door of his apartment the next morning and was immediately greeted by the delicious aroma of bacon cooking and coffee brewing. A man goes for an early morning run along the Embarcadero and comes home to find his new resident chef has breakfast on the table. Not a bad scenario.

Except that said man had spent the night tossing on a sofa, consumed by frustration imagining the resident chef asleep in his bed wearing a skimpy black nightgown and a barely there thong. And in his fantasy, she would not have had her passion extinguished by Brutus puking at just the wrong moment.

As he shut the door behind him, the dog in question came hurtling down the hallway, yapping excitedly, jumping up, and scrabbling against his bare legs. "Down, boy," Tom ordered, "and be quiet."

Brutus obeyed immediately. Maybe there was something in

this alpha-male thing—the little guy certainly wasn't as obedient for Maddy. Tom decided to test it out.

He used his most commanding voice. "Sit, Brutus." Brutus stayed exactly where he was, his head tilted, pink tongue lolling.

"Roll over, Brutus." Brutus tilted his head to the other side.

"I said roll over, Brutus." Brutus looked up at him with bright button eyes. He wagged his plumed tail.

"Oh, forget it," Tom muttered. He'd try this again at some other time. He leaned down to pat Brutus. Though he doubted he would ever forgive him for last night, he was glad the poor dog had recovered from his sedative-induced stupor.

Brutus headed toward the kitchen and his food bowl. The kitchen was off the living room—part of the modern, spacious layout Tom liked. It gave him a jolt to see Maddy quite at home and busy at his state-of-the-art stainless steel stove. A warm and fuzzy kind of feeling crept through him—and he wasn't too sure how to handle it.

"Good morning," Maddy said in a chirpy voice.

She'd obviously had a good night's sleep, he thought a little sourly.

"You've been running?"

She looked ready for exercise herself in shorts and a crop top. Hmm, resident chef wearing revealing, sexy sport outfit in kitchen—the scenario was getting better and better.

He tried not to stare—difficult when he now knew exactly how gorgeous her body looked without any clothes. He forced himself not to think about how she'd looked standing nearly naked at the door of the bathroom last night.

He nodded. "I left early, didn't hear a sound from your

room." Her room that was really his room. His room that he'd spent half the night fantasizing about sharing with her.

"Yes. I heard the door shut. Prompted us to get up and go out, too."

"Us?"

"Me and Brutus. Um, I mean Bruce."

He felt a stab of alarm. "You went out? With Brutus? Maddy, do you think that was wise? Stoddard—"

"I didn't think Jerome would be out and about this early. He doesn't strike me as the early-rising type."

He groaned. "Who knows what the guy is capable of? Did you have Brutus—I mean Bruce—in the basket?"

"I tried, I really did try. But it was impossible to keep him still. In the end I slid him under my big jacket and held him tightly against me."

"And that worked?"

"I got away with it. I just looked fatter."

"But what if he'd barked?"

"I kept my hand over his mouth until we got away from the building. I wasn't taking any risks."

Tom breathed a sigh of relief. He didn't want to draw attention to his apartment while Maddy and Brutus were in hiding, lest Jerome or the press get a whiff of her whereabouts.

He watched Brutus nudge his already-licked-empty food bowl around the kitchen floor, just in case there was something he'd missed.

"Where did you take him? There's not much down there for dogs."

"No. It's definitely city-dweller territory."

He'd chosen this apartment for its proximity to the Financial District. And then there was the bonus of the AT&T Park. What guy wouldn't want to live just a stroll away from the home of the San Francisco Giants? "Great, isn't it?"

"For humans, maybe. Not so great for dogs. There are nice restaurants. But all the trees are blocked in with cement and there's only one well-used patch of grass nearby."

"Lucky you found it."

"Thankfully for Brutus's bladder. Nora, your next-door neighbor, pointed me in the right direction."

"Nora, my next-door neighbor? You told my neighbor we've got a dog here? Maddy, you know it's strictly no—"

"No pets. Yes, I know. Let me explain. We were going down in the elevator together. She introduced herself—she's very nice by the way. Then Brutus growled at her . . ."

Tom swore. Then noticed Maddy's eyes dancing and her lips twitching with a smile she was having trouble suppressing.

"Go on," he said.

"My heart stopped. Then I noticed her shopping bag was moving."

"*Her* shopping bag was moving?"

"Yes. Because she smuggles Max, her cat, downstairs inside it."

"She's got a cat?"

"Yes. Nora is a widow, and she moved here from a big house in Oakland. But she couldn't bear to leave Max. You should see him, he's beautiful, a brown Burmese."

Amazing how women knew each other's life stories within minutes of meeting. He'd been living next door to the older lady for a year and had never gotten past a polite nod.

"Right. Maddy, I don't really care what color the cat is, I just want to know what Mrs. Green—Nora—is going to do now she knows we're hiding a dog in here."

"Nothing. You keep her secret; she'll keep yours."

"Sounds fair."

"And the good news is she's happy to dog-sit for us if we need her to."

"Dog-sit?"

"Yes. We might have to take her up on the offer. I can test recipes and write copy here early in the week but I have to be dog-free on Wednesday for the audition."

"Audition?"

She smiled a megawatt smile. "In all the Brutus drama last night I forgot to tell you. I've got the audition for the television show."

"Maddy, that's great." He was so pleased for her he wanted to lean across and kiss her, but he wasn't too sure of his current status.

Had she put a limit on kissing occasions again? Last night had been amazing—more than amazing—and he didn't want to wreck his chances of moving on to step six—and beyond, at some later stage. Preferably some not-too-much-later stage.

"That's great," he repeated.

"And I've been appointed food editor of *Annie* magazine. It's official."

"Congratulations. Everything you wanted." He felt genuinely happy for her.

"I'm still buzzing," she said. Then her mouth turned downward. "But if the press keeps painting me as some kind of money-hungry skank, the editor in chief might reconsider."

"Another reason we *have* to keep your whereabouts secret." He opened the newspaper he'd carried in with him. "Did you see this when you were out?" He showed her the headline. "Nephew to Contest Secret Millionaire's Will." It accompanied yet another photo of Stoddard.

Maddy groaned. "Will it never end?"

"Yes. When some new celebrity scandal or another erupts. But in the meantime the millionaire mutt is news. And so are you."

"I'll call my editor and ask her if I can do my work from here. I've done my photographic shoots. I'm sure she'll be okay about it."

"That would be wise."

She turned to face the kitchen countertop. "I hope you eat cantaloupe. And how do you like your eggs? I thought scrambled might be good, but if you want them fried or poached I can do that, too."

Tom groaned. Eggs and bacon. Right on the cholesterol hit list. And his favorite breakfast.

"Maddy, I don't eat eggs for breakfast."

Her face fell. "I thought men liked a hearty breakfast. My fathers and brothers do."

"They work on the land, they probably need it."

"There was hardly anything in your fridge, just low-fat milk and some bran cereal."

"That's what I usually have in the mornings."

She pulled a face. "And for your other meals?"

"I can eat at a different restaurant every night of the week."

"Not while I'm staying here you won't," she said. "I bought

the bacon and eggs at the convenience store up the road near where I was walking Brutus. I'll cook for you while I'm your guest."

Both his heart and his stomach warmed at the thought of it. "Maddy, you don't have to do that."

"Of course I do." She looked up, her eyes wide and sincere. "Tom, I really appreciate you helping Brutus and me. The least I can do is keep you well fed. What's the point of having a chef as a guest otherwise?"

"Maddy, that's sweet but—"

"No buts—"

"But—"

She smiled. "Okay, maybe one but."

He didn't feel comfortable talking to Maddy about why he was so careful with what he ate. It might make him seem weak to her. Eggs on the occasional morning wouldn't hurt. But he couldn't make a habit of scarfing down brownies and the rich foods Maddy seemed to favor cooking.

That said, he didn't want to hurt her feelings. He knew from when he'd lived with his mother and sister that rejecting their food made them think he was rejecting them.

He pushed his hand through his hair. "Maddy, I have to watch what I eat."

"I'm beginning to realize that. What's the problem, high cholesterol?"

"Yes, I mean, no." Hell, he didn't want her to think he was a heart-attack candidate at age thirty. "I don't actually have high cholesterol myself, but my father did and he died of a heart attack before he was fifty."

"I'm sorry," Maddy murmured. "I ... uh ... read about your dad in that sleazy newspaper story. And you're worried you might inherit the problem?"

"The doctors figure I'm fine. But the way I look at it, it doesn't hurt to increase my odds by eating well and keeping fit."

His father had smoked like a chimney, ate what he felt like, and had tried to keep up with his gold-digging young second wife. No way would Tom make the same mistakes. No way would he ever be so thoughtless of the people who counted on him.

Maddy's eyes narrowed thoughtfully. "Hmm. This is quite a challenge. Low fat but still satisfying ... Not what I'm known for, but I'll do my best." She grinned. "Mind if I experiment on you?"

"Experiment all you like," he said, trying not to think of other ways he'd like her to experiment on him—and he on her. But he wasn't going to try to get her back into his bed—that is, back into his bed with him also in it—until she gave the word.

Maddy went to put the eggs back in the refrigerator. Hang on, what was Serena's favorite low-cal breakfast? She shuddered at the thought of it. "Right, Tom, first up is an egg-white omelet. Maybe with some of that celery chopped through it. I'll give the bacon to Brutus."

She almost laughed out loud at the look on Tom's face. "No need to do that. Today the bacon will be just fine. And you could poach a couple eggs for me."

"As long as you're sure."

"I'm sure. Do I have time for a shower first?"

He indicated the running gear he was wearing. She had to force herself not to ogle him. Hot, sweaty, and 200 percent male, in shorts and an athletic singlet that clung to every muscle, Tom O'Brien had a body to die for. In a business suit he was a ten out of ten. Out of a suit his rating rocketed off the scale.

The entire time they'd been discussing Brutus, Nora next door, and high cholesterol, she'd been sneaking surreptitious glances at his magnificent physique. This morning was her first sight of his bare legs—they were long and leanly muscled and just as gorgeous as his top half.

Turn around, Tom, turn around so I can check out your great butt again, she thought. What would he do if she actually said that?

It was a crime to tie this man up in a business suit. No, it was good to cover him up in a suit so other women couldn't see him and lust after him. Maddy felt seared by jealousy at the thought.

Tom and another woman. She couldn't bear it. Especially after last night and the bliss of his kisses.

Afterward, alone in Tom's enormous bed, she hadn't known whether to be grateful or not to Brutus for his ill-timed barfing. How many heat-fuelled steps might she have climbed with Tom otherwise? And what about his last words? He was planning on other kissing occasions, a step-by-step seduction.

And she? She still wasn't sure she wanted to risk the inevitable pain of getting involved with a man whose life was so rigidly organized.

He was an ambitious lawyer, yes. She respected that. Yet living his life to a preset plan seemed at odds with a man who admitted to liking animated movies. Who appeared to be so pleasingly protective and yet so feared commitment.

But that dichotomy of character was one of the reasons she was so attracted to Tom. So attracted that her heart was singing at the thought of spending the next eight days living with him in his apartment.

"I think you look good in your running shorts. But if you'd feel more comfortable taking a shower, go for it. Just move my undies out of the way from where they're drying over the bathtub."

"Women's panties in my bathroom," Tom grumbled. But she actually thought he looked pleased.

"And don't use my lavender body wash," she called after him. "It's French and it's only for girls."

When Tom returned, hair damp from the shower and brushed back from his face, he was dressed once more in his corporate uniform of dark suit and tie.

"I have to go straight into the office," he said as he sat down at the table for breakfast.

Maddy couldn't help a stab of disappointment. "That's a shame," she said, keeping her voice light as she took whole-wheat toast from the toaster. No butter for Tom.

He went to shrug and then did that curious no-shrug thing again.

"I notice you seem to have some trouble with your shoulder," she said. She slid his plate of melon in front of him, then set down her own.

"I . . . uh . . . I'm trying not to shrug as you hate it so much."

She hated it so much? "Oh. You mean Jerome." He wasn't shrugging because she didn't like it? What a sweetie. She liked him more every minute she spent in his company.

"Tom, don't stop shrugging on my account. I just don't like Jerome's totally insincere way of doing it."

She sat down opposite him, looking into the brown eyes that had grown so familiar. Brown eyes that were warm with passion when he kissed her and that could also be bright with humor. "Shrug away as much as you please."

"Okay," he said and shrugged those broad shoulders in a big, exaggerated way. Maddy laughed and so did he.

"It's a shame I have to leave you here by yourself," he said as, after they'd eaten their melon, she got up to change their plates.

"Well, not quite by myself. I do have Brutus to talk to."

"Of course. Do tell me the day he talks back, won't you?"

"Of course," she echoed.

Brutus had given up snuffling around the kitchen for snacks and was sitting at the window looking plaintively out at the marina. There wasn't even half a wag in his tail. He was a dog used to a certain amount of freedom.

She slid Tom's poached eggs onto a plate with his bacon. He gave a what-the-hell shrug and ate with gusto.

"I've got a busy day ahead," he said. "Stoddard's decision to contest the will makes a lot of extra work. I want to make sure I cover all bases for the probate court. Knowing Stoddard, he'll fight dirty."

Maddy stared at her piece of toast, suddenly completely without appetite. "Like he already has with that stuff about me in the newspaper."

"And me. I've got over most of the hurdles to make partner. But the senior partners didn't care to see a photo of me kissing a beneficiary of a controversial will splashed all over the front page."

Maddy flushed. "The photographer must have been in the car that drove by and yelled at us."

"These days anyone with a cell phone can be a paparazzo."

"Tom . . . I'm sorry."

He paused, fork halfway to his mouth. "About kissing me?" He held her gaze. "I'm not."

"You don't wish you'd never heard of Walter or Brutus or me?"

He put down his fork. The look he returned her was heart-stoppingly serious. "No. It's my job, Maddy."

His job. It always came back to that. Was she crazy to think it might become something more personal for him?

"I guess . . ." she said, her voice trailing away.

"Though I never thought I'd see the day I'd stand up in court to defend a canine client."

"You're kidding me? Will Brutus have to go to court?"

"Of course. And so will you. The probate court hears any challenges to a will."

She could feel the color draining from her face. "I was afraid you'd say that. Tom, I've never been near a courthouse."

Tom leaned over the table. She thought he was going to take her hand but his rested on the table halfway between them. "Don't worry. You won't be on trial."

"Oh yes, I will. I'm already on trial by the press." She couldn't help the note of bitterness from entering her voice.

"The court hearing won't be about whether you had sex with Walter. It will be about whether you used sex to coerce an old man into making you a beneficiary of his will."

She winced. "That sounds so ugly."

"It's best that you're prepared for what they'll throw at us.

Stoddard's attorney will also try to prove Walter was mentally incapable at the time he signed his will."

"But that's a lie."

"And I'll prove it to be a lie. Maddy, I don't want you to worry about the hearing. Walter's will was always going to be controversial. Trust me, I anticipated a challenge and I worked to bulletproof that will from the word go."

"You mean you're sure we'll win?"

"We can't be sure of anything until we hear the judge's decision." His eyes narrowed. "But that jerk Jerome will be in for a shock."

She smiled. "This is a battle for you, isn't it?"

"You bet it is. And I intend that the best man—or in this case, dog—will win."

"So Brutus has to testify?"

"He just has to sit there and look cute. Uh, as cute as Brutus can look, that is. Walter's love for his dog is what this defense is all about."

Maddy looked across at the forlorn little figure by the window. "Then I'd better get him groomed so he makes a good impression on the judge."

"Correction. You groom him yourself. You and Brutus are in hiding, remember."

"As if I could forget." She pulled a face. "Okay. I'll do my best." Hmm. Shampooing Brutus in Tom's immaculate bathroom would be fun. Not. "I guess his red bandanna could be cute to wear in court. I—"

"No red bandanna."

"But he looks adorable in it."

Tom groaned. "Maddy, we're talking a court of law here. A

witness doesn't look"—he made quote marks with his fingers—
"'adorable.' He looks sober, reliable, trustworthy."

"Even if he's a dog."

"Especially if he's a dog involved in any kind of litigation."

She could not help her mouth from twitching upward in the
corners. "So no bandanna."

Was that a twinkle in those chocolate brown eyes? "When a
young hoodlum stands in front of the judge, he's not wearing his
baggy jeans with half his underpants showing, is he? His counsel
puts the defendant into a respectable suit and tie."

"So we're talking the criminal canine equivalent of a gray
suit?"

Tom nodded. She thought she caught a glimpse of dimple
but could not be sure.

"So . . ." she said. "I'm thinking plain black collar. No studs.
No bling."

"Think corporate."

"Discreet, good-quality leather. Simple silver buckle."

"Now you're talking," he said. And this time the dimple was
well in evidence.

"And how—as Brutus's attorney—are you planning on getting him to behave in a courtroom?"

"I've decided to give him some personal training."

She laughed. "You seriously think you'll succeed where
puppy school professors failed?"

"If there's anything to this alpha-male thing . . ."

"Maybe you'll surprise me. But right now you'd better finish
those eggs before they get cold." She got up from the table. "Let
me top off your coffee."

Tom finished the last of his breakfast and pushed away his

plate. "Today I want to organize some security at Walter's house."

All humor at the thought of dressing Brutus for court fled. Maddy felt chilled at the thought of guards patrolling her home. She swallowed hard. "Security. I hadn't thought of that."

"I have a bad feeling about Stoddard. There's something not right about that guy. He's dug for dirt on us, so I'm digging for dirt on him."

Maddy swallowed hard. "What kind of dirt?"

"Maybe a criminal record in England. Outstanding warrants. That kind of thing."

"A criminal record?" She felt a cold shiver down her spine.

"Just a hunch."

Tom's eyes were drawn and she noticed how tired he looked. As if his job wasn't pressure enough, now he had to worry about her and Brutus. And that was besides the poodle paternity suit.

She vowed to look after him as best she could while she was hiding out in his home. "Tom, I feel bad that I took your bed last night when you have to go to work. Tonight I'll sleep on the sofa."

"No, Maddy, it's fine. Honestly. I'm used to the sofa. My sister stays in my room when she comes to visit."

"Your sister?"

"Anna. She lives in Big Sur with her husband and my two nieces."

"The ones who like *The Lion King*?"

"Those are the ones." Tom suddenly looked serious. "You know, Maddy, I was thinking about my sister when I told you that for some women a career isn't as important as it is to men. Remember, you seemed to get upset about it."

Upset about it? She'd chalked up a big black mark against him because of it. "I thought—"

His dark eyes were intent. "You took it the wrong way. Anna and her husband both had high-flying careers working all hours. Some days she only saw the girls for fifteen minutes. Ultimately, she decided that spending time with the girls was more important than her career."

"I can understand that but—"

"I'm not saying that's for everyone. But it works for her."

Maybe he wasn't the chauvinist ogre she had thought him. And he had been prepared to stop shrugging his shoulders just to please her.

"I . . . I think I get your point," she said. "I've only got this new job because the former food editor wants to spend more time with her baby."

"Yeah. Your job is everything to you now, and I understand that because it's the same for me."

"But maybe I might feel differently in the future."

"You might, you might not."

"Having kids might change things." She dashed from her mind the sudden vision of a little boy with chocolate brown eyes and unruly dark hair.

Tom looked thoughtful. "If we beat Jerome and Brutus inherits, you won't need to work at all."

"We *have* to beat him. If he were a nice nephew who'd been good to Walter and would love Brutus, I wouldn't mind. But Jerome doesn't deserve a cent. Not after what he tried to do to an innocent little animal."

"As the custodian of the millionaire mutt you won't lack for money."

She'd dreamed a little about Walter's money and moving into the big house; she wouldn't be human if she hadn't. "But I can't imagine not working. I'm passionate about my work."

"I think you match me on that score."

But he wasn't the one who would be bearing the children when and if he ever married. "I guess there's nothing about babies in your five-year plan?"

"There isn't. However, I'll be writing a new plan at the end of this five years."

But nothing would change in his current plan, she thought, unable to stop herself from feeling wistful. No serious girlfriend, no fiancée, no wife. *No her.* Her heart contracted in an unexpected spasm of pain.

"What about your sister's husband?"

"He needed some convincing to give up his job in San Francisco, but now he's living his dream and running a small sound recording studio."

"That sounds like happy endings all round," she said. "So what's your dream, Tom?" Did he have any ambitions that didn't relate to work?

His mouth set tight. "To make partner at Jackson, Jones, and Gentry. I'll do whatever is necessary to reach that goal."

Maddy took a deep breath. "Well, Brutus and I will do our best to stay out of your way."

She was so grateful to him for giving them refuge here. It was nothing to him that Brutus survived the twenty-one days. He was just hiding them out of kindness. To make things easier for her.

"You don't have to stay out of my way, Maddy." He leaned across the table and this time he took her hand. She trembled at the memory of how exciting him caressing her body had felt last night. "In fact, the closer you are the happier I'll be."

She met his eyes and was stunned by the warmth she saw there. He wasn't offering anything permanent. But was she sure something permanent was what she wanted or needed? And she still hadn't ascertained whether Tom expected his underpants to be ironed.

She answered the pressure of his hand with her own. "I'll keep that in mind, Tom," she murmured. In fact, his words would probably never be far away from her mind. They might help her decide how far to take things the next time he kissed her.

· Fifteen ·

"**Don't** let anyone in, okay?" Tom told Maddy as he left the apartment for his office.

"Yes, Grumpy. I'll be on full alert for witches with shiny, red poisoned apples."

"Be serious, Maddy. Please."

But she noted a hint of dimple as he spoke that told her he appreciated the joke.

"Can I go out if I'm very, very careful not to be seen? I love the gourmet food stores at the Ferry Building and it's so close."

Tom's hand dropped from her shoulder. "Go to the Ferry Building? Maddy, haven't you heard anything I've been saying? Think of those headlines. You need to stay out of sight of reporters. Not to mention Jerome."

"You mean I'm confined to quarters? It isn't just Brutus who's behind bars?"

"I wouldn't put it that way but that's exactly what I mean."

"But there's no food in this apartment except the stuff I brought with me for Brutus. I guess you wouldn't want canned dog chow served up to you on toast for dinner. I couldn't guarantee it's low fat."

"Ha-ha," he said with a complete lack of dimple. "Order food on the Internet. Use my computer. The password is Buzz20."

"Buzz?"

"As in Buzz Lightyear."

"So your nieces like *Toy Story*?" She injected a teasing tone to her voice.

"They do," he said, refusing to be drawn.

"How can I get stuff on the Internet when I can't let anyone into the apartment? You know, on Grumpy's orders."

"The doorman will call up so you'll know the delivery is okay."

"But you said I'd be safe here."

"Yes, but why risk being seen? You've been on national television now. Someone might recognize you."

"Okay, Grumpy," she said, conceding defeat.

Tom put his finger under her chin and tilted her face upward. "You know it's only in your best interests—and Brutus's."

But before she could say anything in reply he kissed the breath from her and was gone.

Maddy showered and dressed. The apartment seemed very quiet without Tom. She wandered aimlessly through the rooms. Brutus trotted along behind her, his tags clinking companionably.

Hmm. Should she sneak a peek and see if Tom's boxers were neatly ironed and folded? No. Raiding his underwear drawer would definitely be an invasion of privacy. More important, careful as she would be, he might know she'd done it.

Finally, she settled herself at his computer. She accessed the Internet and ordered the stuff she needed for the next few days. Including a selection of corporate-style dog collars.

Then she opened up a document to jot down notes and recipes for the audition.

Annie was a young women's magazine and she assumed that the readers didn't have much time to cook. They cooked to impress, with as little effort as possible. Recipes had to be fast and easy but look fantastic. How could she give that a different twist?

Brutus came up to her, nudged his head against her leg, and whimpered deep in his throat. Poor little thing. He was used to Walter's garden. And the freedom of the streets whenever he got the chance. Becoming a millionaire wasn't much fun for him so far.

She tickled him behind his ears and he snuffled his appreciation. He must be bored. Maybe she could think up some dog-friendly new recipes for him. If truth be told, she wasn't happy with feeding him stuff from cans and packets all the time.

But that was distracting her from the main game. The audition. Competition would be tough. It would be a matter of luck if she hit on something that would appeal.

Luck! She froze with her hand on the mouse. Then she jumped up from the computer and dashed down the hallway to Tom's bedroom. Frantically she burrowed through her suitcase, emptied her handbag out on the bed, pulled out the pockets of her jacket. No lucky pony. Not anywhere.

No wonder she hadn't been struck by inspiration. Without her lucky pony she never would. Think, think, think. She'd taken it to Serena's and put it on the bookshelf in her bedroom. But had she packed it last night in the rush to decamp to Tom's apartment?

Maddy grabbed the phone and punched in Serena's number. "Please be home, Serena. Please be home," she whispered as it rang. She whooped when Serena answered.

"Yes, the pony is still in your room," Serena said.

Maddy clutched the receiver. "Thank heaven. I'd die if I'd lost it."

"How come this pony thing is so important?"

How could she explain to anyone the significance of the mass-produced china figurine? "My mother gave it to me when I first started competing at pony club. I won my first blue ribbon that day. Ever since it's brought me luck. And . . . and my mom's presence."

Serena was silent at the other end of the phone before she spoke again. "Right. I'll go get it for you."

"No! Don't touch it."

"I'll be careful, Maddy." Serena now sounded affronted.

"That's not what I meant. Only I can touch it. That's part of the luck."

"Huh? I don't get it."

"The last person ever to touch it but me was my mom. It's . . . it's kind of like a link."

"Now I get it," said Serena. "But if I can't touch it, how can I get it to you?"

"You can't. I'll have to come and get it myself."

"What? Now?"

"Yes," she said, casting her eyes around for her car keys. Her Honda was in a parking garage a few blocks away.

"Maddy!" Serena's shout came through so loud it hurt her eardrum. "You're supposed to be in hiding. You can't come here. What about the press?"

"Are any reporters outside your house?"

"No. But what about Jerome?"

"I told him I was going away on a shoot, remember. I think we're okay for a few days."

"As if he believed you."

"You don't understand, Serena. I haven't got a hope of getting anywhere in that audition without my lucky pony. I have to have it. Now."

"What about Brutus?"

"I'll ask the lady next door to watch him while I run out."

"Isn't Tom worried about you as well as Brutus?"

"Yes. But I'm a big girl. I can look after myself. I have to have that pony, Serena. Nothing else is more important."

Serena still sounded very dubious.

Maddy thought for a moment. "I'll call from my cell as I drive into your street. Then I'll double-park in front of your house. You hold your front door open for me, I dash upstairs and get the pony, come straight back down, jump into the car, and drive off. I'll be in and out in seconds. That will be perfectly safe."

"I'm not so sure."

"Trust me, Serena. It'll be fine. I'll go crazy with worry here if I don't have that pony."

"Well, okay." Serena's reluctance was obvious. "I'll wait for your call."

Tom wouldn't approve. Maddy knew that but she pushed his reaction to the back of her mind. She wasn't putting Brutus at any risk. He was Jerome's real target. Not her.

This plan was foolproof. She'd be out and back again in thirty minutes. Tom wouldn't even have to know she had gone out.

But some of his caution filtered through. From Tom's closet she pulled a blue chambray shirt off of its hanger and threw it on over her T-shirt, rolling the sleeves up to her elbows. It hung practically to her knees. What else? She grabbed a cap from the top shelf. The beer logo and the "Goof-Off Golf Day" slogan weren't really her thing but it would have to do.

She stuffed her hair right up under the cap, forcing the loose tendrils inside. Her hair color was a giveaway but this camouflaged it nicely.

She waved to the doorman as she rushed through the lobby. Nothing would work out for her if she didn't get that good-luck pony.

· Sixteen ·

Tom lounged back in one of the big, squishy chairs his mother, Helen O'Brien, kept in her boutique on Fillmore Street. The chair was there specifically for the comfort of long-suffering males who waited while their female folk shopped.

Tom wasn't there to shop. He had come directly from his office to ask his mother to be a witness in the probate court hearing that had been set for Tuesday morning. She agreed without a moment's hesitation.

"I spent quite some time with Walter in his last weeks," she said as she twisted one of a pile of silk scarves on the counter into an elaborate knot for display. "I'm happy to swear hand-on-Bible that he was totally in command of all his senses."

She flicked the tail of the scarf well out of reach of her cat, Pixie. The fluffy princess was, as usual, snoozing in her basket on the countertop. Tom often wondered how customers with allergies felt about that.

His mom stopped folding the scarf she was holding. "I can testify to Maddy Cartwright's innocence as well if you need me to."

Tom sat up straighter in his chair. "What do you mean?"

"I'm sickened by all that poison in the press directed at the poor girl." She shook her head in disapproval. "Why does she deserve that? All she did was be kind to Walter and make sure he ate properly. You know that as well as I do."

Tom shifted uncomfortably at the memory of what he'd put Maddy through at their first meeting.

His mother continued. "Someone seems hell-bent on destroying her reputation. And swiping at yours at the same time."

Tom's gut knotted as it did when he thought about Stoddard. The senior partners had hauled him over the coals because of the adverse publicity. If it weren't for that bonus in the offing, he might have lost his job. "It's the nephew from England. Watch me hammer him in court." He slammed his fist into his open hand.

"I hope you do. Maddy was clueless about Walter's fortune. But the nephew knew its value to the last cent."

Tom's eyes narrowed, "How do you know that, Mom?"

"I . . . I heard people talk. That's all."

Something about her reaction didn't seem quite right. It came as no surprise when she quickly changed the subject. He filed a mental memo to ask her about it again before the probate hearing.

"Maddy's a marvelous cook, you know. But I've told you that before, haven't I?"

"Yes, Mom, more than once," he said with the long-suffering-son look that always made her laugh. He then filled her in on Maddy's and Brutus's move to his apartment.

"Oh." His mother raised her immaculately groomed eyebrows. "Is there something you want to tell your dear old mom?"

Tom snorted. Slim and elegant with her sleek bob of silver gray hair, Helen O'Brien was about as far from a "dear old mom" image as you could get. "No, Mother. There is not."

"You're sure about that?"

"Sure, I'm sure."

"So that photo in the newspaper of you and Maddy kissing was . . . ?"

"Nothing."

The part of him that would always be six years old in the presence of his mother ached to ask her advice about the inconvenient, unscheduled feelings Maddy aroused in him. But thirty-year-old Tom was way too used to keeping his own counsel to take that step.

Her voice gentled. "There's no shame in admitting you find Maddy attractive, son. She's a very special person."

"She is that." He folded his arms in front of his chest and refused to be drawn any further.

His mother sighed a long, exaggerated sigh. "You get so cranky with me for what you call my 'damn matchmaking.' But life is so much more fun when you have someone to share it with. I'd hate for you to wake up one day middle-aged and alone."

"Like you did after Dad left?" Tom couldn't keep the bitterness from his voice.

Helen put down the scarf, came around the glass-framed counter, and sat down in the other chair opposite him. "That was a difficult time for me. But the situation wasn't as black-and-white as you seem to think."

A woman pressed her nose to the boutique's plate-glass window and waved to get his mother's attention. She waved back and pointed to the watch on her wrist. The store didn't open until eleven o'clock.

Tom was glad they had the place to themselves. He had never actually asked his mother the question directly. Adult to adult. "Why did you take him back? I've never understood it."

A rueful smile twitched around his mother's mouth. "Because I loved him. It's as simple as that. Because every moment with that man was a moment lived to the max."

"You thought that even after the way he treated you?"

"Tom, no one but the two people involved ever knows what truly goes on inside a couple's private moments. Not even their kids."

He shrugged. "Especially not their kids." He'd never seen his parents' marriage as anything but a template to avoid at all costs.

"I knew your father was . . . shall we say 'high maintenance' from the moment I met him. But I willingly signed on for that until death did us part."

"He didn't seem to have taken the same vows."

"Raymond paid a high price for breaking them." She sighed. "So did I. So did you and your sister. That didn't ever stop me loving him. It stopped me *liking* him for a while. But it didn't stop my heart from singing the day he came back. Or from cherishing every new hour I had with him."

"I still don't get it."

She laughed. "Neither do I. You can't explain love. You can't analyze it. You just open yourself to feeling love and enjoy where it takes you."

He shook his head. "You know that's not how I live, how I've always lived."

She threw up her hands. "I know, darling. But maybe you need to rethink things. You were such a sunny little boy. Now you're so . . . so relentless."

"Relentless? That's harsh. Determined, maybe. That's what's gotten me to where I am."

"True. But maybe you don't need to be quite so determined anymore. Have you ever considered that what used to work for you might not be right for you now?"

He remembered the day his shattered, angry self mapped out that first five-year plan of action. His pen had stabbed right through the paper. Could his mom be right? Was he still reacting like an eighteen-year-old? Had he boxed himself in with a framework constructed from the green, unseasoned timber of adolescence?

His mom leaned closer. "Tom, I know you had issues with your dad. But wasn't it fortunate we were granted the time to mend bridges before he was taken from us?"

Tom remembered the stilted discussion with his father just weeks before his death. "I guess. But he still thought I was doomed to be a wage slave. Kept suggesting alternate ways I could use my law degree."

His mother leaned over and patted him on the knee. "He was stubborn. I'll grant you that. There was his way or the highway. But he would be so proud of what you've achieved."

Tom thought back to the horseback-riding excursions with his father. He remembered how they'd end with a furious gallop back to the stables. How his dad had whooped and hollered his approval on the occasions when Tom had beaten him. How he'd boasted to anyone who would listen of how well his boy could handle a horse.

"Did I tell you I started horseback riding again?" Tom asked, knowing full well that he had not said a word to anyone.

Her face lit up. "Tom! That's wonderful. It was something you and your dad loved to do together. I envied you those wonderful times."

"Except you're terrified of horses."

"They're beautiful creatures. I admire them, but at a distance." She reached up to stroke the silky gray fur of her cat. "I'm much happier with an animal that's smaller than me."

She paused. Her eyes glazed with the matchmaking look he loathed. "Did you know Maddy loves horses? She has the cutest china pony in her living room. I went to admire it, and she wouldn't let me touch it. Why don't you—?"

"Mom . . ." Tom warned.

"So taking Maddy horseback riding would be a bad idea?"

He had to laugh. His mother was incorrigible. But at the moment he leaned over to hug her, his cell phone rang. "Sorry, Mom, I have to answer that. It could be the office."

It was the doorman from his apartment. The supermarket delivery had arrived but his friend had gone and couldn't collect it.

Tom cursed.

Where the hell had Maddy gone? What was so important that she'd ignored his advice and left the apartment?

He apologized to his mom as he ran out of her boutique, knocking a freestanding rail of dresses askew.

Maybe he was overreacting. But the threatening gesture and the gutter-dirty way Stoddard had talked about Maddy and Serena played over in his head.

He called Serena on his cell. At first she was evasive. Then she admitted Maddy was on her way over. Something about her damn lucky pony.

"I tried to stop her, Tom," said Serena, "but she insisted."

"Is Brutus with her?"

"She said she was leaving him with a dog sitter next door."

Thank God at least the dog was out of harm's way. Despite his somewhat disgusting personal habits, Brutus was a cute little guy. He didn't deserve to meet a horrible end at the hands of a poisoned-T-bone-wielding maniac like Jerome Stoddard. And for the sake of his bonus, it was vital that the dog be kept alive for the full twenty-one days.

The bonus. He should tell Maddy about it. Right away. With the press speculating that she was a gold digger, and he was in on the scheme to grab an old man's money, his fee structure should be totally transparent. Especially to her.

But right now he had to make sure she was safe. He hailed a cab to take him to Serena's house.

Maddy left the engine running as she opened the Honda door and took the stairs from the sidewalk two at a time up to Serena's front door. Serena stood by the open door.

Maddy slapped her friend a high five and a breathless "thanks" as she rushed past her and up the stairs to the bedroom. She expelled a breath in deep relief. Her pony sat on the bookshelf just as she'd left it. She picked it up and lovingly stroked it. Then kissed it on its cold, china nose.

From a ten-year-old's perspective she'd thought the pony the most beautiful thing she'd ever seen—a chestnut with a flowing tail, two white socks, and a white blaze just like her beloved first mare, Lady.

With an adult eye she could see it was a cheap piece of mass-produced china, chipped now on one ear. But the pony was as precious to the adult as it had been to the child.

Exhilarated by the success of her mission, Maddy tore down the stairs. She'd jump into the car and be back at Tom's apartment with Tom none the wiser.

Then she saw Jerome.

He stood just inside the door and he had Serena, one hand over her mouth, the other holding her beautiful friend's hands behind her back. Serena's eyes were wide with fear and anger.

Maddy skidded to a halt.

Jerome's voice was as beautifully modulated as ever. "Ah. Madeleine. At last. I've been watching for you. Glad you could make it. We can deal with this in a civilized manner. Or . . ." He tightened his grip on Serena who moaned her fear and discomfort.

"Let her go," Maddy shouted.

"Hand over the damn dog."

"He's not—" she started to say but then Snowball set up a furious barking at the back door.

Jerome laughed a laugh totally without humor. "Don't try and tell me it's not here. I can hear the miserable cur yapping. Get it. Now."

Maddy thought quickly. Snowball, though small, white, and fluffy, was a ferocious watchdog.

"Sure," she said to Jerome and backed down the hallway, not daring to take her eyes off Serena for a second. She opened the door.

A flash of white sped up the hall, took one look at his beloved mistress in peril, snarled, and launched an attack on Jerome's thigh.

Jerome cursed as the Maltese terrier bit deep into his flesh. He let go of Serena and started frantically kicking his leg to shake off his furry attacker. "Where's Brutus?" he demanded. "I'll throttle this one if you don't get Brutus."

Maddy pushed Serena out of the way. "Go," she screamed.

She thought she was seeing things when Tom burst through the doorway and rushed to her side. "What the hell—?"

"Snowball!" cried Serena. She ignored Maddy's efforts to get her out the door. Instead Serena grabbed Snowball's collar from behind and managed to pull him off Jerome.

Thwarted, Jerome turned after Tom and hit him square in the back. Tom, bigger, stronger, but taken by surprise, got the full impact of Jerome's fist. Winded, he staggered forward.

Anger at Jerome burned through Maddy. How dare he hurt Tom in a coward's attack from the rear. What could she do to protect Tom from being attacked again? She needed a weapon. But there was only one thing in her hand. Her beloved good-luck pony versus Tom's safety?

She only had to think for a second. With all the strength she could muster she threw the china figurine at Jerome. The pony hit him sharply on his chest. He lunged at her, cursing a stream of profanities. Tom, recovered now, shoved Jerome away from Maddy, then grabbed him in an armlock.

The two men struggled. Then Snowball wriggled out of Serena's grasp and, baring his sharp little teeth, went for Jerome again. Jerome sidestepped and Tom tripped over the wildly barking little white dog. In the second Tom took to right himself, Jerome twisted away from Tom and headed for the steps.

"You'll pay for this, you bitch," he shouted at Maddy. "When I slit the throat of the old man's dog, you'll be watching."

Maddy felt like throwing up. "When you're in jail, I'll be laughing."

Tom was only one step behind him but Jerome took advantage of his lead to limp down the steps, leap into Maddy's waiting Honda, and drive off in a squeal of tires.

"My car!" cried Maddy.

"Forget the car, what about you? Are you all right?" Tom turned and put his arms around her.

She shuddered at the thought of the venom in Jerome's voice. "I'm . . . I'm fine. You?"

"His marshmallow fist will be hurting more than my back."

Tom's solid chest was a haven. For a moment, she allowed herself to lean against him panting in shock but feeling strangely victorious. Jerome had gotten away but they'd put up a good fight.

She pulled away from Tom. "Serena, are you okay?"

Serena hugged Snowball to her. "Never better. Did you see my little Snowball go for that creep Jerome?"

"Little dog, big teeth. Did you see the way Jerome was hopping around on one foot?" Maddy knew her laughter was tinged with hysteria but she couldn't stop.

"And did you notice the way he referred to Brutus as 'it'? I hate that."

"Me, too, I think—"

Tom interrupted. "Does it really matter if a dog is referred to as 'he' or 'it'?"

Maddy and Serena both turned on him at the same second.

"Okay, okay, he's a 'he,'" Tom said in response to their combined glare. "But there are more serious issues at stake here. How did Stoddard get in?"

"He must have been lurking around outside. Watching for Maddy. And I had the door open."

Tom glared at Maddy. "I'll ask you later to explain what you were doing here. I told you Jerome was dangerous."

Maddy swallowed hard. Now she didn't feel one bit like laughing. Tom's eyes were blazing. He had every right to be angry with her. She'd put not only herself but also Serena in serious danger. And all just for her lucky pony.

Her pony! After all this, had it shattered on the floor?

Frantically, she scanned the floor to find the precious figurine sitting forlornly on the carpet where it had bounced off Jerome's shoulder. She bent down to examine it.

"Oh, Maddy, is it broken?" said Serena, her voice warm with sympathy.

Carefully, Maddy turned it over in her hands. She let out a breath of relief. "There's a chip off the end of her tail but otherwise, I think she's all right."

Tom sighed and he didn't care who heard him. Not only did Maddy think it worth debating whether to call a dog "he" rather than "it," she now called a china figurine "she." This was even odder than talking to animals.

And, he had to admit, even more endearing. He was so glad she was safe that he was finding it difficult to chastise her for her foolishness in being at Serena's house. At Serena's house, wearing his shirt and cap and looking utterly adorable.

Serena confronted Tom. "I hope you realize what it meant for Maddy to risk breaking her pony to protect you from Jerome."

Tom stared back. These girls were missing the point. Here he was trying to ascertain the circumstances surrounding an attack on two women and all they could mumble on about was a china figurine.

Maddy was now quietly stroking the horse from mane to tail. "My pony. It touched Jerome. That's broken the link." He could see she was close to tears, which wasn't surprising considering the shock she'd had. It was hard to stay angry with her.

"Link? What link?" Tom looked from Maddy to Serena and back again.

"The only other person to have touched this horse was my mother." She sniffed. "It's . . . it's . . ."

"Almost sacred to her," said Serena.

The importance of what had just happened dawned on Tom. Maddy had risked breaking her pony to help him. That was some sacrifice. He realized now that what looked like a cheap china figure to him was something invaluable to her. And it got the privilege of being stabled in her underwear. Lucky, lucky pony.

"My pony. It will have lost its luck." Maddy looked up at Tom and her eyes were misty with tears.

"I don't get it, Maddy," he said. "Because it touched Jerome?"
She nodded.

He thought quickly. "But . . . but it only touched his sweater, not his body, not his skin. Your hands and your mother's hands are still the only hands that have touched it. The luck will still be there. I promise you."

He couldn't believe that he, corporate attorney, aspiring partner of Jackson, Jones, and Gentry, was uttering this kind of superstitious nonsense. But putting Maddy's smile back in place was more important than anything else. "Don't you agree, Serena?" he asked.

"Absolutely," her friend agreed. "In fact, I think that after the pony has been so . . . so . . . heroic, it will be luckier than ever."

She. The figurine is a *she*, not an *it*, Tom mentally urged Serena. But Maddy didn't seem to notice her friend's error.

Maddy sniffed again. "Yes. You could be right."

"We are right," said Tom, drawing her close to him. He breathed in the familiar lavender smell of her. She was warm and soft in his arms. "Look how lucky you are right now. You're safe. Serena's safe. Serena's dog is safe."

Maddy's eyes were huge. "And you're safe, Tom. That's lucky, too. Lucky for me. And for Brutus. What would we do without you?"

She snuggled in next to him. His heart started to beat faster. Not from sexual arousal, though that was never far away when Maddy was around.

No, it was a potent mix of relief, protectiveness, and tenderness. A feeling that he'd never felt before for anyone. He liked it that she was wearing his shirt and cap. It made him feel like she belonged with him.

Maddy had been thrust unexpectedly into his life. Today's episode had forced him to confront what life might be like if she was just as suddenly taken out of it. And he didn't like that scenario at all.

Serena coughed. "I hate to break up this little scene but there's something that isn't so lucky around here—Maddy's car."

"Ohmigod, yes," said Maddy, drawing her warmth away from him. Tom could have cursed Serena.

Maddy ran to the top of the stairs. "My Honda is at the end of the block. He's left it there double-parked. And it's getting a ticket."

Tom cursed. "He's a clever bastard. Now we can't get him for car theft." He turned to Serena. "But we witnessed his assault on you."

Serena shook her head. "I don't want to report him. I'm not hurt, and I don't want to have to face him again." She looked pale and shaken.

"Are you sure? He shouldn't be allowed to get away with it."

She nodded.

"Do you want to come home with Maddy and me?"

"I'm fine," said Serena.

"Home?" said Maddy.

"I mean my apartment," he said gruffly, wondering if he'd given himself away by that slipup. Because he suddenly realized that his apartment only seemed like home with Maddy in it.

"Ohmigod," Maddy said again. "I told Nora I'd be back in forty minutes for Brutus. I've gotta get the car."

"I'm coming, too. Do you think I'd let you out of my sight after what's happened here today? Haven't you learned a thing?"

Her mouth quirked. "I guess not. Grumpy rides again."

"You've given me good cause to be grumpy. This is serious, Maddy."

She looked suitably contrite. "Okay. Fortress South Beach it is."

· Seventeen ·

Maddy thought Nora Green seemed quite pleased to hand Brutus back over to her and Tom. Apparently Brutus and Max had not gotten along as well as anticipated. But the older woman assured them she was quite sure the two animals would get used to each other with a little time—and separate living spaces.

And, yes, it was still quite okay to leave Brutus with Nora on Wednesday, audition day. Only could Maddy please pack a muzzle in her dog's playdate kit?

Maddy lingered, chatting to Nora for way longer than was necessary. From where he stood behind her she could sense Tom's edgy impatience. Truth was, she was using the chat to stretch out the time before she had to face him alone and explain why she had left the apartment against his advice.

Finally, Tom politely terminated the conversation with Nora. She could tell he was speaking through gritted teeth. He took her by the elbow and steered both her and Brutus firmly through the door and into his apartment.

"Ouch!" she said, pulling her arm away from him as soon as he had banged the door shut behind them. Brutus took off up the hallway. Maddy made a big show of rubbing her elbow. "That hurt." She looked up at him through eyes narrowed with bravado. "I don't like your caveman tactics."

"I don't like your airhead tactics," he said, back in full grim mode.

"Airhead?" she spluttered. "I don't know—"

"You know exactly what I mean. I couldn't have been clearer about you not leaving this apartment. *Under any circumstance.*"

Maddy knew she was in the wrong. Of course she did. And if Tom had given her a chance to apologize, she would have. But instead he was bossing her around. Again.

Her chin jutted out. "I made a decision based on what I thought was right at the time. I need the pony for my audition. I *have* to have it with me or there's no point in going."

"So you not only risked your own life, you also risked Serena's."

"You think I don't realize that? I even risked Snowball's life, for heaven's sake. Do you think I won't live with that guilt?" Her voice rose with each word.

"How do you think it was for me, Maddy? I didn't know where you were, what had happened. I thought you'd been abducted." His jaw was so tightly clamped he looked as if he were in pain.

Pain caused by her irresponsible behavior. He was right. She hadn't really thought it through before she'd made her mad dash for the pony. She took a deep breath.

"Tom, I'm sorry I messed up. I know you're furious, but I—" She didn't get a chance to finish her apology. Tom pulled her hard against his chest and kissed her, knocking her borrowed cap off her head and onto the floor in the process.

"Tom, I—" she mumbled against his mouth in surprise but he just kissed her harder. His mouth was firm and warm and delicious. She stopped trying to talk and started to kiss him back, relax against him, enjoy it. Until he broke the kiss.

"Hey," she said. "Don't stop. *That* kind of caveman tactic I like."

His hands gripped her shoulders so tightly she winced. "Maddy, this is not something to joke about. I'm just so thankful that you're all right." He dropped his hands from her. "I wonder if you truly appreciate the gravity of the situation. When I saw you there with that madman Stoddard . . ."

His deep, husky voice trailed away and he paused a moment to collect himself before speaking again. "As it was, everything turned out okay. Comical, really, with Snowball the hero of the day. But you heard him threaten to slit Brutus's throat. I believe he's capable of it."

"With me . . . with me watching." Nausea rose in her throat as she remembered the look in Jerome's eyes.

"What if Stoddard had had a knife with him or—God forbid—a gun?"

A gun! Maddy shuddered. A poisoned T-bone. An oversized block of chocolate. All weapons with an element of buffoonery. But she hadn't thought of Jerome carrying a gun.

"Maybe . . . maybe I underestimated Jerome."

Tom looked searchingly into her eyes, his expression intense and unreadable. He skimmed his thumb over her cheekbone and down the side of her face as if to reassure himself that she really was unhurt. "Don't ever pull a stunt like that again. Okay?" His voice wasn't quite steady.

Tom could tell from Maddy's pallor and the way she was chewing on her lip how bad she felt about the Stoddard fiasco. He wanted to pull her into his arms but he didn't dare. He wasn't sure he could stop comfort from flaring into passion. And she'd made it quite clear she wasn't ready for that yet. Though he'd had to—just had to—kiss her.

"I won't," she said. "Pull a stunt like that again, I mean. I realize how out of order I was. I'll never, never forgive myself for putting Serena at risk."

Tom knew she wasn't faking the meekness of her tone. But he wanted to make sure she really understood his worry.

"And you, Maddy. How do you think your friends would have felt if anything had happened to *you*? Imagine how your father would feel if I had to convey that news to him? Your grandmother." He paused. "Me."

She flinched at his words and he felt immediately contrite. But he felt she had to know how it had felt for him to see her in danger. How it had jolted him into a realization that he was developing feelings for her.

Her flinching didn't last long. The pretty chin rose again. "My grandmother would have done exactly the same thing. She wears all her lucky charms around her neck so she's never without them."

Tom forced his eyes not to turn heavenward. *All* her lucky charms? Was Maddy a chip off an older and equally eccentric block? "So that would have made it easier for her if something happened to you?"

"Of course not, but—"

She was exasperating. Adorable, but exasperating. "Maddy, I don't think I'm getting through to you. I'm trying to tell you how I felt seeing you in danger, fearing I'd gotten there too late to help . . ."

She stilled. "Oh, but you are getting through to me. Loud and clear." She chewed on that lip again. Her eyelashes fluttered. "When I saw Jerome hit you I was so frightened. Terrified. Didn't know what I'd do if you were hurt. I . . . I felt so powerless."

Tom was unexpectedly shaken by her words. He sought the right thing to say in response. "So . . . so you risked destroying your priceless china pony to come to my aid."

She turned her face away from him. "Don't mock me, Tom," she said in a voice that wasn't quite steady. "I know it's far from priceless to anyone but me."

He couldn't bear the hurt that crumpled her features. With two fingers under her chin he turned her back to face him again. "I'm not mocking you, Maddy. Please don't think that. I appreciate what you did. What throwing that thing meant to you. I just thank God it didn't break."

The air seemed charged between them and he thought they were actually saying more to each other than the words they were exchanging.

"You would really have seen murder then," she said.

"Who? Me or him?"

"Never you, Tom," she said. A tentative smile danced around her mouth.

"I'm glad to hear that," he said. Her smile spread wider, became more endearing, became—

"I wish you wouldn't do that!" he said.

"Do what?" she asked, bewildered.

With his finger he traced the freckles scattered across her nose. "Screw up your nose in that cute way you do."

"I do?"

"You do. It makes it impossible to stay cranky at you."

"It does?"

Maddy tried wrinkling up her nose but it didn't have quite the same endearing effect as before.

Tom shook his head. "No, not like that. Maybe you can't do it on purpose. Maybe it just . . . happens."

Maddy tried again. Only to make herself cross-eyed trying to look down her nose to see if it was working.

He laughed. "That isn't quite so cute." In fact, she looked downright ridiculous. But even looking ridiculous she was the cutest woman he'd ever seen.

"Well, you were the one making me do it," she said, this time her forehead doing the wrinkling.

Tom laughed but his laugh turned into a groan. "You have no idea what you do to me, do you?" He took a step back from her. He raked his hair with his fingers. "I didn't mean to get attached. God knows I've fought it."

"Attached? Attached to what?"

"Dammit, you know what I mean. Attached to you. Feeling like this about you isn't in—"

"The plan," she finished for him, nodding thoughtfully. "Feeling like what, Tom?"

★   ★   ★

Maddy's heart started thudding double-quick time. She felt the same breathless anticipation as when she was about to pull a soufflé from the oven. Would it be puffy and perfect or disappointingly flat? Was Tom about to tell her he was falling in love with her? And if he was, how did she really feel about it?

He turned and paced a few steps away, then turned back to face her. "Feeling responsible for you. Feeling like if anything had happened to you ... Feeling, I don't know ..." He shrugged. "It's hard to put into words."

Responsible? Was that all he felt for her? Like he was the busy attorney and she the nuisance client? Was that what he was trying to tell her?

Her mental oven door shut with a slam, her spirits as deflated as her most unsuccessful soufflé.

"You don't have to feel responsible for me, Tom. I've looked after myself for a long time now. It's only eight more days and then—"

His hair stood up in spikes by now. "I didn't mean that, Maddy. I meant something more personal. That you've become ... well, special to me."

He flushed under his tan.

Maybe the soufflé could be saved. As she smiled at him Maddy could feel her spirits rising. "You've ... uh ... become special to me, too, Tom."

She moved toward him but was stopped by paws scrabbling on her legs and a sad, attention-getting whine. Brutus. Of course. The canine master of interrupted intimate moments.

Tom glared down at the dog. Brutus held his paw up to shake. His pushed-in face was tilted at an angle.

Maddy couldn't help a giggle. "You see," she said to Tom. "It was the tone of my voice. He thought I was saying nice things. Which I was, but not to him."

"Well, he can forget it. It's my turn now."

"I'll tell him that, shall I?"

Tom's grin was broad, the dimple back in full force. "You did the nose thing perfectly when you said that," he said, stroking her hair. Shivers of awareness ran through her.

"Did I? I'll try again and see if I—"

"Don't try," he said. "The cross-eyed thing isn't quite so alluring."

She went to huff, but—at last—he kissed her, hard and swiftly as if sealing an agreement. The best kisser in the universe back in action again. She wound her arms around his neck in anticipation. What other romantic thing might he say?

Brown eyes bored down into hers. "So don't even think about leaving this apartment when I go back to the office."

"Wh ... what!" she spluttered, her arms dropping to her sides. "You're going back to work?"

"No choice, I'm afraid. Some reports from London came in overnight. Stoddard's known to the police in Britain, under another name."

"You mean he's not part of Walter's family?"

"Stoddard is his real name and he is related to Walter. He operates under aliases for his borderline criminal activities."

"Borderline?"

"Fake diet schemes, get-rich-quick frauds, that kind of thing. Preying on the gullible. Despicable really."

"Does that mean he can't challenge the will?"

"He's a blood relative. He has the right to contest."

Maddy cringed as she remembered how attractive she'd first

found Jerome. Misled again by her weakness for handsome men. "And to think I liked him when I met him. Does that make me gullible?"

Tom absentmindedly tucked a stray wisp of hair back behind her ear, as if he wasn't aware of doing it. "Don't beat yourself up about that, Maddy. He's a con man, he trades on making a good first impression. He didn't fool you for long."

"And he didn't fool Brutus for one second." She compared Brutus's instant liking—no, adoration—for Tom to his animosity toward Jerome. There was something to be said for animal instinct.

"Stoddard is a bad guy. You have to stay in hiding."

"Yes, Grumpy," she said, with exaggerated repentance that masked her genuine remorse that she hadn't taken his warnings more seriously.

"And reporters from all around the country are flooding my office with calls. Stoddard contesting the will is keeping the millionaire mutt story alive. Which is all the more reason for you to stay put."

"Yes, Grumpy."

"And don't call me Grumpy."

"Yes, Gr—"

"Maddy!"

"Okay—Tom."

"So do as you're told and don't move from this apartment!" he said, giving her one brief, hard kiss before he opened the door then slammed it hard behind him.

· Eighteen ·

After Tom left, Maddy found she couldn't stop smiling, a ridiculous grin that kept tugging at her mouth. A warm happiness bubbled around her heart. She felt like singing, dancing, whirling Brutus around the apartment in her arms. She was special to Tom. He'd said so.

As she ballroom danced with Brutus, she kept thinking about Tom's words. And what about the wrinkled-nose business? What did he mean by that?

She popped Brutus down on a chair and tried out the nose thing in front of the mirror. Tom thought *that* was cute? Hmm.

Maybe it was like making perfect meringues; if she tried too hard, they always flopped. It had to be effortless, unrehearsed. She tried again. And again. And could only conclude that the scrunched-up nose and crossed eyes was not a good look.

But who cared what she looked like? There was no one to see her except a little dog who made his devotion to Tom slavishly apparent. She and Brutus, Tom's two-person—no—one-person-and-a-dog fan club. She dropped a kiss on the little dog's head. "What do you think Brutus? Me and your alpha male?"

He cocked his head on one side and she could have sworn he was grinning. He barked. She laughed. "Yes, you're absolutely right. I should be preparing for that audition. Like now. Not moping around the place getting all dreamy over your master."

First on the stop-grinning-like-a-cat-who'd-gotten-the-cream agenda was to unpack the supermarket order. She was pleasantly surprised at the quality of the delivery. Even the flowers were market fresh. A room wasn't a room without fresh flowers, and they'd do something to personalize Tom's arid living space. She couldn't understand how he could be happy in a place that was so . . . gray.

Carefully, she unpacked a whole fish that had been fastidiously packed in ice. What was that thing Grandma used to say about the way to a man's heart? To show Tom how special he had become to her, she wanted to cook something really nice for him tonight. Something that fit his healthy eating habits.

That would be a challenge. Although she preferred cooking lavish, forget-the-calorie-count foods, she could see how people with dietary restrictions or watching their weight might want something lighter but with the same flavor and appeal.

She paused, a bundle of asparagus in her hand. Could that concept work for the television show? Gourmet recipes but with the "thinner version" as well. Hmm, yes. Though, hard as she might think, she couldn't think of a light version of her triple-chocolate macadamia brownies. Maybe that was it. She could show which recipes could be "thinned down" and which couldn't.

Fired with ideas she raced into the kitchen.

Several hours later she flopped exhausted but pleased onto the sofa. She had the whole format worked out for her audition. The lucky pony had done her stuff again.

Brutus jumped up next to her and laid his head on her lap. Would Tom approve of a dog on his leather sofa? She thought she knew the answer to that but she wasn't going to boot her little pal off. Not when he was so obviously miserable being locked inside.

The little pet needed a treat. Before she did Tom's fish she'd create some new Brutus-friendly doggy delights. No onions, no grapes or raisins, no macadamias, and definitely no chocolate. It could be fun . . .

Why not include some healthy dog recipes as a backup for the audition? Just in case they asked for more ideas. Treats dogs love that are good for them. It could work.

She scratched behind Brutus's ears. "Only eight more days 'til you go home to your own yard," she crooned. He wagged his plumed tail.

And how did she feel about going home? She'd go stir-crazy locked up for much longer in this gray room with a view. But although she'd been happy in her little apartment, it wasn't the same since Walter had died. And maybe she wasn't the same since she'd met Tom.

For a moment she closed her eyes and entertained a very warm and fuzzy fantasy of moving upstairs into Walter's big house with Tom. Making a cozy home. Wild sex every night. Cooking him and Brutus healthy meals. Ironing . . . Her eyes snapped open. No way would she iron his underpants. Or even his shirts. She hated ironing. He could send them out to a laundry.

She tuned out of that particular fantasy and headed for the television. Would she allow herself just one daytime soap until she got back to the kitchen? But sliding open the drawer beside the TV she found Tom's DVD collection—filed in alphabetical order. How very Tom. And there were a number of animated films mixed in with the standard guy assortment of action flicks and screwball comedies. Surely all these weren't just for his nieces?

The Lion King was there. "One of my favorites," she told Brutus. "Let's watch it. Though there are no dogs in it, I'm afraid, only nasty old hyenas." Brutus licked her hand, liking the attention.

She hummed along to the Elton John song "Can You Feel the Love Tonight?" and by the time she had sung the refrain for the third time the truth struck her and she stopped mid-bar. *That's* why she was smiling to herself in such an inane way. Because that's what she was feeling. The love. The wonderful, bubbling warmth of being in love with Tom O'Brien.

In love with his sense of humor, his kindness, even his lawyerly stuffiness. And that wasn't counting his best-kisser-in-the-universe-type qualities.

She thought about the big fiberglass sculpture of Cupid's bow and arrow in Rincon Park along the Embarcadero. They'd passed it on the way to Tom's apartment. She'd been shot all right, fair and square in the heart.

She went to jump up, grab the phone, tell him. But reality jerked her back and she stayed put on the sofa.

Did she really want to take the risks involved in loving Tom? What about his plan? His rigid five-year plan. The no-serious-girlfriend, no-serious-kissing plan.

He'd said she was special. He hadn't recoiled in horror when she'd said she thought he was special, too. Could she convince him to write her into the plan as some kind of amendment? Or was it addendum? He would know the correct terminology, she giggled to herself.

Yes. She'd make a big bowl of popcorn and finish watching *The Lion King* before she finalized preparations for the steamed Thai-style fish she would cook Tom for dinner. He'd like that, she was sure. And then maybe she could nudge the conversation toward the love stuff.

Tom arrived home to find the apartment in darkness. Fear grabbed him with icy claws. *Maddy.* Had Stoddard found her?

Then he saw by the light of the empty, flickering screen of the television that Maddy was asleep on the sofa. He sagged with relief. Brutus was snuggled into the crook of her knees, and there was a bowl with a few lone kernels of popcorn on the floor nearby. Brutus pricked up his ears.

"Stay," Tom whispered to Brutus. He didn't want to disturb Maddy. After today's traumatic episode a good sleep was probably just what she needed.

He could tell her later that he'd discussed the assaults on both Serena and himself with the police. He wasn't sure that he'd ever repeat what the police officer had said about self-defense with a china pony. Not in the cop's exact words, anyway.

He caught his breath. Maddy looked so beautiful sprawled on his sofa. One arm was tucked around her head exposing the lovely line of her neck, the other trailed on the carpet. Her hair seemed to shine with a light of its own, her skin luminous in the semidarkness. She was still wearing his blue shirt. He envied his shirt for its closeness to her.

Thank God she was okay. His fear when he'd thought she was gone from the apartment had jolted him into realizing that all barricades against her had been destroyed.

The curtains were open, framing the view of the marina and the city lights. As his eyes got used to the light, he looked around him and noticed a few subtle changes. A jug of roses sitting on the coffee table, an artfully arranged bowl of fruit, some magazines fanned open. Assorted dog toys were scattered around the floor, some exceedingly well chewed. Maddy's shoes lay where she'd kicked them off.

The room smelled differently, too, the sweet scent of the roses mingling with Maddy's own lavender and the unmistakable hint of dog.

Three weeks ago he would have hated the disruption to his designer-perfect room. Now he sat and relaxed into it. Reveled in it, in fact. Even the doggy smell.

His perfect bachelor pad. Infiltrated now by a beautiful girl and a not-so-beautiful mutt and he, the bachelor, in willing defeat.

He turned away and walked quietly into the kitchen. She'd packed away the shopping. In the fridge was a whole fish marinating in some spicy stuff and some finely sliced vegetables. Looked like she'd been planning dinner but it didn't seem like she'd wake for it.

He padded down the hallway and into the bedroom. Again, her presence was inescapable, her scent part of the air he breathed.

Her ridiculous lucky pony was sitting on the bedside table. He didn't dare touch it. Just in case he screwed up her luck.

The bed was neatly made and draped across the foot was a short, lacy black nightgown. He resisted the urge to pick it up and bury his face in it. That would be too weird.

He heard the sound of dog tags clinking and glanced up to see Brutus trotting into the room. The dog stopped, cocked his head, and looked up at him expectantly.

"So you're hungry, too, Brutus? We'll have to fend for ourselves, I'm afraid, old buddy. I saw some cans of—"

Tom stopped himself, horrified at the sound of his own voice. He was actually talking to the dog. Talking to the dog in the same eccentric way Maddy did.

He shook his head in disbelief. Thank God she hadn't heard him. He'd never live it down. The final bastion had been breached. Time to pack up the defenses and fly the white flag.

He picked up the phone and dialed an order to his favorite noodle restaurant just a block away. It would be ready by the time he got there to pick it up.

He went back into the living room and stood looking down at Maddy for a long time. He could easily carry her into the bedroom where she could sleep more comfortably. But what if she woke up? Woke up and accused him again of caveman tactics?

After last night, he didn't want to scare her off by coming on too strong. He wanted . . . he wanted something more than no-strings sex with Maddy. She was worth way more than that to him.

He needed to know if she was totally serious about the two-date thing. Was she still hurting from a past relationship? The fiancé maybe? Or did she only see him as Brutus's attorney? If so, he would have to convince her otherwise.

He shook out a soft gray throw that usually lay immaculately folded on the sofa and laid it lightly over her. Then he looked at her some more. Just soaking up the sight of her and musing on the changes she'd brought to his well-ordered life. Changes he wondered just how to incorporate into his plan.

While he ate his solitary noodles he'd plot how he was going to keep this wonderful woman in his life after the twenty-one days expired next Thursday.

· Nineteen ·

Maddy woke up feeling totally disorientated. Morning sun filtered on unfamiliar pale gray walls. The slide of a leather sofa beneath her. Her shirt twisted around her. The rich smell of coffee. She sat up. Ah, Tom's living room. And Tom in the kitchen brewing coffee.

Blinking, still a little dopey with sleep, she watched him head toward her bearing a large mug.

"Thought you might like to start the day with coffee." He was wearing jeans and a T-shirt and his hair was slicked back from his face as if he had just showered.

She stifled a yawn. "Great. Thanks." She took the cup from him. "It's not some healthy type of coffee, is it?" she asked, unable to hide the suspicion from her voice.

"The full caffeine hit," he assured her.

She took a few sips. It was not as strong as she liked her

coffee, but she appreciated his gesture and didn't want to hurt his feelings.

"I had to guess," he said. "I actually prefer it stronger but—"

She laughed. "I can live with it stronger. Next time make mine the same as yours."

Next time? Did she just say *next time*? Next time Tom brought her coffee in bed? This being in love thing was making her careless with her words.

To cover her confusion she started to apologize. "I'm so sorry. Last night. The dinner. I was going to cook for you. I had fish—"

"Don't worry about it. I ordered takeout."

She swung her legs off the sofa. "You weren't supposed to do that."

"My personal chef was asleep. Snoring her head off."

Her hand flew to her mouth. "I wasn't."

He laughed. "No, you weren't. But Brutus was. That dog needs to go back to puppy school."

"I don't think they teach dogs not to snore at puppy school. I certainly didn't notice it on the brochure."

"What about his other seriously bad personal habits?"

"Not them, either. Besides, they won't have him back. His report card reads 'delinquent dog.' He flunked all his classes."

"I told you he needs some homeschooling. Of the tough-love kind. What was that Mrs. Green said about a muzzle?" There was a hint of dimple so he probably wasn't serious but she couldn't be sure. Not after the BMW upholstery incident.

"Nothing. Nothing at all," she said, getting up. She took her mug over to the dining table. It was time to change the subject. "I guess you were glad to have your bed back last night."

His bed. Her hands clenched around her coffee mug yet she scarcely felt the heat. So why did she have to mention the bed?

"Uh, wh . . . where is Brutus?" she asked, changing the conversation again before Tom had a chance to reply to her inane question about the bed. Before she had time to conjure up images of him in it, his tall, muscular body sprawled across the same place where she'd lain the night before, his body imprinted on hers. The same place where he'd kissed and caressed her all the way to step five.

"Still asleep in the bedroom," said Tom. "He had an active night—snoring, scratching, clanging his tags together, you know, that kind of noisy stuff. He obviously passed Insomnia for Owners 101. With honors."

Maddy shook her head in sympathy. "Poor you. He was too zonked to disturb me the night before. That was after you . . . after we . . ."

"After he barfed in the bathroom you mean. After—"

This conversation was heading into uncomfortable territory. She didn't want to analyze or discuss what had happened so spontaneously between them. Not now when she was still getting used to the idea of being head over heels in love with him.

Luckily Brutus chose that moment to trot into the room, heading straight for his food bowl.

"Here he is now," she said, trying to keep the relief from her voice. Saved by the dog. "Good morning, little guy." She gave Brutus a vigorous pat down. "Were you a naughty boy again last night? Keeping your alpha male awake."

She cast a sideways glance at Tom. Strangely, he didn't react to her calling him Brutus's alpha male. Even stranger, he didn't tease her for talking to the dog as if he were a person. In fact, she could probably describe the look on his face as indulgent. Maybe he was mellowing.

Tom leaned down to scratch Brutus behind the ears. Their hands brushed. Tom took her hand and squeezed it. She squeezed back. The simple, affectionate gesture made her feel ridiculously happy.

Brutus looked adoringly up at Tom with his black button eyes. When the twenty-one days were over and she was back home, she supposed she'd have to organize some sort of visitation rights. But what about visitation rights for her? She couldn't bear the thought of not seeing Tom on a regular basis when their imposed time together came to an end.

"So," she said, "is it back to the office for you today or do they allow you Saturdays off?"

"I have to bill a lot of hours but I won't work all weekend. I thought . . . I thought we could spend the day together today. If that suits you, of course."

"I have no plans. Just lonely incarceration in your apartment." The mournful tone of her voice was only half a joke.

Tom finished his own coffee. He put the mug down on the table. "Maddy, there's something I'd like to ask you."

He looked so serious, his brows drawn together. What could be so important? Her stomach knotted with apprehension. Then Tom coughed, a little dry clearing of the throat that let her know he was nervous. Tom nervous? Of her?

"Fire away," she said.

"I'd like to . . . to ask you on a date."

She spluttered into her coffee.

"A date?" was all she managed to get out as she got her breath back.

"Yes," he said, still looking very serious and lawyerlike and—curiously for a soccer hunk—vulnerable, his brown eyes wary. "We've had kissing occasions and we've had French kissing occasions. But we haven't had a date. A proper I-ask-you-out type of date."

"No, we haven't," she said, smiling at his overly formal tone. When she first met him she'd have thought it unbearably stuffy. Now she knew he was just being Tom. And along with the stuffiness went the sincerity and honesty she found so appealing. "And . . . and I would like to go on a proper you-ask-me-out type of date."

His relief at her acceptance was apparent in the breadth of his smile and the depth of his dimple. "It's late notice, I know, but I'd like to ask you out on a date today."

"Today?" She looked out the window. The sun shone from a pale blue sky. Lunch at a bayside restaurant? A ferryboat to Sausalito and a leisurely browse through the galleries there? "But I'm not allowed outside."

"If the coast is clear of reporters and if you lie down on the backseat so you can't be seen, we could get right out of San Francisco. To a place where they know me and our privacy would be respected."

"And what would we do?"

"Horseback riding," he said.

She stared at him. "Horseback riding? I didn't know you liked horseback riding."

"I used to ride as a boy. I started again last fall at a ranch in Marin County."

She jumped up from the chair. "I couldn't think of anything I'd rather do. I miss my horse so much—thank you, thank you, thank you!"

Hmm. Maybe she'd overdone the enthusiasm some. Tom looked bemused at her reaction. She backpedaled. "What I'm trying to say is that's a great idea for a date. You know, no clichés like lunch or romantic picnic or—"

"The picnic idea is good," he said. She noticed he didn't pick up on the word "romantic" but she wouldn't really expect that from Tom. In her experience, men ran from the word. Ran screaming.

She gave her enthusiasm full rein. "I ordered tons of stuff from the supermarket yesterday. I can fix the picnic."

"Excellent. We can pick up extra things on the way if we need to."

"But what about Brutus?"

"We'll take him with us. He could probably do with some exercise."

"In . . . uh . . . your car?" She quailed at the memory of the chewed upholstery.

"I'll cover the seats with some rugs."

"That might be wise. But what about when we get there? I mean when we ride the horses?"

"The woman who manages the ranch likes dogs. I'm sure she'd be happy to look after him and keep him out of mischief. Though we'll have to remember to call him Bruce, not Brutus. Just in case someone has been following the millionaire mutt story and puts it together."

"Oh, Tom, this is a great idea. I can't thank you enough." She wanted to throw her arms around his neck and hug him but stopped herself from giving in to the impulse.

She could have easily done it before she realized she was in love with him. But somehow that secret new knowledge made her self-conscious about touching him.

He looked pleased at her words. "There are some good horses out at the stable. I'll call and book."

"But what about clothes? My breeches and boots. My helmet. They're at my apartment."

Tom frowned. "That poses a problem. I could drive over and get them. But if there are press camped outside I can't risk them following me here."

Maddy's spirits plummeted to the level of her toes. She felt overwhelmed by sheer hatred of Jerome for putting her in this position.

"Tell you what," said Tom. "You get the picnic ready. If I can't get into your apartment, we'll eat right here."

"A picnic on the living room floor?" It wasn't the same as horseback riding. But it could be a romantic option. "Okay," she said. She started to plan the picnic menu. Did she have time to whip up some muffins?

Tom shifted from foot to foot. "Before I go, I'd like to ask you something else."

"Yes?" she said, her mind still with the muffins.

"Keeping in mind your two-date rule, I'd like to ask you on another date."

"Another date?" Caught off guard, it was all she could think to say.

"Yes. Late notice again. Thursday night?"

"A nighttime date?" A date after eight was serious stuff. In her book, a date after the sun set equaled two daytime dates.

He cleared his throat. "Dinner with the senior partners of Jackson, Jones, and Gentry."

"Wow," she said, again caught off guard. "Sounds, uh, impressive."

What she really wanted to say was, "Sounds boring—really, really boring." Not boring being in Tom's company, never that. But dinner out with a bunch of stuffy lawyers was not exactly her idea of a hot date. But if Tom wanted her company, did the occasion matter?

"It's kind of the last round of my bid for partnership," said Tom. "Dinner with them and their wives. I'd like you to come with me as my date."

This really was progress. She'd be his official date, not just a nuisance client he was keeping out of trouble. "Fine," she said. "I'm, uh, fine with that. Thank you."

But what on earth would she talk to these men about? And would their wives be as stuffy as the guys were sure to be?

Still, she knew how important Tom's goal of partnership was to him. She'd do anything she could to help him. "I'd better be on my best behavior then."

"Just be yourself. That's your best behavior," he said, warming her with his words.

Panic set in. "But what will I wear? I—"

"You want me to pick up a dress for you at the apartment as well as your riding gear?"

"Let me think." Mentally she reviewed the contents of her purple suitcase. "No. I think I have something with me that will suit." What sixth sense had made her pack her favorite black party dress and the shoes that went with it?

After he left Maddy found herself singing as she prepared her muffins. Two dates with Tom. A daytime date—and a nighttime date.

Was she seeing a variation to his plan? She hoped his master plan was like her basic muffin recipe—able to stretch to accommodate new developments.

She could add blueberries, pistachios, grated lime peel, or chocolate chips and the recipe would still work. It was just a matter of adjustment. Maybe she should see herself as the chocolate chip in his muffin mix of life.

She sang a little louder as she stirred the muffin mixture—adding oat bran for Tom's cholesterol—but quickly switched to another tune when she realized she was warbling the words to "Can You Feel the Love Tonight?" with way too much feeling.

· Twenty ·

Tom thought Maddy looked sexy in jeans. Sensational in a skirt. Words failed him as to how she looked in her riding gear as she strolled toward the stables. It was a good thing the reporters had given up on her apartment and he'd been able to get her stuff.

Her tight cream breeches clung to her curvy bottom and her slender legs, but it was her T-shirt that was like a magnet to his gaze.

Long-sleeved and dark green, it was embroidered with plump "hungry ponies" galloping toward a bunch of carrots stitched on the pocket. The pocket that just happened to be placed over her left breast. He'd like to dive into that pocket and feast, too.

"Cute T-shirt," he said, trying to be as casual as he could, forcing himself not to focus on the pocket and how provocatively it curved.

"It is, isn't it? I've got another one that's just as cute with frisky ponies kicking up their heels."

Tom groaned inwardly. He felt more than frisky himself. Being in such proximity to her and holding back was beginning to tell on him.

"After years of formal dressage stuff, I like wearing something fun," she explained unself-consciously stroking the pony nearest to her breast.

Fun. Tom gritted his teeth. Fun like the sexy underwear she chose to wear under her chef's uniform. He wondered what underwear she had on now—and it wasn't the first time he'd thought it today.

This fascination with her undergarments was bordering on obsessive. Though to be honest it wasn't just her underwear that was constantly in his thoughts. Her smile. The warmth in her eyes when she laughed. That cute way she wrinkled her nose. They intruded as often.

Maddy Cartwright had come so unexpectedly into his life and turned it upside down. So upside down he found himself struggling to keep his balance. But when he thought about her smile, he felt like dancing way up there on that ceiling.

"Where's the horse you ride?" she asked. "I'm dying to meet him."

The big bay nickered as they approached his stall and poked his head over the gate.

"He's magnificent," said Maddy when they reached him.

"Over seventeen hands," Tom said. "He's an ex-racehorse."

"I had no idea you were into horses," Maddy said, her nose crinkling in that delightful, now-so-familiar way.

He shrugged. "My dad was a real outdoorsman. He taught me to ride when we lived in Denver."

Her eyes were thoughtful. "I don't know why, but I think of you as such a city slicker."

"Because I wear a suit and work in a legal firm?"

She tilted her head on its side. "Maybe."

"In that case, I might have some more surprises in store for you." The kind of surprises he'd have to show, not tell.

"I like surprises," she said, surprising him by leaning up and kissing him lightly on the lips.

As she was carrying her helmet in one hand and a bag of carrots in the other, it was difficult for him to do more than pull her to him in an awkward hug. "More on the surprises later," he murmured.

He was acutely aware of the interest he and Maddy were getting from the teenage girl stable hands. He could see a gaggle of them nudging each other and giggling as they watched him from the other end of the stable.

This was the first time he'd brought a girlfriend here with him. The first time he'd thought anyone special enough to share this newly resurrected aspect of his life. This weekend world was important to him. His escape. A link to his father. Up until now he hadn't wanted to share.

The horse he always rode nickered again for attention. Maddy turned to face the big bay gelding.

"What's his name?" she said. "Oh, hang on, I see it on the stable nameplate. *Squiggles.* You're kidding me, right? Don't tell me this big boy's name is Squiggles."

"Yeah, I suppose it's kind of inappropriate. But I think it suits him."

In fact, the thought had never entered his head. What was it with Maddy and names?

She was obviously having some trouble suppressing her laughter as she stroked and patted the big animal. "Okay, Squiggles," she said, feeding the horse a chunk of carrot from the flat of her hand. "I'd think of you more as a Blaze or a Chieftain. Something more . . . dignified."

There she was again, talking to an animal as if it were a human and would answer her back. But after his conversation with Brutus last night, on what grounds could he say anything?

"At least his name isn't Bruce," he commented.

Surprised, Maddy looked up at him. A shaft of sunlight from the window in Squiggles's stall hit her hair and it gleamed like burnished copper in the gloom of the stable.

"Point taken," she said, her eyes creased with good humor.

It warmed Tom's heart the way Maddy could take a joke. He also liked the way she was as at home here in the muck and the straw as she was in a photographer's studio.

"Shall we saddle up?" she asked with a grin. "I don't mind if you help me mount. That will really give those girls ogling you something to giggle about."

The stable hands giggled all right and continued to giggle every time they "accidentally" encountered him and Maddy along the trail ride.

Their surveillance was beginning to bug him. Maddy was an expert on horseback, and they were well matched to ride together.

But—trail ride over—here he was with Maddy on a picnic blanket and not appreciating an audience hiding somewhere in the forest behind them.

Brutus—known for today as Bruce—was snoring peacefully nearby. Tom had had a tough time separating the less-than-discerning dog from the wonderful new toys he'd found lying around everywhere—dried balls of horse manure.

Maddy lay back against the big tree stump they'd used as a table. She stretched her arms out above her head, an action that lifted her breasts enticingly into prominence, the embroidered ponies pulled nearer to their bucket of carrots.

Lucky ponies. From where he sat Tom could reach out and touch them. But as he moved closer, there was a muted chorus of giggles. He swore.

"Be flattered," Maddy said, smiling, "and accept that we're being chaperoned."

He didn't want to be chaperoned. He was thirty years old and he wanted to kiss Maddy in privacy. And maybe explore those carrots. He grumbled some more. This wasn't how he'd planned the day.

"The girls obviously think you're a hottie and are used to having you all to themselves. I'd say they're jealous as hell of me."

"A hottie? Me?" The idea seemed preposterous, although he had to admit to being flattered. "Get real. I'm an old man to them. A boring old lawyer."

"I find you anything but boring. And you look pretty well preserved to me." Her gaze traveled lazily over him. It was as if she had trailed tantalizing fingers over his body and it reacted accordingly.

"As long as you think so, that's all that's important," was all he managed to choke out. He lay down on his stomach to disguise the evidence of his reaction. "But you're a grown woman, these are just kids."

"When I was fourteen I had a mad crush on my riding instructor." A smile hovered around her impossibly sexy mouth. "He scarcely knew I existed and, boy, did that hurt."

He knew she had been engaged, must have had other boyfriends, but he didn't want to think of her being involved with any other man. "I wonder what you were like when you were fourteen."

Maddy pulled a face. "Gawky. Ugly. Covered in freckles."

"Ugly? Never." He moved closer to her and propped himself on one elbow as, with the other hand, he traced the sprinkling of freckles across her nose. "I think your freckles are cute." He leaned down to kiss the tip of her nose.

"Ugh," Maddy said. "I hate 'em. The freckles, I mean. Luckily they faded once I started in kitchens. Working 'til two in the morning with only Mondays off I hardly saw the sun."

"It sounds like a tough life. What made you become a chef?" He enjoyed the play of expressions on her face as she thought about her answer. In the dappled sunlight her eyes shone greener than ever.

"Accident, really. I was at college, living in town with my grandmother. To make some extra money I waited tables at the only halfway decent restaurant there."

He imagined her in a short black skirt, smiling her luminescent smile as she took the orders. Bet she made lots in tips. And not just from the male patrons. He thought back to how she'd handled Mrs. Poodle. The impression she'd made on his mom. Maddy was the kind of girl other women liked, too.

Maddy continued. "One night the chef turned up drunk, totally incapable. The owner was desperate. I volunteered to cook and somehow managed to get through all the orders."

"So . . . they gave you the job and a star was born."

"Nothing as fairy tale as that. The chef stayed sober from then on, and I finished my journalism degree."

"And . . . ?" he prompted.

"I got a taste of being a professional cook. When I graduated, I moved to San Francisco and trained as a chef."

She sat up, rolled back her sleeve, and flexed her bicep. "See? Muscles. They're from hauling industrial-sized saucepans around a kitchen." She pointed to a small scar on her forearm. "That's a burn from the grill."

"Hard work," he said, admiring both her spunk and her shapely arm.

"Yes, but worth it. At *Annie* magazine I get to be both journalist and cook. The best of my two worlds. Now if I can just get this television gig . . ." Her eyes became hazy with dreams.

Maddy was on the brink of her dream job; he was on the way to his partnership.

She was as ambitious as he was. So how did he factor in her job, her goals with his master five-year plan? Could he successfully amend it and still ensure they both got where they wanted to go? And what would he do if he couldn't?

Rethink things. That's what his mother had urged him to do. Was his rigid life plan grounded in an adolescent reaction to a set of adult actions he hadn't, at the time, fully comprehended?

It was time to shed that self-imposed stricture. Rid himself of something he'd long outgrown. Open his no-longer-bombproof heart to the possibilities this wonderful woman brought into his life.

The sun warmed his shoulders and Maddy's scent intoxicated his senses. He filled his lungs with the sharp, pine-tangy air and felt a rush of the most exhilarating sense of freedom.

★   ★   ★

Maddy sat up, pulled her knees up to her chest, and hugged them. "That's enough about me. How about you, Tom? Was there some"—she sought the right words—"significant event in your life that changed it forever?"

Tom looked so relaxed, his big, hunky body sprawled on the picnic rug. To Maddy, he appeared a man born to wear riding gear. His tight breeches molded the long, lean muscles of his legs and hugged the contours of his butt.

A good butt meant a lot on a man, and so did a good set of broad shoulders. Tom had both. She'd been appreciating them all day.

His handsomeness was not in doubt. But she ached to know more about this man she'd fallen so unexpectedly in love with. When she asked him the "significant event" question, he tensed. Immediately she regretted it, wondering if she had breached a no-go zone.

He pulled himself up to sit near her. "I can't come up with anything as interesting as a drunken chef." His mouth twisted into something that was neither grimace nor grin. "But I guess my father leaving us for a girl the same age as my sister could count as significant."

Maddy snatched her hands to her mouth. "Oh, Tom, I'm so sorry. Of course they mentioned your parents' divorce in that horrible newspaper article. I didn't mean to . . . to reopen old wounds."

He picked up a fallen eucalyptus leaf and worried it between his fingers, releasing its pungent odor. "That's what they are, old wounds. I've put all that behind me now."

Had he? The pieces of the puzzle that was Tom began to slide into place. His five-year plans, for instance. Maddy was no psychologist, but she wondered if he used those plans to exert control over a life that had for a while been thrown out of kilter.

Yes, that must have something to do with it. The knowledge made her feel she had moved to a new level of understanding and it served only to strengthen her feelings for him. She'd had her own way of dealing with her mother's death that might not have been much different.

"Thanks for sharing with me, Tom," she said.

He gave the leaf a final squeeze, tore it in two, and threw it onto the grass. "It's no big deal." He turned to meet her gaze. She was surprised at the expression of mingled relief and triumph that shone from his eyes and lit his smile. "I really mean that, Maddy."

She slid closer to him on the picnic rug and snuggled against him. With her finger she traced that wonderful dimple, the sexy curve of his upper lip. Then she kissed him.

There was an immediate chorus of muted giggles and she broke away, giggling herself. "We've still got an audience."

"Unfortunately."

"No more kissing then," she said, and laughed at his grim expression. She looked teasingly up at him. "But we've managed to talk and find out things about each other and that's good, isn't it?"

"Really good. But not as good as kissing. Never as good as kissing."

Kissing—and much more than kissing—was what she wanted, too.

He got up and pulled her to her feet. "Let's gallop. I'll race you back to the stables."

· Twenty-one ·

Tom scanned the corridor outside the door to his apartment, trying not to appear too furtive. Thankfully the coast appeared clear.

He, Maddy, and Brutus had safely negotiated the journey from basement garage to doorway without any of the other apartment owners detecting the presence of a dog. Brutus had again refused to be confined to Maddy's shopping basket, and she had him clutched to her chest, hidden under the picnic blanket.

Brutus was protesting at his confinement, wriggling and squirming and trying to fight his way out. From beneath the plaid blanket came the beginnings of a growl.

Suddenly a door opened down the corridor two apartments away. Maddy swiftly clamped her hand over the dog's mouth as Tom pushed open their door. They fell through the doorway as Tom slammed the door behind them.

"That was close," she said, getting her balance. Then she snatched her hand away from Brutus. "Ouch! You get down right now," she said to the dog, plunking him on the floor.

Without a backward glance Brutus scrabbled away from her then waddled up the hallway, progressively freeing himself from the blanket until one final shake of his back leg left it lying on the floor behind him as he scampered toward the kitchen.

"Straight to his food bowl," Tom observed. By now he had figured out Brutus's priorities.

Maddy was still shaking her hand and wincing. "Did Brutus bite you?" Tom said. He threw down the bag with the picnic stuff.

"No, his teeth just grazed my hand when I was trying to keep him quiet."

"Show me."

Her pale hand, long fingers topped with short, practical fingernails, lay in his much larger one. He turned it over but couldn't see any marks, just a slightly reddened area. But he held on to her hand, anyway, enfolding it in his.

That brought Maddy very close to him, the hungry ponies in their eternal quest for embroidered carrots just stroking distance away. "I really am fine." Then she sighed. "But I'll be glad when this is all over and Brutus can run around freely again."

Her words reverberated through him with a pain that surprised him. "Will you?" He searched her heart-shaped face for answers. "I won't be. Glad when it's over, I mean. I, uh, I've gotten kind of used to having you around."

There was a long, still silence between them. "Me, too," she said, "gotten used to you, I mean." A pink flush appeared high on her cheekbones.

Tom cleared his throat. "You and Brutus, well, you've made your mark . . ."

"On your car upholstery. Yes. Don't forget to bill him for that. That's assuming we win the court case, of course. I suppose he'll have a bank account but what about signatures and ID and—"

Maddy was talking way too fast. He took her other hand so both were captured in his. Her face was only inches from his.

"Don't try and change the subject, Maddy. You're very good at doing that."

"I am?" Her eyes widened.

"You know you are. I'm trying to be serious here . . . I . . . uh . . . dammit, this isn't easy. I'm trying to say I don't want this—you, me—to end after twenty-one days. I want us to . . . well, I want there to be an 'us.'"

Hell. That didn't come out very well. At work he was known for his eloquence. Yet he couldn't find the right words to tell this special girl that she'd gotten under his skin and how he couldn't imagine a life without her. Or, in fact, without that pesky little dog.

But, hold on, her eyes had gone all misty, and that delightfully bow-shaped mouth was trembling. Maybe she had gotten the message after all.

"Tom, I feel the same way," she said in a soft little voice that made his heart beat faster. "Yes, it's no fun having to stay inside, keeping Brutus locked away, but it's . . . I . . . well, I'm really enjoying being with you. I don't want that part to end."

"So, what does that mean for the two-date rule?"

Maddy didn't hesitate, looked straight into his eyes. "Forget the two-date rule."

"And kissing occasions?"

She nodded in the affirmative. "Forget them, too." Then wailed, "Oh no, that's not what I meant." She tried to pull back from him but he held her hands firmly.

He smiled. "You meant, I think, forget any limitations on kissing occasions."

"Yes, Mr. Attorney, that's exactly what I meant," she said. And the pout to her lovely mouth made it very clear that she expected a kissing occasion right now.

Oh, oh, oh, this was turning out *so* right, Maddy exulted to herself as Tom's mouth covered hers. He hadn't said he was in love with her. Not exactly. But she was sure he must be close. He just couldn't say it.

Well, who could blame him? It was hard to utter those three words, darn near impossible, in fact. She'd had her chance, and she hadn't murmured, "I love you," either.

But, oh, how she was feeling it. After their blissful day together she felt so close to him, so confident that they could be happy together. That they understood each other.

So they hadn't talked long term, but didn't short term have to come first?

And if this was short term, she was in heaven. Tom's arms around her, his mouth on hers, his heart beating against her breast, beating so fast she knew he must be thinking the same way as she was. His hands slid down her back, cupped her bottom, pulled her even closer.

Tom kept kissing her and she kept kissing him back.

It felt so good. But there was another dimension to the

physical contact. With his arms around her she felt like she could deal with anything. The press intrusion. Jerome. Tuesday's courtroom appearance. Her fear of Jerome harming Brutus.

Brutus. Where was he? She pulled away from the kiss and looked around.

"Where is Brutus?"

"In the kitchen. I told him to stay away. And as his alpha male he listens to me."

Maddy whipped around to face Tom. "Say that again?" she asked, delighted at his words.

"I said—"

"So you're finally admitting you are Brutus's alpha male?"

"I'm just—"

"Go on, admit it," she teased, loving how uncomfortable he looked.

"Okay, dammit." He raised his hand as if swearing an oath. "I admit that I am Brutus's alpha male."

"And with all the responsibilities that entails . . ."

"And with all the responsibilities that entails," he intoned. "But that doesn't mean cleaning up after any of his 'little accidents,'" he hastily amended.

Maddy laughed her agreement. He'd come a long way from his grumpy attitude toward her at their first meeting. Of course, at the time he had thought she and Walter were having an affair. She remembered the bitterness in his voice when he'd spoken of his father's second wife.

If there were any traces of those suspicions still lingering in his mind, she needed to know.

Maddy paused before she spoke, choosing her words carefully. "You never seriously thought my relationship with Walter was . . . was anything improper, did you, Tom?"

She realized she was holding her breath for his answer.

Time to step up to the plate, thought Tom. Silence hung between them for a long moment. Maddy's eyes were questioning, unguarded. Tom knew any kind of future he might have with her rode on him giving the right answer the first time.

Knowing her now as he did, how could he ever have doubted her innocence?

"Not after I got to know the real you, Maddy," he said.

Maddy's sigh of relief was audible.

"Before that day you opened the door in your apron, I had built up quite a different picture of Madeleine Cartwright, believe me."

To his relief, she giggled. "Tell me. Go on."

"We-ell," he said. "Bleached-blond hair—"

"Big boobs," she prompted, laughing. "Go on. I bet you thought big boobs."

"And tons of makeup. You know, completely fake."

Maddy put up her hands to her makeup-free face.

"Everything I'm not," she said, her voice a little unsteady.

It was true. There was no artifice to her. What you saw was what you got. She looked so cute in that childish T-shirt with its chubby ponies, her hair mussed, her freckles standing out from her pale skin after a day in the spring sunshine.

So entirely different from that gold-digging Madeleine Cartwright he had envisaged.

He had to kiss her. Her lips were warm and yielding as she

kissed him back, pressing her delicious curves against him. She smelled intoxicatingly of lavender, a touch of hay, and warm, lovely woman. His woman. Maddy. Beautiful. Funny. Generous. His woman.

He kissed her harder, parting her lips with his tongue, savoring the feel and the taste of her. Enjoying her enthusiastic response, the throaty little murmurs of appreciation as he slid his hands down her arms and pulled her tighter to him.

In response she slid her arms around his waist, hugging him hard. Tom couldn't help but wince at the pressure.

"You're hurt," she said, alarmed.

"Not really," he said, releasing her to rub under his shoulder blades. "It's just where that idiot Stoddard thumped me. After a day on horseback I'm feeling it."

She slid her hands under his shirt, her fingers delicate but firm. "Can I rub your back for you? I'm quite good at massage."

There was nothing he'd like better than her warm, slender hands on his bare skin. His body's response was instant.

"I'm sure you are," he said. "But, Maddy, you start massaging my back, and I won't be responsible for what might follow."

"You mean, step six?" she whispered, looking up at him, her green eyes lit by a provocative gleam.

"Step six and all the steps after it," he said.

She smiled a mischievous, catlike smile. "I've never been afraid of heights," she murmured.

"You really are the best kisser in the world, Tom O'Brien," Maddy murmured on a sigh of contentment sometime later. She always liked to give credit where credit was due.

"I'm glad you think so." Tom pressed a trail of hot little kisses down her throat that sent shivers of pleasure coursing through her.

"In fact, I'd say the best kisser in the universe," she amended in a whisper.

"Let's not get into any more semantic debates. I'm far more interested in exploring what those hungry ponies are after."

"I—" she started, then gasped as, with his fingers, he traced the shape of the carrots embroidered on the pocket over her breasts. Her nipple peaked immediately in response.

"I've been wanting to do that all day," he said, cupping her breast. "Poor old ponies, doomed forever to never getting nearer to their target."

"Whereas you . . ."

"I'm right where I want to be." He dipped his head and nuzzled at the pocket, taking her nipple into his mouth through the fabric.

"Right where I want you to be," she said, suddenly short of breath. She pushed her fingers urgently through his hair.

"The next place I want to be is under the carrots," he said, tugging at her T-shirt and pulling it from the waistband of her breeches.

He slid it over her head, stood feasting his eyes on the sight of her in her bra. "Ah, good enough to nibble on," he said in a voice husky with appreciation.

He caressed her over her bra until her breath came in short gasps and her nipples were so hard they ached.

"You always surprise me with your underwear," he said, sliding the straps over her shoulders.

Lucky she'd worn a pretty, lacy set and not some utilitarian sport bra.

"You mentioned surprises yourself," she murmured. "You've got me wondering what they could be."

"They wouldn't be surprises if I spoke about them, would they?" he said, his voice roughened with impatience.

She wound her arms around his neck and kissed him, pushing her tongue through his lips, breathing in the delicious scent of him, more male than citrus after a day on horseback. Now she wanted more than kissing. "So why not show me?"

"You can start by riding me," he suggested.

"What? Here? Now?" she stammered.

"Not that kind of riding. Not yet."

"I don't get it," she said, aware that she was crinkling up her nose in the way that seemed to charm him. He was right, the nose thing only worked when she didn't think too hard about it.

"Take off your boots," he ordered, then helped her pull them off, followed by her socks. Mmm. She hadn't known her feet were an erogenous zone until he made sliding off her horseshoe-patterned socks into an exciting caress.

He lifted her up from under her arms and lowered her bare feet onto the toes of his riding boots. "I still don't get it," she said but gripped his boots with her toes to keep her balance.

"It's easy. Just hold on and ride me," Tom said, then started to walk her toward the bedroom.

Maddy hung on tightly around his neck and laughed in delight as, step by step, he moved her backward. "Now I get it. Silly me, how could I have imagined any other kind of riding?"

To keep her balance she had to press her body intimately to his, so closely she could feel the powerful muscles in his thighs working as he stepped forward. So close, she was aware he was as aroused as she was.

She took the opportunity to rain urgent little kisses down his throat. To kiss again the dimple that had fascinated her from the get-go.

"But what about Brutus?" she asked as they neared the bedroom. Behind them, the little dog lay asleep in his favorite spot near the big windows overlooking the bay.

Tom stopped. "What about Brutus? That crazy mutt ran around so much today—not to mention barking out of the window for most of the journey home—I doubt we'll be hearing from him."

"I'm just thinking of other occasions . . ." Her voice trailed off. "You know, unwelcome interruptions."

"We'll shut the bedroom door," said Tom. "Brutus can spend some quality time with the view."

"But what . . . ?" Whether he barfed or barked she was determined the little dog didn't upstage Tom yet again.

"Maddy, quite honestly, I don't give a damn what Brutus does. All I'm interested in right now is his mistress."

He closed the door behind them, walked her over to the bed, and lowered her onto it. "Now you're exactly where I want you to be," he growled.

Maddy lay on his bed before him, exactly as he had fantasized her, her hair bright against the silver gray of the cover, her face flushed, her eyes expectant and just a little nervous.

Had riding gear ever looked so erotic? Well, if you counted just tight breeches and a lacy, see-through bra as riding gear.

Tom allowed himself to feast his eyes on her. He was overwhelmed by the strength of the feelings she aroused in him. She was so beautiful, so special, and here she was in his bedroom.

Just him and her with that pesky little dog snoozing out in the living room behind a firmly closed door.

It was taking all of his self-control not to tear through steps one to whatever and straight to the ultimate step that would make her his.

Impatiently he pulled off his boots, threw them on the floor, and knelt astride her. She wiggled beneath him and made little purring noises of anticipation that did nothing for his self-control.

"Maddy," he said. He bent and made himself kiss her slowly, leisurely, wanting to make this special for her. Not wanting to rush their first time.

She kissed him back, murmuring with pleasure deep in her throat. Her bra was a greenish blue color, see-through in places, revealing tantalizing glimpses of milky skin and pink nipples puckered into sexy, tight peaks.

In seconds the bra was off and he was stroking her breasts, in awe of their perfection, her beauty. When he lowered his head and took each pink nipple in turn in his mouth, Maddy's breath came in quick gasps, her hands gripping his shoulders.

"Step three already," she murmured, "and I'm loving it."

Impatiently, she wiggled her way out of her breeches, leaving only the briefest of tight, lacy French panties that left him in no doubt that she was a natural redhead. He wanted them off, too, pronto.

But as he tugged at the elastic, she stayed him with her hand. "I think things are kind of one-sided here, me wearing only my panties and you fully dressed for riding of yet another kind."

So who was he to protest when she proceeded with much laughter and sexy innuendo to divest him of his polo shirt and breeches?

Maddy could hardly breathe at the sight of Tom clad just in his boxers—made of a fine knit fabric that didn't need ironing, she couldn't help but notice. Those magnificent shoulders looked even better naked, the dark hair on his marvelously muscled chest just the right amount, his six-pack belly totally awesome.

"I promised you a massage," she murmured, starting to explore the ridges and hollows of his body.

"Later," he said.

"You promised me surprises," she said, scarcely able to talk as his hands slid down from her breasts to her tummy and around to stroke the top of her bottom.

"We could talk about the various ways of moving from step four to step six or we could do them," he said hoarsely as he pulled her to him, bare skin to bare skin. Her breasts ached with pleasure at the contact with his hard chest, the tickle of his hair. "What would you prefer?"

"Uh, trick question." She gave up on trying to make a witty reply as he slid her panties off, somehow making the act a caress of her legs from thigh to ankle. Her ankle—just another erogenous zone Tom had discovered on his sensual exploration of her body.

As he kissed her, she tried to remove his boxers in as exciting a manner. Her fingers weren't as skillful, but if his moans of appreciation were anything to go by, she was succeeding in some measure.

Then they were naked—skin to skin, softness to strength. "Tom, this is wonderful," she whispered, unable to keep a tremor from her voice. "I can hardly believe we're here together like this, can you?"

"Believe it," he said, cupping her face in his hands and kissing first her forehead, then each cheek, then her nose in a way that was as tender as it was passionate. "And yes, it's wonderful."

For a long moment she gazed into his eyes, dark as bitter chocolate in the subdued lighting. The warmth she saw there only served to underline the sincerity of his words, the passionate yet respectful way he touched her body.

There was still so much unknown on this journey she was about to take. But even if this were all there ever would be with Tom, she wanted it. Now.

"Now about those steps . . ." she murmured on his mouth.

Step five was every bit as amazing as she remembered from last time as he stroked her intimately until she was melting with want.

She was too light-headed with desire to even think about whether it should be labeled step six when his tongue worked even more magic. Or did that count as one of his surprises?

Was it step seven when she returned the favor, his deep moans transmitting his pleasure? Or step eight when she pushed against him in urgent need?

Step nine, step ten, who cared anymore about counting or keeping track of steps? All she could think of was Tom and how much she wanted him as he took care of the protection and slid deep inside her.

Exquisite pleasure pulsed through her body until her whole being was centered on attaining the ecstasy that was so nearly in her reach.

Their rhythm became faster, more urgent. Then Maddy's last conscious feeling was of looking up to see Tom's face above her, focused, intent, until he let go, calling out her name, and she went with him in a kaleidoscope burst of sensation.

· Twenty-two ·

Judge Irene Eaton was not happy to have a dog in her court-room. Maddy was aware of her skewering glances of disapproval from the bench every time Brutus so much as shifted on her lap.

Despite his perfectly groomed coat and smart new black collar with coordinating leash, the little animal did not appear to have gotten off on the right paw with Her Honor.

Maybe the steel-haired judge with the piercing gaze did not approve of Brutus's celebrity status. Maddy and Tom had had to run quite the gauntlet of press just to get him into the court-house. The photographers had gone crazy to get a new shot of the millionaire mutt.

The judge's gimlet eyes turned to Tom, who sat to Maddy's right on the defense table. "Counselor, is the dog entirely neces-sary to your case?"

Tom stood up. He cleared his throat. "With due respect, Your Honor, the case hinges on the relationship the dog had with the testator, the late Walter Stoddard. This dog must have his day in court."

Maddy felt a warm buzz of pride. Tom was a hotshot corporate lawyer. This was the first—and he'd vowed the last—time he'd represented a dog in the San Francisco County superior court. She knew he feared he would expose himself to ridicule in the legal community.

Yet for Brutus's sake he was determined to defend the authenticity of Walter's will against Jerome's challenge. That showed honor. And she loved him the more for it.

The judge nodded. "All right, Counselor, I'll allow it. But the first sign of trouble and the dog is out."

Tom settled back in his seat. Maddy didn't dare look at him. Jerome was sure to malign her as a woman no better than a hooker. She didn't want to send out even the faintest signal that she'd spent last night in opposing counsel's bed. And the night before. And the night before that.

Instead she bent her head to Brutus's ear. "Please behave, little guy," she whispered under her breath. "Don't let your leader of the pack down."

Short of doping him again with Snowball's leftover tranquilizers, she'd done everything possible to ensure Brutus would make a good impression in court.

She'd groomed him with a soothing lavender and chamomile spray. She'd dosed him with a calming herbal tonic. She'd even considered the doggy diaper route in case Brutus decided to make his mark on the courtroom. But the logistics of fitting him with a doggy diaper for the first time seemed way too daunting. Instead she'd walked Brutus around the Civic Center Plaza outside the courthouse and let him lift his leg until there could not possibly be a drop left.

Her precautions appeared to have worked. Against all expectations, Brutus sat as docile as could be on her lap. He didn't even chew on his toy gorilla. Rather, ears alert, he rested his head on his front paws and looked straight ahead.

Maddy could only wonder if her canine buddy felt as intimidated as she did by the scary new experience of being in court.

She shivered, in spite of her long-sleeved jacket. She hated the fact that the probate court was open to the public and the gallery behind her was packed with press. What scandalous new headlines could she expect? What innuendo-laden television reports?

Worse, every time she looked up, she seemed to catch Jerome's eye from where he sat at the next table. And each time he smiled, with a polite baring of those toothpaste-commercial-perfect teeth. Did no one else notice that the smile never reached his too-blue eyes?

Jerome Stoddard was sly as a fox all right, thought Tom. No way would the court guess what kind of guy the Englishman really was. The mask of courteous charm fit so perfectly in place it forced from Tom a kind of grudging admiration for his opponent. Followed by a fierce determination to wrench it away and expose Stoddard for the contemptible lowlife he was.

The judge called on the plaintiff's attorney to make her opening statement. Zoe Wong was whip thin with a sharp, intelligent face framed by a cap of glossy black hair. Tom knew her by reputation—and it was excellent.

She addressed the bench. "Your Honor, my client, Jerome Anthony Stoddard, contends he was unfairly excluded from the last will and testament of his great-great-great-uncle, the late Walter Stoddard. He contests the will on the grounds that his uncle lacked mental capacity at the time it was executed."

She paused for dramatic effect before she continued. "He also asserts that his uncle was under the undue influence of the major beneficiary of the will, Madeleine Grace Cartwright."

Maddy gasped out loud. Tom shot her a warning glance. There would be worse to come and he had briefed her to try not to react. He wished she didn't have to hear the hum of interest from the public gallery.

The judge addressed Tom. "And what is your position, Counselor?"

Tom stood. "I intend to prove that the late Walter Stoddard was of sound mind when his last will and testament was executed, that it reflected his true wishes for the dispersal of his estate, and that he did not consider Jerome Stoddard to be in any way his heir."

Tom took his seat at the defense table, as careful as Maddy had been not to make eye contact. He waited for the judge to call the first witness for the plaintiff.

Not surprisingly, it was Jerome Stoddard himself.

He was dressed in an immaculate, judge-pleasing dark suit. Tom noticed, with no small degree of satisfaction, that he was limping—no doubt from Snowball's killer grip on his thigh.

When Stoddard took the stand, his crisply modulated voice oozed sincerity. "I met my uncle Walter for the first time just six weeks before his death."

"Did your uncle appear in good health?" his attorney asked.

Stoddard assumed an expression of gravity that made Tom grit his teeth with disgust at his hypocrisy. But he suspected it looked good to the judge. "Sadly, no. Physically he appeared quite robust for a man of his years. However, his mental health was another matter altogether. Quite frankly, I considered him to be stark raving bonkers."

Again Maddy gasped audibly. Tom thought he also heard the beginnings of a faint, menacing growl rumbling from Brutus.

"What made you draw that conclusion, Mr. Stoddard?" Zoe Wong asked.

"On the afternoon we first met, he had just held a birthday party for his dog. With a cake and candles. And a number of canine guests. At the time of my visit the dog was still wearing its party hat."

"So?" Tom heard Maddy hiss under her breath. "That's hardly a sign of insanity in California."

"He was forgetful. Vague. Unable to recall details of his earlier life. I had a feeling he was not all there. Sad, really."

"Any further evidence of your uncle's instability, Mr. Stoddard?"

"Surely the wording of the will is evidence enough? He left his millions to a dog, for God's sake. How much crazier can you get?"

Tom leapt to his feet. "Objection! Under law a dog is considered property. Property cannot be bequeathed property. Mr. Stoddard left his residuary estate in trust and appointed a guardian to administer for the care of his dog and to inherit the remaining funds when the trust expired."

"Objection sustained," said Judge Eaton.

Zoe Wong resumed her examination. "What can you tell us

about your uncle's relationship with Madeleine Cartwright?" she asked Stoddard.

"I didn't actually meet the woman. However, I very quickly became suspicious that she was using sexual favors to manipulate him."

"Did you see any evidence of that?"

Jerome pulled a fastidious face. "Please. A man his age with a girl like that. Just the thought nauseated me, let alone the idea of actually watching—"

Tom leapt to his feet again. "Objection."

"Objection sustained," said the judge.

"So sorry," said Jerome with a saccharine smile. "I withdraw my comment."

"No further questions," said Zoe Wong. "Your witness, Mr. O'Brien."

Tom was more than prepared to do battle. He squared his shoulders, drew himself up to his full height, and set his expression to stern. Then he started his cross-examination. "Mr. Stoddard, how do you explain this clause in Walter Stoddard's will?"

He read out the exact words. "To my distant relative Jerome Stoddard I leave nothing. For years I financed his tuition at an elite private school in England. Recently I gifted him the sum of ten thousand dollars. I consider I have discharged any obligation to him."

Stoddard shrugged. "I see that as further evidence of my uncle being coerced by his young mistress to ignore the rights of a legal heir. He was a foolish, mad old man."

The sound of deep, vicious growling was now unmistakable. Alarm gripped Tom. He whipped around to see Brutus straining against Maddy's hold. Hackles raised and ears flat, the dog's gaze was directed at Stoddard. His lips were pulled right back in a snarl. Even on a comical little dog like Brutus, the wolflike effect of his teeth was frightening.

There was a collective gasp from the court.

Maddy's eyes were huge with an appeal for help as she pulled desperately on the leash to hold the enraged animal. But before Tom could reach her, Brutus broke free.

He jumped over the defendant's table and, trailing his leash, scampered on his stumpy, turned-out legs to the base of the witness stand. There he looked up at Stoddard and erupted into loud, rapid-fire barking.

Stoddard's mask slipped momentarily. His eyes glittered with hostility and his lip curled in an approximate imitation of Brutus's snarl before his urbane expression slid back into place. Then he rolled his eyes heavenward in a blatant attempt to discredit Tom. He affected a laugh.

Judge Eaton banged her gavel. "Control your witness, Mr. O'Brien, or it will be evicted from this courtroom."

Tom marched toward the dog. "Brutus," he said in his most commanding, alpha-male voice. Brutus stopped barking and looked up at him. Then he turned back to Stoddard and started to bark again.

"Brutus. Heel."

Brutus ceased his racket. He whined. He looked up at Tom with mournful button eyes. He put up his paw to shake. He whimpered. Then he rolled over on his back, showing his brindle tummy, tail thumping on the courtroom floor.

Tom heard a smothered laugh from Zoe Wong and titters

from the gallery. He would never, ever live this down. What did this performance mean for his hopes at Jackson, Jones, and Gentry?

The only person who didn't seem to find Brutus's performance amusing was the judge.

Tom gritted his teeth and picked Brutus up. He nodded to the bench. "My apologies, Your Honor." He would look more and more ridiculous as the hearing went on if Brutus continued to object like this to Stoddard's answers.

"No further questions," he said. Then he stalked back to the defendant's table and dumped Brutus back in Maddy's lap.

To Maddy's horror the plaintiff's next witness was a middle-aged man of Walter's acquaintance.

She'd met him just the once. She had been upstairs at Walter's house cooking dinner. His visitor had followed her into the kitchen and attempted to fondle her ass. When she'd slapped his hand away, he'd made lewd suggestions that made her want to swing a saucepan at him. Now she felt sick to her stomach as she heard the man swear on oath that she had enjoyed a sexual liaison with Walter.

Cheeks flushed scarlet, she could only do exactly as Tom instructed and keep her head down. Thank heaven she had Brutus to hug close for comfort and her lucky pony in her purse. She swore she could hear the collective scratching of the reporter's pens on paper as they recorded her humiliation. This was so unfair. Not for the first time, she cursed Jerome.

She longed to stick her fingers in her ears to block out the testimonies of the rest of Jerome's witnesses. Where had he dug up these horrible people who were so willing to swear she was a ruthless, gold-digging skank?

But finally the hearing took a turn for the better. Tom's witnesses were altogether of a different ilk.

First was Walter's family doctor, one of the witnesses to the will. In brisk, no-nonsense terms he attested that Walter's official cause of death was bronchial pneumonia. But while his patient had faded physically, in the doctor's opinion Walter was mentally alert and fully compos mentis until the very end.

"Walter played bridge until the last week of his life and did the newspaper crossword every day."

Tom asked the doctor if Walter was on any medication.

"Yes," he said, "for several years Walter took medication to control high blood pressure."

"Were there any side effects of this medication?"

"Yes. A common side effect is impotence." The doctor glared at Jerome. "Walter was not capable of having an affair even if he'd wanted to."

Yes! Maddy took great pleasure in the chorus of indrawn breaths that greeted the doctor's statement.

Poor Walter, imagine having an intimate health detail like that broadcast in court. But personally she felt like cheering at its vindication of her. She brightened even more when she noticed a corresponding lack of cheer on Jerome's face.

Tom's next expert witness was a prominent psychiatrist, the other witness to the will. He also testified to Walter's mental competence.

Things were definitely looking up for the good guys.

Tom called his third witness. Much to Maddy's bemusement, it was Helen O'Brien, elegant as ever in a gray silk suit.

"Mrs. O'Brien," Tom asked, "how much time did you spend at Walter Stoddard's house in the last weeks of his life?"

"Our church drew up a rotating roster so Walter was never left alone. I was often there."

Maddy wondered how Tom could keep a straight face, addressing his mom so formally. And how would Helen refrain from mommy speak when answering her son's questions?

Still, who else had taken such a Christian interest in Walter's welfare? Helen had filled twice the number of slots on the church care roster than anyone else.

"Did you observe Mr. Stoddard's relationship with his dog?" Tom asked his mother.

"Brutus was Walter's dog kid. He adored him. I firmly believe caring for Brutus was the reason Walter kept going for as long as he did."

"Did he ever refer to his fears for Brutus's future once he, Walter, had passed away?"

"He was very concerned."

"What was Mr. Stoddard's relation to Madeleine Cartwright?"

"Maddy was his tenant. She lived in the apartment below his house. Maddy was a breath of fresh air in Walter's life. In my opinion, the vitality of youth is very refreshing for a person nearing the end of their years."

"Did you suspect a sexual relationship between Mr. Stoddard and his tenant?"

Tom's mother flushed. "Certainly not!" She waved her arm to indicate Jerome. "That . . . that creature should be put down for suggesting it."

"Objection!" said Zoe Wong.

"Objection sustained," said Judge Eaton. "Counselor, please ensure your witness confines herself to answering the question."

"Then I'll repeat it," said Tom, his jaw set. "Did you suspect an intimate physical relationship between Mr. Stoddard and Ms. Cartwright?"

"No. Walter considered her a surrogate granddaughter. His wife and the little girl he lost had red hair. Maddy was not related to them, of course not. But she brought a special kind of light to Walter's last years. Not to mention a great many delicious meals to tempt his appetite." She turned to glance at the judge. "She's a chef, you know."

"What was Madeline Cartwright's relationship to the dog, Brutus?" asked Tom.

"She was marvelous with him. And Brutus is not . . . well, he's not an easy dog to love."

Maddy put her hands over Brutus's ears. "You don't want to hear that," she whispered.

"What did you consider to be the most important things in Mr. Stoddard's life?"

"Objection. Relevance," said Zoe Wong.

"I will prove the question relevant, Your Honor," said Tom.

Judge Eaton fixed him with a look. "Make sure it is, Counselor. Objection overruled."

Helen took a deep breath. "It certainly wasn't money. None of us knew he had any."

Maddy was amused to see Helen tick off the points she made on her fingers, just like Tom did.

"The three most important things in Walter's life were, first, Brutus. Second, his church." She waved at the gallery. "Sorry, Father Andrew, to list you second to a dog, but it's a fact." She faced Tom again. "Third was Maddy, who brought him a grand-fatherly joy he thought he'd never have."

Maddy's heart turned over. She had been so fond of Walter. He had been such a good, kind man. He did not deserve this public raking over of his life. All because of Jerome's unscrupulous greed.

"Were you surprised at the contents of Mr. Stoddard's will?" Tom asked.

Helen O'Brien shook her head. "No. It was exactly how Walter would have wanted things."

Maddy sensed that the mood in the courtroom had subtly shifted—just as the smug complacence had all but vanished from Jerome's face. It was the doctor's revelation about the side effects of Walter's medication that had done it. Now she could hold her head high again. The only damning looks coming her way were from Jerome.

Then it was her turn to take the stand. Even though Tom had coached her on what to do, her heart was pounding and her mouth dry.

She left Brutus with Helen and approached the witness stand on leaden legs. Her voice didn't want to work as she swore the oath and the court official had to ask her to speak up. She kept her hands clasped together to stop them from trembling.

"Ms. Cartwright," said Tom, "were you aware that Walter Stoddard was a multimillionaire?"

She shook her head. "No. I had no idea. Nobody did."

"Did you at any time discuss with him the terms of his will?"

"Never." Her voice grew stronger with each answer. All she had to do was tell the truth.

"Did you agree you would adopt the dog Brutus after Mr. Stoddard's death?"

"Yes. Walter was terrified Brutus would end up being euthanized at a shelter."

"Did he discuss financial recompense for your care of the dog?"

She shook her head. "No. It was my understanding I would feed and look after Brutus using my own money. I was happy to do that."

"That will be all, thank you, Ms. Cartwright. Your witness, Ms. Wong."

Maddy swallowed against a suddenly dry throat. In her own way, Jerome's attorney was as formidable as the judge.

"Ms. Cartwright, do you consider yourself to be a close friend of the O'Brien family?"

"No! I mean . . . well . . . Mrs. O'Brien was a friend of Walter's and . . . she visited him along with the other church ladies. I met her then." Her eyes darted to Tom and back to Zoe Wong.

"Isn't it true, Ms. Cartwright, that in the weeks before Walter Stoddard's death you plotted with his attorney, Tom O'Brien, to influence the old man to leave—?"

"Objection!" Tom leapt to his feet. "That's an unsubstantiated allegation."

"Objection sustained," said the judge. She directed her beady gaze at Zoe Wong. "Be very careful of where you're going, Counselor."

Maddy's cheeks burned scarlet. "I had never even met Tom O'Brien."

"And now, Ms. Cartwright?" said Zoe Wong. "Are you dating your attorney?"

Before Maddy had a chance to stutter an answer, Tom was on his feet again. "Objection," he said. "Irrelevant."

Maddy heaved a sigh of relief that turned into a gasp at the judge's next words.

"Objection overruled," said Judge Eaton. "Answer the question, Ms. Cartwright."

Now even the tips of Maddy's ears burned. She ached to look to Tom for guidance. But that would only add fuel to Zoe Wong's accusation.

Instead she took a deep, steadying breath. *Just tell the truth.* "Tom and I . . . Yes. We've gotten close. But only very recently."

"So how do you explain the newspaper photograph of you and Mr. O'Brien kissing passionately just days after Walter Stoddard died?"

Maddy felt paralyzed by panic. Damn Jerome and his gutter press pals. "But I'd never met him before Walter died. I swear I—"

"No further questions," said Jerome's attorney.

Maddy made her way back to her seat, took Brutus from Helen, and sat down. She felt bad about the way she had answered the last question. Had she made it worse for Tom? She chewed on her lower lip. Surely that must be it for their case? Would the judge take long to make her decision?

But Tom was not finished yet.

Tom approached the bench. "Your Honor, my final evidence is in the form of a video presentation."

A gratifying murmur of interest hummed through the courtroom. Court officers adjusted a large, flat-screen monitor at the front of the courtroom and a number of smaller monitors throughout.

Tom made his voice very grave. "Your Honor, when Walter Stoddard discussed his final wishes with me, I knew any resulting will could be contentious. I took the precaution of interviewing my client on the day the will was executed."

That was the "bulletproofing" he had mentioned to Maddy. In hindsight it was the smartest thing he'd done all year.

He pointed a remote control at the monitor. The screen flickered into life. "Your Honor," said Tom, unable to completely suppress a note of triumph from his voice, "my final witness, the late Mr. Walter Stoddard."

The courtroom went deathly still. Tom could not help a very unprofessional inner gloating at Jerome Stoddard's ashen expression. But when he saw the grief etched on Maddy's face as Walter appeared on the screen, his heart went out to her. He sobered and turned back to the screen.

The professional video producer Tom's firm had employed had done an excellent job. The opening shot was of Walter in animated discussion with Tom and the two expert witnesses, the doctor and the psychiatrist. Then it cut to Walter, sitting at the boardroom table of Jackson, Jones, and Gentry.

The old man turned to look directly into the camera. Tall, but stooped with the burden of eighty-two years, he was thin from the ravages of the illness that would claim his life just four weeks after the filming. But intelligence shone from his eyes and determination from the set of his jaw.

When he spoke his voice was strong and confident. "Good morning," he said. "If you're watching this, you know I'm long gone."

A stifled sob came from Maddy's direction. Tom couldn't help turning to her, saw her wiping tears from under her eyes. Brutus sat statue still, his back paws resting on Maddy's knees, his front paws balanced on the edge of the table. Ears pricked up, he stared intently at the screen and whimpered deep in his throat.

Walter's image continued: "I'm here to prove I'm not a crazy man." He chuckled. "And that I knew exactly what I was doing when I made my will." He leaned closer to the camera. "I'm leaving some money to my church, and the rest in trust to the best young friend a man and his dog could ever have. I know Maddy will look after Brutus, and I hope she will use the money to give herself a good life, too."

Tom saw Jerome in urgent, whispered consultation with his attorney. He was gesticulating wildly with his hands. The veneer was definitely cracking.

"You might wonder why I never told any of you that I had money," said Walter. "It couldn't help me save my daughter's life, so I never made a whole lot of fuss about it."

The old man coughed, then reached for a glass of water from the table. He sipped and put the glass back. "And I don't want another penny of it going to that Jerome. Why, I put that boy through private school with never a word of thanks. Then he shows up here two weeks ago with his slimy ways trying to squeeze more out of me. I gave him ten thousand bucks to get him out of my hair." He leaned forward. "Not another penny, Jerome. Find some other scheme to pay your debts."

Jerome leapt to his feet and cursed viciously.

"Control your client, Ms. Wong," said the judge without taking her eyes off of the screen.

In the final scene of the video, Walter leaned back in his chair. "Maddy, honey, this is a message just for you."

Tom couldn't take his eyes off Maddy. Eyes reddened with tears, she was staring, entranced, at the screen. Brutus strained forward toward the monitor. A low but audible whimper vibrated through him. Tom wondered why the judge let that go without comment.

"Maddy," continued Walter, "the money will change your life, and I'm sorry I couldn't warn you about that. But remember what I always told you. It's not right for a special young lady like you to live her life alone. You go find you that good man."

Walter's image faded from the screen. But before Tom or anyone else had a chance to say anything, Brutus threw back his head and howled at the top of his doggy voice. The desolate cry echoed eerily through the courtroom.

Judge Eaton stared at Brutus. Tom tensed, expecting another reprimand. But the judge surprised him. "Amen to that," she said to the little dog.

Maddy gathered Brutus back into her arms. Tom was aware of her comforting the little animal throughout his and Zoe Wong's closing addresses. The video would have been a shock to her, too. He wished he could hug and comfort her.

By the time the judge prepared to speak, Brutus had settled down into the occasional snuffle.

With her short, gray hair and piercing eyes, Judge Eaton was a formidable presence on the bench. "I intend to make an immediate ruling on this case," she pronounced, again to Tom's surprise. He expected her to take more time to deliberate.

"It appears to me," she said, "that there is proof by a preponderance of evidence that the late Walter Stoddard was in sound mind at the time his will was executed. He was not coerced into any decisions. Therefore, I rule that the will is held valid and shall proceed to probate. My decision is final." She banged her gavel.

"All rise," intoned the court official.

The courtroom erupted into a cacophony of sound. Brutus leapt out of Maddy's arms and sat at her feet, his tail thumping the ground. Tom pulled Maddy into a hug and swung her around in the air. "We did it," he cried.

But Stoddard crossed the room in just a few quick steps. The moment Maddy let go of Brutus, the Englishman pounced. With a roar of outrage that distorted his features from any semblance of good looks, he grabbed the startled animal. Brutus yelped but Stoddard pressed him to his chest with one hand while the other yanked back on the dog's new collar.

"No one cheats me out of what is mine. Especially a filthy mongrel. I'll finish you off this time, you cur."

"Let go of the dog," shouted the judge, "or I'll find you in contempt of court."

Stoddard ignored her. Brutus started to choke and splutter as the collar tightened around his throat.

For a split second Maddy stood paralyzed by shock. Then she grabbed the metal water jug from the defense table and whacked Jerome over the shoulder with it. Icy water cascaded down his back.

"You bitch," he screamed. But he loosened his hold on Brutus. The little dog seized his chance to turn his head and bite his captor on the hand. With an outraged bellow, Jerome dropped him. Maddy lunged forward but only managed to deflect Brutus's fall, not stop it. He landed on his back with an audible thud on the hard courtroom floor and lay very still.

"Brutus!" She fell to her knees.

Jerome didn't even glance at the prone dog. "This is all your fault, O'Brien," he spat. "You and your damn whore."

Maddy looked up and gasped as Jerome made a wild swing at Tom with his left, unbitten hand. But Tom rocked back out of range of Jerome's flailing fist and it slid ineffectively past his chin.

Then Jerome struck at Tom with his right. Tom reacted so fast it was like a blur to Maddy. Sidestepping effortlessly, Tom parried the blow and simultaneously grabbed Jerome by his right wrist. Jerome grunted.

"Go, Tom!" Maddy urged under her breath.

Jerome yelped as Tom twisted his arm until it was outstretched with the elbow locked straight. Then Tom used his free hand to push against Jerome's straightened elbow, forcing his opponent to hunch down toward the floor. "Move and your elbow will snap," said Tom.

Maddy didn't usually like to see another human being held helpless and humiliated. But in this case she rejoiced. If she hadn't been tending to the seemingly unconscious but still breathing Brutus, she would have joined in the fray.

She longed to kick Jerome with her stiletto right where it hurt a guy the most. Once for the cemetery stunt. Once for the T-bone. Once for the chocolate bar. And once more just for good measure.

By this time the armed court deputies had reached the bench. "You're welcome to this dog-murdering scum," said Tom. He steered Jerome toward the waiting arms of the law.

But Jerome stumbled, slipped on the spilled water, and fell to the ground on all fours. The deputies immediately secured him. But before they could drag Jerome to his feet, Brutus suddenly made a miraculous recovery and went for him. With a magnificent growl, he leapt onto Jerome's right butt cheek and latched on tight with his teeth. He worried and tugged at his prey.

Jerome screamed with pain and begged the deputies to get the dog off of him.

Watching with secret delight, Maddy recalled Walter's comments about Brutus's Heinz heritage. In among those fifty-seven varieties was almost certainly bulldog. And Brutus was hanging on to that butt cheek with bulldog tenacity.

"Your dog, ma'am?" asked a deputy.

Maddy turned to Tom. "Maybe it's time for some alpha—"

"Don't say it," said Tom. But his dimple was back in place.

"Brutus. Get off," he ordered.

Reluctantly, Brutus let go of his quarry. But he gave Jerome one last good bite, adding another dose of doggy drool to Jerome's torn and bloodied designer suit pants. Then he turned and trotted to Tom, nudging his head against Tom's leg.

The judge spoke from behind Maddy's shoulder. "Is he okay?"

Fear clutched her as she turned to answer. "You mean Jerome?" To get through all this and then have Brutus arrested for attacking his would-be murderer would be unbearable.

"No," said the judge. "I meant the dog." She bent down to pat Brutus. "He's a cute little guy. I have pugs, you know." Brutus enthusiastically licked her hand with his long pink tongue.

"So you're not . . . ?"

"A clear case of self-defense, I would say," said the judge. With that she strolled away, wiping her hand on her judicial robes. Maddy was too stunned to even thank her.

Leaning back against Tom's solid chest, Brutus by her feet, she watched the deputies drag Jerome away. "I hope that's the last we see of him."

Tom started to tick off a list on his fingers. "Not only will he be charged with contempt of court but he'll also have to face U.S. immigration officials, a representative from the British Consulate, and San Francisco's finest for his accumulation of driving and parking citations." Tom's voice was rich with both satisfaction and vindication.

Maddy twisted back to face him. She smiled her admiration. "Wow. You did dig up some dirt." It had been so worth him going to the office and leaving her alone all those hours in Fortress South Beach.

"And then there are his friends in the gutter press," said Tom. "They'll go to town on him." He made no attempt to hide his relish.

"Tom, I'm really, really impressed. You were awesome in court." *Boring* and *lawyer* were two words she would never again link together.

"Brutus was the star. Not only did he make a great impression on the judge but he also guaranteed Stoddard an uncomfortable flight when they deport him back to England. I imagine he will have to travel standing up."

Maddy laughed. "Brutus had his revenge, didn't you, little guy?"

"That he did," said Tom, squeezing her hand. "All in all, I think we could call this day a howling success."

· Twenty-three ·

On Wednesday morning, audition day, Maddy was awake well before the time she'd set for her alarm. Well, it was actually Tom's alarm clock and she was using Tom's alarm clock because for the last four nights she'd slept in Tom's bed. With Tom.

Now she was lying entwined with him in the warm, rumpled sheets, her head resting intimately on his shoulder. Tom didn't stir. Maddy turned her head so she could enjoy the private luxury of watching him, unguarded in sleep.

In repose, his face lost the tense look he often wore when awake. His mouth curved in a sensual half smile, his dark lashes fanned against his cheek, and his jaw was darkened with a night's growth of beard. There was just a hint of dimple. He seemed younger somehow, more Tom the cartoon fan than Tom the ambitious corporate lawyer who had won so resoundingly in court the other day.

Would she have him more one way than the other? No.

Grim Tom and Funny Tom were just aspects of his personality—as was Amazing-Lover Tom. And Maddy knew there were more aspects to discover as she fell more and more in love with him.

It was a thought that was both exciting and frightening at the same time.

She was wondering how she could extract her leg from under his without waking him to get up and fix breakfast when the doorbell sounded.

Darn! Maddy slid her leg out from under Tom's, slipped cautiously out of bed, threw on her filmy robe, and tiptoed down the hallway.

Through the peephole she could see it was Nora Green from next door. She tightened her robe, wishing it wasn't so short and sheer. She jumped as she felt Tom put his arms around her from behind.

She twisted around to face him. He was wearing his thick, white toweling robe and his hair was all mussed up. Her heart missed a beat at how gorgeous just-out-of-bed Tom looked. He felt warm and strong and she wished she were back in bed with him.

"It's Nora," she whispered. "I don't know why she's here this early. I wasn't planning to take Brutus next door until just before I left for the television station."

Tom yawned. "Well, see what she wants." His voice was all husky with sleep. He nuzzled up against her, his chin deliciously rough with overnight growth.

"I feel weird answering the door dressed like this. I mean, it's pretty obvious that I'm naked underneath."

"So?"

"She'll know that I slept with you."

"So you did." Tom pulled her to him. "And I wasn't ready for you to get out of bed yet."

"Hmm, I can feel that," she whispered, melting against him, wanting him again. She kissed him, loving the rough feel of his chin against hers. Loving the morning intimacy. Loving him.

The doorbell rang again. "I'll leave this to you," said Tom.

Reluctantly, Maddy pulled away from Tom to open the door. Nora Green twisted her hands together in agitation. "Ah, Maddy, I'm so sorry to wake you but I'm afraid something dreadful has happened. My daughter has tripped over one of the kids' toys and badly twisted her ankle."

"Oh," said Maddy, "I'm so sorry for your daughter."

Tom's next-door neighbor looked distressed. "I'm the one who's sorry, my dear. Because it means I've got to get over to help her with my grandchildren. They're only toddlers. And of course that means I can't dog-sit Brutus for you today."

Can't dog-sit Brutus. The words sunk into Maddy's brain like fists punching down bread dough. Today of all days. Not only her audition but Tom's interview with the most senior of senior partners regarding his partnership.

"Oh, I understand, Nora," she said, "of course I do." What else could she say? That she could curse Nora's daughter for spraining her ankle so inconveniently?

"What about Max?" This was a two-way deal; she felt she had to offer to cat-sit. Even though she was clueless about what she'd do with Brutus today, let alone another animal.

Nora pointed to her basket sitting at her feet. "Max is coming with me. The kids love him, though he's not so sure about them. Hates being dragged along by the tail."

"Who could blame him," said Tom from behind her.

"Thanks so much for letting us know, Nora," said Maddy, not daring to look at Tom. "I'm sure we'll find some other arrangement for Brutus. I hope all goes well for your daughter."

After the older woman had gone, Maddy leaned back against the door to brace herself against a panic attack. "Think, think, think," she said on a rising intonation. "Who can help out with Brutus?"

"Serena?"

"She's on a shoot today." Maddy glanced at her watch. "Right now she would have already spent an hour modeling bikinis on a beach." She shivered, wrapping her arms around herself in sympathy. Although it was spring, the mornings were still cool.

"What about his vet? Brutus's vet, the radio shrink. Could we take him there?"

"Good idea," said Maddy, racing for the telephone in the living room. She spoke to the night nurse on duty as it was too early for the regular staff. "Their boarding kennel is completely booked." She knew her voice was rising in hysteria. "Tom, what am I going to do?"

"There's no chance you could take him to the television studio with you?"

"No way. Not if I don't want to blow this audition completely. It would be totally unprofessional. And there's a hygiene thing, too. You can't have dogs around food."

Tom grabbed the telephone directory. "There must be other vets, other boarding kennels. Professional animal sitters even."

Maddy started to pace up and down the living room. "The boarding kennels are out of town. I don't have time to call around to all the vets. And, even if I knew where to look for an animal sitter, how could I get one with this kind of notice? The television studio car will be here to pick me up in an hour."

Tom's brow creased. "There must be someone."

She faced him. "Tom, I'll only be away for half the day. Surely I could leave Brutus here in the apartment? I could barricade the furniture or something."

"And have him bark the place down? His presence would hardly be a secret then. Apart from that we shouldn't take any risks with him so close to the end of the twenty-one days. There's still a real threat of kidnap after all this publicity. He needs to be supervised."

She was desperate. "Your office? Could you take—?"

Tom shook his head. "No way. Not possible. Not if I value my job. Especially after Brutus's performance the other day in court."

Maddy blinked down hard against tears, bit her lip to keep it from trembling. "Well, there's only one answer, isn't there? I'll have to pull out of the audition."

She felt nauseous at the thought. Competition was fierce. There wouldn't be a second chance for the audition. She knew that. But what else could she do? "I . . . I'll stay here and look after Brutus."

"I?" said Tom, his dark brows drawn together in a frown. "What's all this talk about 'I'? Maddy, isn't the word 'we' in your vocabulary?"

"We?"

"Yes, 'we,'" he said, tight-lipped. "As in 'you and me.'"

"You and me?"

"Maddy, haven't the last four nights meant anything to you?"

She stared at him. Wasn't that understood? "Tom, of course they have. They've meant everything."

With every kiss, every laugh, every confidence shared, she had fallen more deeply in love with him. Even allowed herself to cautiously dream about something more permanent with Tom, something more than being a mere chocolate chip in his life.

His expression became less granitelike. "We're in this together. Don't you understand that? The Brutus problem isn't all yours to shoulder."

"It . . . it isn't?" she asked, her heart singing. She wasn't used to this kind of support from the males in her life.

"No."

"Thank you. That . . . that means a lot." Because she wasn't used to being given support, she wasn't quite sure how to accept it. "But we've discussed all the options. What can you do that I couldn't do?"

Tom clenched his hands together and held them under his chin. "I can postpone my appointment with the senior partner and stay at home with Brutus. Then you can go to your audition."

Had he really said that? Tom was almost as incredulous as Maddy at the words that had slipped out of his mouth.

No way should he be jeopardizing his future partnership by missing this long-anticipated appointment with the most senior partner at Jackson, Jones, and Gentry. When Clive Gentry said "jump," you jumped and asked how high on the way up.

But her disintegrating dreams were visible on Maddy's woebegone face and the sight moved him more than he'd thought possible.

"No," she said, shaking her head. "No. I won't let you do this. I know how important your interview is to you."

"And your audition? How important is that to you?"

She looked somewhere in the direction of his feet. Her mouth twisted. "Very important. Once in a lifetime. You know that."

"Yes. I do know that. That's why I'm offering to do this." He turned and it was his turn to do some pacing. "Maddy, I've never missed a meeting, hardly had a sick day since I joined the company. For once, just this once, I'm going to ask them to change an appointment to suit me because . . ."

He paused, planning to say, *because for the first time I've found something—someone—that's more important to me than my job.* But somehow he just couldn't say it. The time wasn't right. When he talked to Maddy about how he felt, he didn't want it to be a rush job. Instead he finished, "Because being flexible is important."

Maddy looked up at him, her eyes huge. He noticed her face was reddened from stubble burn but didn't dare point it out. She was freaked out enough already. Hopefully the television station had makeup to cover it for her screen test.

"If you're absolutely sure," she said.

"I'm absolutely sure." And, to his own amazement, he was. He wanted to succeed at Jackson, Jones, and Gentry, but if they marked him down for missing one meeting—even if it was with the great god from the executive floor Clive Gentry—how worthwhile was the job, anyway? Besides, he was so close to bringing in that bonus.

Maddy flung her arms around his neck. "Thank you, Tom. Thank you. I can't thank you enough."

The look on her face was reward enough for his decision. It was so worth giving his dream a butt kicking to buy Maddy a few hours to pursue hers.

Maddy burrowed into his shoulder. He nuzzled the bright hair that smelled of lavender and, now, of him. Felt the absolute rightness of it.

He loved her.

That's why he'd suddenly made a compromise in a life that up until now hadn't allowed for compromise. He seriously loved her.

The realization was overwhelming. No subsection of the plan had allowed for this possibility. *You can't explain love. You can't analyze it.* His mother's words echoed in his head. Now, finally, he understood them.

The alarm clock sent up a racket from the bedroom. Maddy pulled away from him. "Ohmigod, it's time to get moving. Breakfast first. I've got fruit salad and a new whole-grain cereal I got from an organic-foods website. I think you'll like it. Then there's—"

Tom held up his hand to stop her stream of nervous chatter. "Maddy, how about I fix breakfast for us as I'm now in no rush to get out to the office."

"Would you? Could you?"

"I think I'm capable of serving fruit salad and cereal," he said.

"I guess so. Thank you." She looked deep into his eyes, traced the outline of his jaw with her finger, shook her head slowly from side to side. "Are you real, Tom?" she asked in a whisper of a voice. "Or just a wonderful dream?"

He laughed, enthralled by the tenderness in her eyes. "I'm real enough. You'll wake up and realize that before too long. But I'd like a shower before I start in the kitchen."

Maddy's mouth curved in that so-sexy way that thrilled him. "I need a shower, too." Her robe had fallen open, revealing a curve of creamy breast and a cheeky pink nipple.

He swooped her up into his arms. "Shower for two coming up," he growled, carrying her toward the bathroom.

Surprisingly, although she squealed a little, she didn't say a word about his caveman tactics.

· Twenty-four ·

If happiness was being with the man you loved, being involved in his life, and having delicious, sneaking suspicions that he might be in love with you, too, then Maddy was the happiest she'd ever been.

Then there was the relief of the news that, one way or another, Jerome would be behind bars for quite some time. Once the authorities here had finished with him he would—as Tom had predicted—be deported back to England. The police would be waiting for him there. And with the criminal record he was rapidly racking up, he would never be allowed back into the United States.

She hadn't realized how heavily the threat posed by Jerome to both her and Brutus had weighed on her until it was lifted.

The press had turned around, too. Now she and Brutus were media darlings rather than villains. And by selling the exclusive, inside story of the millionaire mutt to a national news magazine, she had both freed herself from everyday harassment and earned a substantial sum to donate to Walter's favorite dog shelter.

The frosting lavished on the top of her happiness cake was yesterday's promising audition—she'd heard back already that she was on the short list. A very short, short list. Humorously enough, although the producers had liked her "healthy, new twist to an old theme" concept for the show, it was the dog recipes that had done it. Her unique brand of canine cuisine was the deal maker. She felt very, very confident that the gig was hers.

That achievement had been made possible only by Tom's generous action in giving her career priority at a time when their work commitments clashed.

Never would she forget what he'd done. Though she still hadn't really puzzled out why he'd done it.

Now she sat in the backseat of the taxi heading for his ask-her-out-type date number two, the senior partner's dinner. Tom held her hand as he briefed her about the "inner circle" five senior partners and their roles at Jackson, Jones, and Gentry.

"How will I ever remember all their names? Not to mention their wives' names," she said, chewing on her bottom lip.

Tom gave her hand a reassuring squeeze. "Just look to me for clues. I'll help you out as best I can. All you have to do is to be yourself. How could they fail to be charmed by you?"

"Hey, my ego is going to get out of control if you keep on saying things like that." She leaned over and kissed his dimple, taking great pleasure in the proprietary gesture. He moved his head to connect with a kiss on her mouth.

"I'll do my best for you, I promise," she said. "I just hope I get seated next to a wife who likes cooking. It makes the conversation go so much better."

"Or someone who likes dogs."

"Horses, even."

"Who knows, these ladies might even talk to their pets like you do. You could exchange tips on how to interpret their answers."

"Don't tease me, Tom, I'm nervous enough."

"You've no need to be. Have I told you how beautiful you look?"

Maddy smiled a secret, satisfied smile in the dim light of the taxi. "Several times."

It was a wonder they'd gotten out of the apartment on time after he'd first seen her in her dress. Though only a simple black slip dress with a sheer overlay, Tom seemed to find it incredibly sexy.

It was what it hinted at rather than what it revealed, he'd explained as he'd pulled the dress over her head and carried her into the bedroom. In the taxi, she smiled to herself again as she recalled the passionate lovemaking that had followed. She'd had dessert before they'd even left for the restaurant.

"You know I bought this dress from your mother's boutique."

"You did?"

"Yes. She said it would be perfect for me and I guess she was right."

Tom frowned. "I didn't know you were on such good terms with my mother. Before the probate court hearing, I mean."

"I used to chat with her when she popped around to see Walter."

"So that's when she showed you my baby photos."

She laughed. "To be honest I didn't look at them too closely.

She was pushing her wonderful son so hard on me it had the opposite effect and I backed off."

"I'll have to have a word to her about that," Tom said. "I've told her what I think about her matchmaking."

She put a hand on his arm. "Don't be too hard on your mother. In the end she was right, wasn't she? About us maybe . . . liking each other if we met."

"She certainly was," he said as he kissed her again.

Would she ever, ever tire of kissing Tom O'Brien? By the time they got to the restaurant she wouldn't have a scrap of lipstick left.

The senior partner's dinner was being held in a fashionable new waterfront restaurant at the other end of the Embarcadero.

Maddy knew the chef; they'd been friendly rivals at one stage. She was looking forward to sampling the Cal-Asian fusion menu that was earning him such rave reviews. But tonight wasn't about business, her business, anyway. It was about being Tom's date and helping him to impress the people who counted so much to him.

She stood at the entrance to the restaurant. Tom's hand rested comfortably at her waist. "I'm so proud of you," he whispered. Maddy took a deep, steadying breath before they entered the room.

Tom introduced her to the five senior partners and their wives, who chatted easily with her over drinks. Her nerves began to dissipate. Until she found herself separated from Tom when they were seated.

On one side she was seated next to a beautifully groomed

woman in her fifties, introduced as Vanessa Kent, wife of senior partner Simon Kent. On the other side, another of the senior partners. Opposite sat Clive Gentry, the most senior of the senior partners.

To her dismay, Tom was diagonally opposite her; she'd been counting on him being only holding-hands distance away. He looked across the table at her and discreetly signaled his apology. But the seating plan had nothing to do with him.

Immediately after their orders were taken, Vanessa Kent swiveled around on her chair and leaned close to face Maddy. At her ears and throat Vanessa wore the most enormous pearls Maddy had ever seen. Serious diamonds flashed from both hands. The rewards of partnership were obviously substantial. No wonder Tom was so keen to achieve it.

"First of all, let me tell you I'm a great fan of yours," the older woman said. "I subscribe to *Annie* and love your recipes. They're sensational."

Though the magazine was aimed at young women, Maddy was always delighted to know her features reached a wider audience. "Thank you. I'm glad to hear that."

"Yes, I've cooked your seafood risotto several times—it's become a favorite."

Maddy smiled her thanks. Vanessa moved closer. She lowered her voice. "You know this is the first time we've actually met one of Tom's girlfriends."

"Really?" Maddy schooled herself to be noncommittal.

"Yes. He's always been very cagey about his personal life. Let me tell you, my husband and his colleagues are pleased that he seems to be serious about you. They prefer the partners to be in a stable relationship."

"Really?" Maddy said again. So much for Tom's much-vaunted plan that excluded a serious relationship. Little did he know, but his insistence on staying single might work against him. Would she tell him or let him find out for himself?

Vanessa nodded. "The senior partners believe that not having to worry where the next girlfriend is coming from enables a new partner to focus entirely on the business."

"So what's the partner's, um, wife meant to be doing while the partner is concentrating on the business?"

"Why, getting on with her own career or looking after the family, whatever has priority at the time."

"I just wondered." She couldn't help but puzzle over where she might fit as the girlfriend of a partner in such a conservative establishment.

"I hear you're living with Tom in his apartment," said Vanessa. "My dear, is there an announcement to be made?"

Maddy flashed a desperate look over to Tom but he was deep in conversation with Clive Gentry. She swallowed hard. "No, um, I . . ." This was worse than being on the stand.

Vanessa patted her hand. "You don't have to explain, Maddy. Some things are better kept private for a while. I know you haven't known Tom very long—"

"Yes. That's it. Not long enough to . . . to . . . well, get that serious." She thought about the partners' approval of Tom's "steady" relationship and frantically backpedaled. "Uh, *yet*. Not that serious *yet*," she amended. "We only met because of Brutus. You know, the little dog—"

Vanessa laughed. "You don't have to explain who Brutus is, my dear. We've all been enthralled by the story. The drama of it.

The courtroom uproar. Those juicy articles in the press. So much hanging on the twenty-one days for all of us."

For all of us? Maddy wondered at Vanessa Kent's choice of words. Surely the twenty-one days only mattered to her and Brutus?

But she had no chance to ponder it further as another wife next to Vanessa asked her what it was like to work at a glossy magazine and did she really squirt hairspray on the food to make it look so good for photography. Maddy was only too happy to deny the hairspray allegation.

Tom thought he would burst with pride as he glanced across the table at Maddy. Over dessert, she had her end of the table enthralled by something or other she was saying. Maybe it was the naked-girl-in-the-bath-of-chocolate story. The senior partners would relish that one.

He strained to hear her. "Then just as we were about to shoot this perfect eggs Benedict, the photographer's cat sneaked up, stole the slice of ham from under the hollandaise sauce, and ran away with it," she told her rapt audience, gesticulating with her hands as she embellished the story.

Maddy was adorable. Utterly adorable. Obviously she was a huge hit at the dinner—her girl-next-door appeal combined with the glamour of a magazine career went down wonderfully. Already three of the senior partners had indicated their approval of his date.

The funny thing was that he couldn't care less what they thought. Yeah, it was great Maddy fit in so well, had made such a great impression, probably enhanced his chances for partnership. But it was how he felt about her and how she felt about him that counted. Not his employers' opinions.

He loved Maddy Cartwright and he was hoping like hell that she felt the same way about him.

His shoulders tensed as he realized how devastated he'd be if Maddy didn't stay a part of his life. They hadn't discussed anything much beyond the rapidly expiring twenty-one days—down now to mere minutes. Was she planning to go back home to the Fall River Valley one day? Or follow her career to New York? And what would that mean for him if she did?

Tom drummed his fingers on the tabletop. He'd take no further chances. After dinner he'd take her somewhere romantic—with a view of the bay and the bridge perhaps—and tell Maddy he loved her. Talk about the future.

She must have felt the intensity of his gaze because she looked up and gave him a little wave and pulled a discreet "rescue me" face. Dammit, why wait until after dinner? He rose up from his seat to go to her. But Clive Gentry put his hand on his shoulder to keep him in his place.

The senior, senior partner tapped the rim of his wineglass to get the table's attention. The chatter came to a halt. The older man thanked everyone for coming. He reminded them with witty though ponderous words what it was like for an aspiring new partner to have to undergo such a dinner, the "final trial" as he called it.

Then he turned his attention to Tom. "Tom, the senior partners of Jackson, Jones, and Gentry are pleased to invite you to join us as a partner on the terms we discussed at our meeting yesterday afternoon."

Touchdown. Winning basket. Home run. And the triumph was so much the sweeter for Maddy's megawatt smile and clenched victory fists from across the table.

He started to thank Clive Gentry, though the words of the speech he'd written in anticipation just in case had fled from his brain. But Clive hadn't finished yet.

Maddy was aching to dash around the table and congratulate Tom on his triumph. He looked a little shell-shocked; she was pretty sure he hadn't expected an actual offer of partnership to be made tonight at the dinner.

She'd signaled her good wishes across the table but she wanted to hug her man hard; she knew how much this partnership meant to him. So why was Clive Gentry still rambling on?

The distinguished-looking older man cleared his throat. "You may wonder why we chose this particular evening for our dinner."

He glanced at his impressive wristwatch. "Those of you who have been counting will now realize it has just struck midnight and the dog known as Brutus has survived the twenty-one days specified in the will of the late Walter Stoddard."

Yes, Brutus was alive and well and snoring in Nora Green's apartment—she'd called to check on her cell phone only an hour ago. But why did that warrant enthusiastic applause from the table of Jackson, Jones, and Gentry senior partners and their wives? Politely Maddy clapped, too, without being sure why she was doing so.

Then the table quieted as Clive continued. "I think we can assume the very substantial bonus agreed on by Mr. Stoddard for Tom—and thence to our firm—on condition of the dog living the specified time will be coming our way. Well done, Tom. You've handled this case superbly."

Frozen to her seat, Maddy felt the blood drain from her face. Clive Gentry's voice seemed to come and go in waves. A bonus to Tom? What bonus?

Vanessa Kent nudged her into lifting her glass when Clive asked everyone to toast Tom's success. Champagne glass in hand, Maddy stared over the table at Tom, scarcely registering that he looked as pale as she felt.

Frantically she searched back in her memory. Tom had never mentioned he was due a bonus if Brutus survived twenty-one days. She was positive of it.

Maddy swallowed hard against the nausea that rose in her throat. The whole thing had been a fraud. His concern for Brutus. His concern for her. Working together to thwart Jerome. The court hearing. All along it had been about Tom O'Brien's interests and ambitions.

Dollars were evidently what counted in a law firm like this and no one could have been as motivated as Tom in his quest for partnership. He was a complete and utter phony. And she a total fool for having been taken in by him. How could she ever have let herself trust such a handsome man?

She clenched her hand so tightly around the stem of her glass she was in danger of snapping it. What felt worse—the humiliation or the hurt?

She cringed at the memory of how naïve she'd been. Insisting on cooking for him in return for his giving her and Brutus sanctuary. Admiring his honesty and sincerity. But worst, worst, worst of all—being stupid enough to fall in love with him.

Feeling as though she was moving in slow motion, she

drained the glass of champagne and placed it back down on the table. Through her shock and anger she noted Tom trying to push his way toward her through the throng of people congratulating him.

Pointedly, she turned her back to him and forced herself to smile and make small talk to one of the partners about his wine collection. She couldn't trust herself not to make a scene if she had to confront Tom just then.

But she couldn't hide from Tom for long. As the party rapidly wound down she forced herself to make polite good-byes to everyone, to accept their wishes that they might meet with her again. Until at last she found herself alone with Tom.

At the end of the table in the by-now-emptying restaurant she faced him. "Why didn't you tell me about that bonus?" she said, her hands tightly gripping the strap of her evening purse.

Tom looked rather like Brutus when the little dog had done something wrong and knew he'd been caught. But Tom was too much the alpha male to cower in a corner.

He shrugged and gestured with his hands. "Maddy, I'm sorry, I just didn't get a chance to mention it." He paused. "But from that look you're giving me, I don't suppose you'll believe me."

It was an effort but, conscious of the waiters clearing up around them, Maddy kept her voice low and steady. "You're right. I don't believe you. A huge bonus for keeping Brutus alive isn't something that would easily slip your mind."

"When we first met, it wasn't appropriate to tell you about the bonus and then—"

"Not appropriate? How can you say that?" She could feel a hot flush burning up her neck.

"I was Walter's lawyer. You were . . . well, you were an unknown quantity. I didn't need to disclose to you the details of my fee structure with my client."

She swallowed the hurt that rose in her throat. "Because you thought I was a gold digger on the make."

"Maddy, that isn't fair. You know I—"

"Fair? What was fair about letting me think you were looking out for Brutus and me out of . . . out of the goodness of your heart? Not for a big, fat bonus that would help you make partner." Her voice rose higher with every word.

He winced. "Maddy, the bonus had nothing to do with it."

"So you deny you never thought about your bonus when you told me stop feeding Brutus cupcakes?"

"Yes, of course I considered it."

"And what about when . . . when . . . we became . . . close?"

"The bonus was the last thing on my mind. Maddy, I—"

"Huh!" she said loudly. Then, aware of a waiter hovering nearby, she said more quietly, "I wish I could believe you . . ."

Tom didn't seem to notice the waiter slowly picking up cutlery piece by piece so he could listen in on every word. "Maddy, I honestly intended to tell you about the bonus. Especially when the press started questioning our relationship. But then Jerome became such a threat. When he contested the will, it became a race to prepare for the hearing. I didn't give the bonus another thought."

Maddy glared at the waiter, who by now had stopped making any attempt at clearing the table. Then she shifted her glare to Tom. "And you expect me to believe that?"

Tom's eyes blazed. "Yes, I do. I didn't want to see Brutus or you in danger. Protecting you two became my only motivation."

Tears began to smart her eyes. She blinked down hard on

them. "How can you say that when by lying, all you did was hurt me?"

Tom went to touch her arm but Maddy quickly stepped back from him. He glared at her. "I never lied to you, Maddy. I made a mistake. Okay?"

"Well, it was a darn big mistake."

Now Tom was back in full grim mode. "Yes, it was. And I've said I'm sorry. How many times do you want me to say it?"

The waiter by this stage was making no attempt to hide the fact he was eavesdropping. Maddy glared at him again.

To her astonishment the man put down the water jug he was holding and joined in. "He sounds sorry to me. Why don't you give him a break?"

Maddy stared incredulously at the nosy waiter. "You can stay out of this." Behavior like this would never be tolerated in any restaurant where she was chef.

"Sure. But I think you should kiss and make up."

Maddy felt like whacking the waiter over the head with her purse. "This is none of your business. I know the chef here. I'm going to complain about you."

The waiter shrugged, then stacked plates one on top of the other. He grinned. "Report me. He's my boyfriend." He winked at Tom as, balancing a handful of plates, he sauntered off.

Then he called over his shoulder. "By the way, Brutus is a terrible name for a kid. Why didn't you call him Bruce?"

Maddy felt her face blazing. Now she understood what it meant for someone to say her blood was boiling.

She turned back from the waiter to find Tom fighting a battle to suppress laughter, his face contorted with the effort, his shoulders shaking.

"You! You think that's funny?"

Tom struggled to keep a still face. "Of course not. I . . . uh. Terrible guy. Impertinent. Should be fired immediately. I, uh . . ." He lost the struggle and started to laugh, his dimple out in full force.

"You're laughing at me!"

"No. No. I'm not. Really. It's the waiter. The Brutus-Bruce thing. Maddy, come back!"

Maddy stalked as fast as three-inch heels would let her away from the table and out of the restaurant. A salty breeze from the water cooled her face but did nothing to cool her temper.

Tom caught up with her at the end of the pier, took her arm. Furious, she shook it off. "Maddy," he said.

"Don't you 'Maddy' me," she spat. "You lie to me, you make a fool of me in front of your colleagues—you should have seen the pity in Vanessa Kent's eyes when she realized I didn't know about the bonus—and then you take sides against me with a waiter, a waiter whose boyfriend, by the way, is an old rival of mine and who'll make sure everyone in the Bay Area hears about this."

Completely out of breath, she paused. Her heart was pounding so loudly she felt it would burst from her chest.

Tom didn't look at all like he was laughing now. "Maddy, you're blowing this all out of proportion. Let's go home and—"

"Home? Did you say home? Back to your apartment where you've kept me—and Brutus—prisoner to ensure that you get to cash in on the millionaire mutt? Is that what Clive Gentry meant by the 'superb job' you've done? Is that what . . . ?"

Her words petered out at the look on Tom's face. Shock?

Hurt? Disillusionment? Whatever it was she didn't like it. And she knew she'd caused it.

"If that's what you think, Maddy, there doesn't appear to be much I can do to change your mind." Tom was as grim-faced as at their first meeting, his eyes impenetrable, his mouth a rigid line.

He strode ahead of her toward the taxi rank. In her high heels Maddy had a struggle to keep up with him.

"Tom, wait up," she called.

He stopped just long enough for her to draw up alongside him, then he continued to walk, more slowly this time. And in silence. Huh! So he wasn't talking to her now? Proof of his guilt.

Her footsteps dragged as they neared the line of taxis. Maddy knew without Tom having to say a word that he'd be back on the sofa tonight.

She took in a great gulp of fresh, midnight air. Maybe that was for the best.

For all his apologies for neglecting to tell her about the bonus, Tom hadn't broached the subject of what lay beyond the twenty-one days other than a nebulous reference to "us."

After all, she wasn't written into his famous five-year plan. Even though she and Brutus had—inadvertently—helped him get to his goal of partnership. She'd been forced into Tom's life for the time specified by Walter's will. And now that time had expired.

In silence she waited beside Tom behind another couple waiting for a taxi. There was no one behind them. When the next available taxi drew up in front of them, she stepped away from Tom.

"Tom, I'm going to take this taxi home to my apartment. By myself."

A tightening of his mouth was Tom's only reaction. "That surprises me. But if you think it's a good idea."

"I do," she said, wishing he'd tell her it wasn't. But he didn't.

"Jerome is locked up so you don't have to worry about him," he said. "But take care, won't you?"

She nodded. "I will. I'll . . . uh . . . drop around tomorrow to pick up Brutus and my things."

"It might be easier if I brought him to you." He didn't look anywhere near her eyes as he spoke.

"Whatever."

"Fine," he said.

She slid into the taxi. Wasn't he even going to try to stop her? She gave the taxi driver her address.

Tom raked his fingers through his hair until it stood up on end. He leaned down toward the car door. "So, I'll see you to-morrow sometime," he said.

"Great," she said.

"Great," he said.

She banged the door shut, wounded beyond belief that he hadn't even kissed her good-bye.

As if she would have let him.

· Twenty-five ·

Very early the next morning, Maddy indulged her misery in the best way she knew—by baking. The tray of peanut butter and chocolate chip cookies, salted with her tears, was in the oven. She was beating her hurt and anger into the batter for a coconut and lime syrup cake when she heard a knock on her door.

Tom!

Surely not this early? But who else knew she was back home? At the thought of facing him after the dreadful scene last night, her heart started a furious pounding.

Her hands went automatically to smooth her hair. She must look awful after a night spent alternating between sobbing into her pillow and pounding it in pain and frustration.

Was Tom a calculating, self-serving phony or a warmhearted, genuine guy who had tried to stay on top of an impossible situation? Had he lied about the bonus or had he genuinely overlooked it? Oh, why hadn't she listened to him last night instead of going overboard on wounded pride? She felt like running home to her grandma. But her home was in San Francisco now, no matter what. And, besides, she wasn't too sure her grandma would be on her side.

At dawn she'd given her pillow a particularly hard whack at the thought of the interfering—but quite possibly well-meaning—waiter and then gotten out of bed and started to bake.

How would she handle this? Cool and composed? Yes. She liked cool and composed.

"Good morning, Tom," she would say, not even giving him a hint of how upset she was. "How nice of you to bring Brutus home."

Then she would suggest they sit down and discuss like civilized adults what had happened between them last night.

Forget reckless, remember cool and composed, she told herself before she opened the door. To find a basket-load of puppies thrust at her by an agitated woman dressed all in black.

She didn't recognize Mrs. Porter until she spoke. "Here, take them, they're yours."

The dog breeder looked so different. Her curly hair was cut short and straightened in a spiky, butch style. Dirty yellow streaks swept back from her ears. She wore tight leather pants and a leather top, with a heavy, spiked black collar around her neck. Matching leather bands encircled her wrists. It even seemed like her slim frame had bulked up.

"Thank heaven you're home at last," she said. "This is the third time I've stopped by."

Bewildered, Maddy clutched the basket of wriggling, heaving puppies to her. Little paws reached up to scrabble at her chest and pink tongues to lick at her arms. "Mrs. Porter, I don't—"

Mrs. Porter shot an anxious look up at the road. A red station wagon was parked outside. Maddy could see Coco in the backseat scrabbling against the window, hear the little black poodle's frantic whimpering.

"I'm moving to Vegas. I can't take the puppies."

"Mrs. Porter, slow down. I—"

The poodle lady smiled a smile that transformed her anxious face. "I'm getting back with my ex. But he's got dogs, too. Rottweilers. I can't take these puppies there."

So that was it. Mrs. Poodle had morphed into Mrs. Rottweiler.

Coco was starting to howl, a piteous, heartrending sound that set Maddy on edge. "But what about Coco?"

"I'm into Rottweilers now. Coco's got a pedigree as long as my arm. I have a buyer for her."

"But what about her babies? Aren't they still very little?"

"They're nearly weaned. I've tucked some care instructions into the basket for you."

Coco's frantic howling became louder. Two of the puppies started whimpering hysterically in return. Desperately Maddy tried to jig the basket in a soothing, rocking rhythm, but the puppies would not be consoled.

Maddy thought back to the last time she'd seen Coco, her puppies snuggling contentedly next to her. The poodle was a wonderful mother. And Brutus a proud father. Okay, so maybe she was guilty of humanizing the animals. But the distress she heard in Coco's howl seemed very real.

"Poor puppies. Poor Coco. She sounds heartbroken."

"She's just a dog, Ms. Cartwright. She'll get over it."

"Mrs. Porter, can I buy Coco from you?"

What had Tom said about the dollar signs in Mrs. Porter's eyes? "As I said, I already have a buyer but—" She named what seemed a very high price.

Maddy's initial reaction was to try to bargain her down. But it was Brutus's money. Would he haggle over the purchase price of the dog he loved? "I'll pay it," she said.

"Okay. She's no use to me now. I want to make a fresh start with my ex. He reckons my obsession with poodles is what made him move out in the first place. I can't understand that, but there it is."

"So it's a deal?" Maddy tried to shake hands but found it impossible over the bundle of puppies. Mrs. Porter ended up shaking a little black paw instead.

"It's a deal," said Coco's old owner. "I'll send my new address to Mr. O'Brien's office, you can send the check to me there."

The new incarnation of Mrs. Poodle turned and walked back up the path to her car. She snapped on Coco's leash and headed back down to the apartment with the black miniature poodle.

Coco headed straight for Maddy, sniffing and whimpering and anxiously jumping up on her legs. "It's okay, little mom, your babies are safe," Maddy said, putting the basket of puppies down on the floor.

Immediately Coco nudged each one as if counting them and then settled down to a thorough licking. The puppies clambered joyfully all over their mother.

Mrs. Porter handed Maddy a snazzy red cosmetics bag. "Inside are Coco's hair ribbons, her diamanté collars, and her custom-dyed leashes. I won't be needing them for the Rottweilers."

"Thanks, Mrs. Porter. I appreciate this. Coco will be in good hands."

"I know that or I wouldn't be leaving her with you."

Maddy shook Mrs. Porter's hand, properly this time. "Good luck with your ex."

"Thanks. And good luck with Tom O'Brien. He seems a good man."

"Oh. No. We're just . . . just friends."

Mrs. Porter gave her a sly wink. "Don't give me that. I'm a dog breeder. If there's one thing I'm an expert on, it's animal attraction. You two are crazy about each other. I could tell that when you came around to my house."

"Well . . ." Maddy shrugged halfheartedly. She might be crazy about Tom but there hadn't been too many indications he felt the same way about her.

Mrs. Poodle-now-Rottweiler seemed so callous. But she leaned down to give Coco a long farewell hug. Then she was gone.

Maddy sat down on her pretty blue print sofa and tried to think how on earth she would manage with six dogs. Seven, counting Brutus when he came home. And no Tom to help her with them.

Right up until the minute he knocked on Maddy's door Tom wasn't sure whether he was going to be tough and uncompromising with her or grovel abjectly at her feet.

She didn't give him a chance to do either. "Oh, Tom, thank heaven you're here," she said, grabbing his arm and hauling him into her apartment. "If I ever needed an alpha male, it's right now."

It was hardly the welcome he had imagined. After last night he'd feared she might want nothing to do with him ever again.

Before he had a chance to recover, Brutus set up a frantic barking and pulled so hard on his leash that Tom let it go.

Brutus ran round in circles for a moment, then headed for
another little dog that scampered forward to meet him. Yapping
deliriously, both dogs stood up on their back legs, jumping excitedly around each other as if they were dancing. They did the
doggy sniff-each-other's-bottom thing.

"Isn't that Coco?" Tom asked. He couldn't help feeling envi-
ous at the ecstatic reception Brutus was getting from the little
poodle. "Coco of the litigious owner Mrs. Pood . . . uh, Porter?"

"Yes. I've bought her. Or actually Brutus has bought her. But
he didn't have to pay for the puppies. Not any extra, anyway."

"Puppies?" Tom felt like he'd been transported into some
parallel reality. Not an uncommon feeling when he found himself around Maddy.

"Coco's puppies. His puppies. Oh, Tom, they're adorable but
they're running around everywhere and they won't do a thing I
tell them and—"

Tom threw up his hands. "Whoa! Maddy, can you please start
at the beginning?"

Maddy was flushed pink, her hair all mussed, and there was a
streak of flour across her cheek just like the day he'd first met
her.

How could he ever have thought he could be tough with
her? Last night after they'd parted he'd spent the most miserable
hours of his life. He didn't care to experience any more like
them.

Words spilled from her as Maddy regaled him with the story
of Mrs. Porter's visit. And her remarkable transformation. "So

what could I do? I couldn't break up the happy little family, could I?"

He could barely bring himself to think of the inherent impracticalities of the situation. "Of course not, but I wonder if—"

"Oh, Tom, look."

Tom followed her gaze. Brutus and Coco were lying together on the floor near the puppy's basket. It didn't take much of a stretch of the imagination to think that the two little dogs were cuddling. Three of the puppies were clambering onto their parents, tumbling all over them in unmitigated joy.

"How sweet," Maddy breathed. "Like Romeo and Juliet reunited."

"Romeo and Juliet with triplets," said Tom.

"Triplets? But there are— Ohmigod, where are the other two?" Maddy wailed. She turned and dashed for the kitchen.

The delicious smell of baking intensified as Tom followed her. Peanuts? Chocolate? His mouth started watering. Both?

How he missed Maddy's sinful, cholesterol-laden concoctions. She was doing such a wonderful job feeding him the low-fat, nourishing stuff, but it just wasn't the same. And now, if he didn't say the right thing, the future of his access to Maddy's cooking—low fat or otherwise—and Maddy herself was in jeopardy.

One little black-and-tan creature sat proudly near a puddle on the floor, obviously of its own making. Its black sibling had gotten hold of a set of plastic measuring spoons and was mauling them to pieces.

"Oh no! I've had those spoons since college," Maddy cried. "You naughty little—"

Tom was rather more concerned about the puddle. But he addressed the puppy chewing on the spoons. "No! Drop them." The puppy instantly let go of the spoons and looked up at Tom, wagging its tiny tail so vigorously it nearly fell over. "Good puppy," said Tom.

Gingerly Tom picked up the spoons, bent now and liberally embellished with puppy drool, and handed them to Maddy.

She looked up at him, head tilted to one side. "How did you do that?"

"You just have to be firm with dogs. Let them know who is boss."

Maddy quickly cleaned up the puppy puddle with paper towels. "No, it's not that. I tried firm and they ignored me. It's the alpha-male thing. You're obviously the alpha male to Brutus's entire little pack."

Tom closed his eyes. Please. This couldn't be happening to him. But when he opened his eyes, the puppies were still there. So was Maddy. And although there was a smile dancing around her mouth, her eyes were wary.

He cleared his throat. "So, if I'm the alpha male to them, what does that make me to you?" His voice was gruff with the emotion he was finding it almost impossible to mask.

She chewed on her lip before answering in a voice that wasn't quite steady. "You're my alpha male, too, and . . . and I missed you terribly last night."

"I missed you, too," he said, relieved beyond measure at her words and the yearning expression that accompanied them.

He kissed her, deeply, possessively—breathing in her warm, familiar scent, tasting the tang of lime and the richness of coco-nut, exulting in her feminine curves pressed close to him. The misery of the last hours was eclipsed—eclipsed but not entirely forgotten.

"Maddy," he said, breaking the kiss. "Last night, I'm so sorry. It was unforgivable . . . I want—"

She touched a finger to his mouth. "No, I'm the one who should be apologizing. I overreacted and—"

"I should have told you about the bonus."

"Maybe. But I shouldn't have made such a big deal of it. I didn't even congratulate you on your partnership."

"You did, you waved across the table."

"That wasn't a proper congratulation. I wanted to give you a big hug."

"It's not too late to give me a hug right now."

She wrapped him in as big a bear hug that a five-six woman could give a six-two man. She nestled her head against his shoulder. It felt so good to have her there. So right.

"Congratulations, Tom," she said. "Jackson, Jones, and Gentry are very lucky to have you as their newest partner."

Tom kissed the top of her head. "Thank you. Your best wishes are worth more than the rest of them put together."

She moved away to face him again. "I believe you really mean that."

"I'm not in the habit of saying things I don't mean. I think you know that by now."

"I guess so," she said, still sounding a tad uncertain. She glanced at the clock on the wall. "But talking of the partners, shouldn't you be at work right now?"

"It was more important to come here. Anyway, I'm meeting with my important client, one Brutus Stoddard."

"Who is currently getting reacquainted with his lady love."

"He was miserable last night without you. So was I."

"I didn't sleep a wink."

"Same. Of course it didn't help to have Brutus snoring away on the bed."

"You're kidding me." Her eyebrows rose. "You let Brutus on the bed with you?"

"Yeah. I told him I shouldn't but that, as I missed you, too, I understood how he was feeling. So I let him stay on the condition he slept right down at the end."

Only when the last word was out of his mouth did Tom realize what a disastrous admission he had made.

Maddy stared at Tom for a long, incredulous moment. "Say that again, will you please?"

"Sure, I—"

"Tom, you talked to Brutus. Talked to him like a person. Did you seriously expect him to answer you?" she said, mimicking his own somewhat pompous tones when he'd asked her a similar question.

She expected him to be defensive, argumentative even. Instead he grinned, a big, dimple-revealing grin, and threw up his hands in a gesture of surrender. "Okay, I admit it. Guilty as charged. I've caught it from the Cartwrights. I talked to a dog. Yes, like I expected him to answer me. And do you know what? He did."

"Answer you? Brutus has got the gift of speech now?" This was too big a turnaround for her to easily cope with.

"I'm serious. I think Brutus knows exactly what is going on most of the time. He's not as dopey as he seems. It's animal instinct and if you're on the right wavelength you can tune in to it."

"Like my mother used to say, it's the tone of the voice rather than what you say."

"I don't think your mother's theory is entirely correct," said Tom. "Too many variables."

Maddy shook her head. "Huh? Tom, I'm clueless as to what you're talking about."

"That's obvious. And it proves my point. The—"

"Wait," she said. She'd been watching the dogs from the corner of her eye. "The puppies have gone into the living room. I think we'd better follow them."

"Good idea. Though you do realize that wiping up puppy puddles is not part of the alpha male's responsibilities?"

She looked at him, deadpan. "So why doesn't that surprise me? But is eating peanut butter and chocolate chip cookies on the alpha-male menu?"

"Right at the very top."

Maddy followed Tom into the living room and sat down next to him on the sofa. There wasn't much room so she was forced to snuggle up next to him as they nibbled on the cookies.

"So, what's this about my mother's theory?" she finally asked.

Tom looked very serious and lawyerlike. "The whole misunderstanding about the bonus debunks her theory."

"Explain."

"The truth is, I didn't tell you about the bonus because I was so caught up in protecting you and Brutus from that evil Stoddard that I simply didn't think about it."

"Yes. I can see that. Now."

"But you thought I was just doing it for the money. If

'cashing in on the millionaire mutt' means what I think it means."

Maddy pulled a remorseful face. "Sorry about that."

"You're forgiven," he said with a swift kiss. "But here's the interesting bit. If your mother's theory was correct, you would have known from the tone of my voice—and from what I was doing rather than saying—how I felt about you. But you didn't, and that made you go off on entirely the wrong tangent."

A glorious sense of anticipation made her feel like half-set Jell-O—contained on the outside but all mushy and wobbly on the inside. She remembered his concern for her after the Jerome-and-the-lucky-pony incident. The way he exposed himself to ridicule by defending Brutus in court. How he had risked his important meeting with Clive Gentry so she could make her audition.

And suddenly she was receiving him loud and clear.

"So it was like, actions speak louder than words. Only I wasn't picking up on the meaning behind the actions."

"That is correct." His choice of words was so wonderfully lawyerlike.

She snuggled even closer to him on the sofa. Her voice suddenly didn't work very well and she had to force it out of a dry throat. "So . . . what are the words, Tom?"

They both sat very still for a very long moment. Then Tom twisted her around to face him. He cupped her face in both his hands. "That I was looking after you and Brutus because I . . . I cared for you . . ." His brown eyes had never seemed more sincere and his tone wasn't lawyerlike at all.

"Yes?"

"Because I love you, Maddy."

She swallowed hard. "I . . . I love you, too, Tom." The words, once out, weren't nearly as difficult as she'd imagined. In fact, she felt like singing them over and over.

The kiss that followed was the sweetest she had ever experienced. And not entirely due to the cookie crumbs on both their tongues.

On Wednesday she'd asked Tom if he was a dream. Last night the dream had turned into a horrible nightmare. Now the wide-awake reality was so much more wonderful than any dream could ever be.

"There's something else," said Tom. He reached into the back pocket of his jeans and pulled out a square of white paper. He unfolded it and Maddy could see it comprised two tightly printed pages.

She caught her breath. "Is that what I think it is?"

Tom nodded. "My five-year plan." Then, with great exaggeration, he tore it in half.

"Tom!"

He tore it through again. Then he crumpled up the pieces into a ball and threw it toward her pretty, hand-painted wastebasket. He missed, and the paper ball was immediately pounced on by the nearest puppy.

Maddy knew Tom had lived his life according to that plan and the ones before it for half his life. "Are you sure destroying your plan is what you want to do?"

"Absolutely sure. And I've trashed the computer file. Deleted the BlackBerry."

"Wow. That's serious stuff."

Tom got up from the sofa and paced the tiny area of her living room. "Maddy, I was an idiot to let something like that plan dictate my life. When I think how inflexible I let myself become ..."

The printout of the plan was now being squabbled over by two puppies emitting fierce baby growls as they shredded it all over her floor.

"I wouldn't say inflexible, Tom. More ... focused. Don't beat yourself up over it. You needed that plan. Now you don't. End of story."

He frowned. "What if I'd adhered so strictly to subsection 2c that I'd missed out on loving you?"

"The point is you didn't. And, remember, I threw the two-date rule out the window."

"And the kissing-occasion rule, don't forget."

"That's right. It's all about compromise, I guess."

"That's what my mother said this morning."

"Your mother?"

"I called to tell her the good news about the partnership. She picked up on how miserable I was and dragged it out of me that we'd had a disagreement."

Maddy liked Helen O'Brien. And she wouldn't mind a closer look at those baby photos. "What did she say?"

"She went ballistic. Turned out she and Walter cooked up the twenty-one-day clause and the bonus with the express purpose of forcing us into each other's company."

Maddy started to laugh. "You're kidding me? You heard Walter on the video. He was always telling me it wasn't right for me to be on my own. That I needed a good man in my life."

"We've been manipulated from day one."

"Are you complaining?"

Tom sat down beside her again. He put his arm around her

to pull her close. "No, I'm not. I'm grateful to Walter. Maddy, I couldn't imagine ever loving anyone the way I do you."

Tenderly, he wiped the streak of flour off her face with his finger.

"Me, too. Loving you, I mean," said Maddy. "I—ouch! There's a puppy chewing on my foot." She shook it off and he scampered back to join his brothers and sisters, who were now flopped on top of each other in a heap next to Coco.

"Maddy, you don't intend to keep all of the puppies, do you?" Tom didn't quite mask the undertone of dismay in his voice.

"No. Even when I move upstairs into the big house, it wouldn't be practical. I'd like to keep one, the little girl I fell in love with at Mrs. Poodle's house. I'm going to call her Tinker-belle. We'll have to find homes for the others."

"As long as the new owners sign an agreement to relinquish any claims on Brutus's fortune."

"Yes, Mr. Lawyer. But I'd like to hang on to all the puppies for a bit longer until they're ready to leave their mother. And father, too, of course."

Brutus had joined the heap and within seconds all the dogs were asleep. From the ones that looked most like Brutus emanated puppylike snores.

"We'd never, ever part Brutus and Coco." Maddy sighed. "Hmm. Mr. and Mrs. Brutus . . . Hey, I've just had an idea."

Tom felt himself break out in a cold sweat at the faraway look in Maddy's eyes. "No, Maddy. No. You're not thinking of holding a wedding ceremony for two dogs, are you?"

Maddy's eyes danced with mischief. "It would look cute, don't you think? Brutus in a new bandanna. Blue perhaps? And Coco in her best diamanté collar with ribbons tied in her fur. Hot pink, I think. We could even paint her claws pink to match with nail polish."

Tom groaned. "I think you're getting a bit carried away here," he cautioned.

Maddy narrowed her eyes, deep in creative thought. "I could sell the pictures. Can't you just see the headlines? 'Millionaire Mutt Weds. Makes Honest Dog of Mother of His Puppies.'"

Tom rapidly raked his fingers through his hair. "Don't even joke about it, Maddy. Please. And don't for one minute even think about making our wedding a double service."

Maddy stared at him. She did the nose thing. "What did you say, Tom?"

Where had that come from? Tom had a sudden vision of Maddy gliding up the aisle toward him in a beautiful white dress, her face all misty behind a white veil. Suddenly it seemed the only way to go. The logical conclusion.

"I said . . . I said the word 'wedding.'" He felt dazed, his feelings in free fall.

Maddy looked equally stunned. "What brought that on?" she asked, with the tiniest of tremors in her voice.

He took both her hands in his. "You know how traditional I am, Maddy. First comes love. We're there. Right?" He kissed her gently on her adorable nose. "Then . . . then comes marriage."

"You mean become Mrs. Tom O'Brien?" Maddy's eyes were huge in her heart-shaped face.

"Yes, Maddy. I mean, will you marry me?" He held his breath for her answer.

Maddy was trying to smile but Tom could see her lips were trembling too much for the smile to work. But finally she choked out the words he was aching to hear. "Yes, yes, and yes again. Tom, I love you."

He felt overwhelmed with pride, exultation, and pure alpha-male possessiveness. "I love you, too, Maddy. For always and forever."

Maddy felt as if her entire being was bubbling with joy. She hadn't known Tom long but she'd known him long enough. Nothing could make her happier than to be not just a chocolate chip in his life but his lawfully wedded wife.

He kissed her again. The best kisser in the universe would be hers to have and to hold and to kiss for the rest of her years. She was destined to a life with no lipstick and she couldn't be happier about it.

But there were a few details to sort out before they started talking china patterns. Or in his case, no doubt, china without patterns.

"Uh, Tom, there's just one thing."

"Mmm," he said, nuzzling into her neck and sending delicious little tremors through her body.

"We've got the love, we'll plan the marriage, and then—quite likely—we'll get to the baby carriage stage."

"I hope so," he said, more intent on undoing the tie of her apron from around her waist than on listening to her.

"I'd like to have right of veto over the naming of our children. No Bruces, no Squiggles, no—"

"Maddy." Tom slipped the knot of her apron, released the ties, slid his hands under her T-shirt to the small of her back, and pulled her close to him. "Just be quiet and kiss me, will you?"

And she did.